THE MILLIONAIRE MURDERS

DORSET CRIME BOOK 5

RACHEL MCLEAN

Ackroyd Publishing

ackroyd-publishing.com

 Created with Vellum

THE MILLIONAIRE MURDERS

The garden was peppered with mature trees: shade in the summer, protection in the winter, and the view always stopped her in her tracks. She'd grown up by the beach, but in a house that was nothing like this.

This wasn't Ines's house of course; there was no way she could afford this on her salary. But it was where she worked. Lived too, for now. Susannah Ramsay, Ines's boss, had made her millions as a corporate lawyer in the City of London. She spent part of the year here on the Sandbanks Peninsula, enjoying the fruits of her labours. And it was Ines's job to take care of her every need. This week Susannah was away in Switzerland, so Ines could take care of her own needs.

Feeling Vali's hand on her shoulder, she turned and let him kiss her. She forced her body to soften into the kiss, pushing away her anxiety. Vali was cute, she'd been seeing him for a month since they'd met in a Bournemouth bar. This was the first time she'd brought him here.

Susannah had fired her last gardener after he'd hosted a barbecue on the lawn. She'd attempted to bring criminal damages charges. Ines knew the consequences if she was caught.

Vali pulled away from the kiss and looked into her eyes, grinning.

"This place is something else."

She nodded. "Come and see the living room."

She took his hand and led him through. The double doors opened up into a broad space, illuminated by the moonlight. The beach was eerie in the dim blueish light.

Vali walked to the doors and placed his hands against the glass.

"How much did you say your boss earns?"

Ines approached him. "Don't worry about that now. Let's go upstairs."

He nodded. "Are you sure there's nobody else here?"

"There's a cook when she's in the house, but he's gone with her to Switzerland. I get to stay behind. I work for the house more than I do for her."

She surveyed the kitchen. It gleamed. Ines might not own this house, but she was proud of how beautiful she made it. Especially when Susannah wasn't here to undo all her work.

Vali looked up at the ceiling. It was high, lending an almost cathedral-like quality to the room.

"Lucky house," he said, winking.

Ines smiled. "Come on."

She grabbed his hand and tugged him towards the door. They stumbled through the broad hallway and tiptoed up the stairs. Ines knew the house was empty, she knew there was no one here to hear. She also knew that the thick carpets and concrete steps would muffle the sound of her footsteps. But she still felt like she was trespassing.

They reached the top of the steps and Ines turned to Vali.

"My room's the second on the right."

She felt her skin tingle. Their relationship so far had consisted of meetings in pubs, walks along the shore in Bournemouth and snatched kisses at bus stops. It hadn't gone any further. Until tonight.

Vali put his hands on either side of her head and pulled her in for a kiss. Ines tried to relax, but was aware of the stairs right next to her. She felt untethered, and off balance.

She pulled away. "Come on."

She headed for her room, passing the closed doors to Susannah's bedroom. She paused for a moment. What if her boss hadn't gone away? What if she was in there asleep and not in Verbier?

"We'll have to be quiet," she whispered to Vali.

"You said the place was empty?"

"It is," she said. "But I don't want the neighbours hearing."

He laughed. "You're that loud, are you?"

She gave him a wink. "You'll have to find out."

"Even if you screamed the house down, the neighbours wouldn't hear you here," he said. The next house could be half a mile away, these buildings were so isolated.

He pushed open one of the doors to Susannah's bedroom.

"Why don't we do it in here? I bet her bed's bigger than yours."

He walked through.

Susannah's bed was as wide as it was long, an ocean of silk and velvet. Part of Ines's job was to change it every week. She'd done so this morning, just after Susannah had left.

"No," she hissed. "My room."

"Hang on," said Vali, his voice tense.

"What?" Ines whispered.

She touched his cheek, surveying the line of his jaw. Vali was handsome. She couldn't believe her luck meeting him here.

He turned to her. "Out," he whispered.

"What?" she said.

"There's somebody in here."

Ines's heart clenched. "No there isn't."

He bent down to look into her eyes, his face inches away from hers.

"The bed," he whispered. "There's somebody in the

bed."

Ines felt her muscles tense. "There can't be."

She looked past him towards the bed. Sure enough, there was a shape in it.

When she'd made the bed this morning, she'd smoothed the sheets, pulled them taut. She knew that they would reflect the moonlight. This room didn't have curtains; Susannah liked to wake and look at the view.

But now the smooth lines of the bed were disrupted. There was a shape in the centre of it, darkness disturbing the sheets.

Ines put out her hand, feeling like she might fall.

"I don't understand," she said.

"Has your boss got any pets? Maybe..."

"No. She's allergic." Her heart was racing. "Come on, let's go."

"Turn the light on," he said. "We need to check."

"No! Don't be stupid."

"Look, Ines. You and me have been stood here talking to each other for too long now. If your boss is asleep over there, we'd have disturbed her."

"No. Come on." Ines thought of the gardener.

"Could she be on drugs?"

Ines shook her head. Susannah was into clean living. Vile smoothies with grass and seeds, egg-white omelettes. "No."

"We need to see, Ines. Turn the light on."

She approached the bed, trembling. The shape hadn't moved.

Her foot brushed against something and she yelped. She grabbed Vali's arm and pulled him back to the door. He reached out and flicked the light switch.

"Vali, no!"

She blinked, her eyes acclimatising.

"Shit," said Vali.

Ines followed his gaze.

The bed wasn't empty.

At its centre was Susannah. On the floor in front of it –
the thing she'd touched with her foot? – was another shape.

"What's that?" she said. "It's a..."

"It's a man."

Ines frowned. Susannah was single. No men ever came
in here. "Who?"

"Fucked if I know," said Vali.

Ines whimpered. "Get out. We have to get out now."

Vali turned to her. "We should check on them."

She stared back at him. "I'll call 999."

"We should check on them," he repeated.

"No," she said. "Don't touch anything."

She was a housekeeper, an immigrant. He was a student
on a temporary visa. She knew how things like this could
turn out for people like them.

"Don't touch them," she told him.

Her eyes flicked insistently between the two bodies, on
the floor and on the bed.

Susannah was laid out at the centre of the bed, her arms
out to her sides. In the middle of her chest, staining her silk
dressing gown, was a dark patch of blood.

On the floor in front of the bed was a man Ines didn't
recognise. He had dark hair and looked young. His suit was
covered in blood. On the carpet beside him, a puddle of the
stuff.

Ines retched. She put a hand to her chest and took a deep
breath.

"Vali," she said. "What happened?"

CHAPTER TWO

LESLEY CLARKE WASN'T EXPECTING a buzz on the intercom. Elsa had left for work ten minutes ago and she was about to head out herself.

She yawned as she opened the door. She hadn't stopped to check who it was.

"What is it?" she asked, expecting a delivery driver.

Standing in front of her was a man she didn't recognise. He had dishevelled blond hair and blotchy skin. His suit looked as if it hadn't been dry-cleaned in years.

"Who are you?" she asked him.

"Matt Crippins," he said. "BBC Dorset."

Lesley stiffened. She had an idea what this was about.

"Come in."

He followed her through to the living room. She stood in the centre of the space, not sure whether to offer him coffee.

"You're here about Sadie," she said, "aren't you?"

He nodded. "She was supposed to get back from Malta yesterday."

"And she didn't?" Lesley asked.

"No."

He raised a clenched fist to his chest. "I think you were right. Your colleague DI Finch too. What if Sadie didn't go on her holiday?"

Sadie Dawes was a journalist for local BBC TV. She'd been investigating the death of Lesley's predecessor, DCI Mackie. A week earlier, Lesley had reported her missing, but the man standing in front of her had reassured her that Sadie was on holiday.

"Sit down," she told him. "Tell me everything you know."

He dropped onto the sofa. "She was supposed to be at work yesterday morning. I think her flight back from Malta was two days ago. I've tried calling her mobile, her home phone, her emergency contact number. No answer."

"Parents?" Lesley asked.

"No idea," he said. "She's not from around here, you've heard her accent."

"I have," Lesley replied. Sadie was from Yorkshire.

"We need to find out if she's got family," she told him. "You have to look further into her employment records."

"I was hoping you could help with that."

She shook her head. Sadie had been arrested a few months earlier, but not charged. "You're formally reporting her missing?"

"I think so."

She folded her arms. "You think so, or you are?"

"I am." He licked his lips.

"Good."

"I should have done this a week ago, shouldn't I?" Matt was pale.

Lesley shrugged. "It's OK, Matt. She'll turn up."

"I'll see what I can find about her friends and family."

"Do that," she told him. "Keep me updated. We'll be sending someone round to talk to your staff."

"You can't disrupt us while we're getting today's news out."

Lesley cocked her head. Journalists were like coppers. Even in an emergency the job had to go on.

"I know that," she said. "But we still need to talk to everybody Sadie might have been in contact with. Do you know what she was working on?"

Lesley thought she knew the answer to that herself, but she wanted an idea of how much Sadie's colleagues knew.

He shook his head. "She insisted it was hush hush. Sensitive."

"OK." Lesley dragged a hand through her hair. "I need to talk to my colleagues. But you go back to your office, tell your colleagues what's happened, make sure they speak to us if they know anything."

He nodded and stood to leave.

Lesley waited for him to go. She picked up her keys and bag and headed for the door.

Three days ago, Elsa had said she might as well move in. She was arranging for her house in Wareham to be transferred back to the lettings agency. She wasn't sure she was ready for cohabitation yet. But at the same time, she and Elsa were already as good as living together. And Lesley's ex-husband Terry had bought her out of the house in Birmingham.

It looked like she was staying in Dorset.

Her phone rang as she got into the car: PC Tina Abbott.

"Tina," she said. "I'm just on my way into the office."

"Where are you?" Tina asked. "Wareham or Bournemouth?"

Lesley smiled. Tina knew all about Elsa.

"Bournemouth. Why?"

"You need to go to Sandbanks," Tina told her. "A body's been found."

CHAPTER THREE

UNIFORM WERE out in force at the crime scene. Three squad cars were parked outside, plus DS Dennis Frampton's Astra. Lesley walked into the wide driveway leading up to the house and nodded to the constable at the door.

"DCI Clarke," she told him. "Add me to the log."

"I need you to sign in, Ma'am."

She grabbed the clipboard from him and signed her name then stooped to put on her overshoes.

The heavy front door was open. Lesley stepped inside and took in the building. The hallway was wide, on each side an open door. One led into what looked like a study, the other a dining room. The dining room looked stiff and formal, probably never used.

She continued through an open set of double doors into a wide open-plan living space. There was another dining table: long, made of oak. A kitchen to the left and living area to the right. In any other house, this space would look lived in. There would be dirty dishes, books lying around, shoes on the floor.

But here, there was nothing. It was immaculate.

Lesley turned back into the hallway.

"Where do I need to go?"

The constable at the front door turned to look inside.

"Upstairs, Ma'am. Can't miss it."

"Thank you."

Like everything else in this house, the stairs were wide. Covered with a plush white carpet, no reverberation as she climbed. As she neared the top, she heard voices and movement.

She stopped at the top of the stairs. In front of her, another set of double doors opened into a bedroom. This would be above the open-plan living area downstairs, offering the same view of the beach.

Lesley stood at the threshold. Two white-suited techs were near the bed and a uniformed constable stood by the door making notes.

On the bed was a woman. She had long blonde hair, fanned out on the pillow beneath her. Her arms were outstretched and her legs straight. A browning patch of blood adorned her chest.

In front of her, slumped against the bed, was a man. Lesley looked back at the woman. She looked to be in her forties, the man in his twenties most likely. Her son, or a younger boyfriend or husband?

She shivered. The windows beyond the bed were open.

"Someone close that," she said. "The breeze will contaminate the evidence."

A figure emerged from behind the bed, straightening up: Dennis. He went to the doors, which glided shut in silence.

"Boss." He frowned. "They were open when we got here."

"Dennis. You beat me."

"I was out for a morning walk when Tina called. Shell Bay."

Lesley wondered how Dennis found time to fit in a walk before work. Good for him, though. She should get more exercise herself.

"What have we got, then?"

"Her name's Susannah Ramsay," Dennis said. "She owns the property. The housekeeper found them."

"No ID for him?"

"Housekeeper has no idea who he is."

One of the techs looked up. It was Gavin, Gail's colleague. The one so tall he reminded Lesley of the honey monster.

"Morning, Ma'am," he said. "Gail's on her way."

"Good."

Gail would be getting the ferry across from Swanage.

"What do you have so far?" she asked him.

He looked down at the body on the floor. The man had dark hair and olive skin. Blood pooled beneath him, soaking into the thick carpet. His face was lifted upwards, as if he had been looking at the woman when he died.

Lesley took a few steps in. Susannah's eyes were closed. Light crow's feet lined the edges of her eyes, but a smooth forehead betrayed Botox use. She lay on the bed with her arms flung out to the side, as if she was being crucified, her legs straight out beneath her. Blood bloomed in the centre of her chest. Her expression was calm. There was no blood elsewhere on the bed, no sign of a struggle. The sheets were smooth.

Had she been posed like that after death?

Or had she died willingly? A suicide?

"Any sign of a weapon?"

Gavin walked to a chest of drawers so far from the bed it was almost in another time zone. He picked up an evidence bag. "Kitchen knife. No sign of prints to the naked eye, but we'll run the usual tests."

She took it off him. The knife was clean: no blood, no visible prints. But even the most thorough killer would leave traces of themselves.

"Excellent," she said. "I want this processed as soon as Gail gets here."

He nodded.

She went back to the bed. "Angle of the wound?"

Dennis stood at a diagonal from her, looking down at the woman.

"Not consistent with suicide, if that's what you're thinking."

"You reckon?" She turned her head to get a better look. It was difficult to tell where the wound was, with all that blood. "Has Whittaker been called?"

"Whittaker is still off sick," Gavin said. "It'll be Dr Brightside."

"OK."

Lesley had worked with Fiona Brightside on a previous case. The woman was efficient, if brusque. Unlike Whittaker, who was slow and plodding.

She stood back, looking down at the man. "What about him?"

"Defensive wounds on his palms," said Gavin.

Lesley squatted beside the man's body. He lay at an awkward angle, his back half up the bed, his legs twisted to one side. "Maybe he came to her defence."

"That's a very old-fashioned concept for you, boss." Dennis was next to her.

"Maybe he was an old-fashioned man."

"He's young."

"Doesn't necessarily follow." She looked up at the woman. "We need to find out who he is, what their relationship was."

"There may be photos around the house, boss."

Lesley sniffed and looked around the room. It was austere. Not a sign of personalisation. "The housekeeper found them?"

"Ines Perez," said Dennis. "She's outside."

"Let's take a look around, then talk to her. Gavin, keep me updated please."

"Ma'am."

Lesley bristled.

She walked towards the door, her gaze on the carpet.

"What's this?" she asked.

There was an object on the floor, reflecting the CSIs' lights. Gavin followed her. He reached down, placed it in an evidence bag, and held it up to the lights.

"Looks like a fingernail," he said.

Lesley looked at Susannah. "One of hers by the looks of it."

The woman had a fingernail missing, her left ring finger. Lesley went back to the bed and bent over.

"Not much bleeding."

"Post-mortem, perhaps," said Dennis.

"Perhaps. The finger could be significant. We need to know if she was married, or engaged." Lesley checked her watch. "Where is Dr Brightside coming from?"

"Dorchester, Ma'am," Gavin replied.

She sighed. "You don't have to Ma'am me, you know. You're a civilian."

"Sorry, habit. DCI Mackie preferred it that way."

"Well, I'm not DCI Mackie."

"What's happening?"

Lesley turned to see Gail standing in the doorway holding a pilot case.

"Morning, Gail," she said. "You come over on the ferry?"

"Got here as fast as I could. You've made a start I see."

"Two victims," Gavin said, "IC4 male, mid-twenties, IC1 female, mid-forties. Stab wounds to both."

Lesley listened as he finished recounting the injuries to the crime scene manager.

"Check under their fingernails," Gail said. "Remaining ones, in her case. Clothing and carpet, for fibres. And the bed. We'll need internal swabs from the woman once the pathologist is here, and analysis of bloodstains." She turned to the second CSI. "Brett, cover the rest of the house. Dust for prints, use UV on the carpets. Find out how the killer entered and exited."

Lesley smiled. It was good to see Gail take charge.

"What's your theory about the woman?" she asked.

Gail turned to her. "You mean, did she kill herself?"

Lesley nodded.

"We'll need the pathologist's analysis, but I think not. The angle of the wound. There are no practice wounds. And if she was going to kill herself, why would she do it with him here?"

"Double suicide pact?" Gavin suggested.

"If it was," said Gail, "he wouldn't be like that on the floor. We need to do more work here, but..."

"Someone went for her," said Lesley. "He came in while it was happening, and was killed trying to protect her."

"Even with her laid out like that?" Dennis asked.

Gail looked at Susannah's body. "It's unusual, one body posed like that and the other not. But that's why she was probably the intended target. He was collateral damage."

Dennis winced. "Poor fellow."

Lesley looked down at the man. "We need to confirm his identity. Dennis, let's go downstairs."

CHAPTER FOUR

LESLEY HEADED DOWN THE STAIRS, Dennis behind her. Brett, the junior member of Gail's team, was already down there dusting the doorknobs.

"I take it you don't want us touching anything?" she asked him.

He looked up and nodded. "Please."

"What about the floors?"

She stood on the bottom step of the stairs. The stairs were covered in a plush cream carpet. She had no idea how many people had already been up and down. The bedroom at least had had protective plates on the floor, safe spots for them to stand.

"Just go carefully," he said. "And keep your overshoes on."

She nodded. She and Dennis had both brought gloves and overshoes from their cars.

They walked through to the living room. The doors leading to it were already open, so they didn't have to touch anything. Even so, Lesley took care to stand away from walls and doors.

She stood at the centre of the room, Dennis next to her. Ahead of them was a long dining table, the kitchen to one side and a living area on the other.

"Nice work if you can get it," Dennis said.

Lesley raised an eyebrow. "We'll need to find out what Susannah Ramsay did. This could be work-related."

"Professional rivalry?" Dennis asked.

"Possibly. Or she might have been up to no good. Embezzling money, defrauding clients."

"What was her job?"

She shrugged. "We'll ask the housekeeper that."

"We can get Tina and Mike looking into the victims. Shall I call them?"

"You do that," Lesley told him. "Get Tina on background for Susannah, Mike can work on identifying the man."

She called through to the hallway.

"Brett, can you send photos to DS Frampton's mobile?"

"No problem."

Lesley nodded at Dennis and turned back into the living room. This room was pristine, recently cleaned or rarely used.

She stepped towards the living area, expecting to find photographs on a surface, but there was nothing. Maybe the house was rented out as a holiday home. Susannah would keep the personal knickknacks to a minimum.

Lesley shivered.

Susannah looked to be in her forties, the man in his twenties. They could be mother and son. Lesley's instincts told her that they weren't. She was blonde, smooth, expensive-looking. Her remaining fingernails were perfectly manicured, and her skin looked as if she received regular facials.

The man, while smartly dressed, looked nothing like her. He was Asian for a start, shorter than her. His suit was cheap. A boyfriend, a casual acquaintance? Hopefully Mike would be able to find out.

Dennis came back in, plunging his phone into his inside pocket.

"Tina's been looking into Susannah. She lives in London most of the time."

Lesley wasn't surprised: most of the houses along this stretch of coast were second homes. She wondered what kind of place the woman owned in London to be able to afford a holiday home like this.

"What about the man?" she asked. "Any ideas?"

"Nothing," Dennis said. "Mike's got photos, Gail's team will be sending prints through shortly. We'll see if there's a match on the system."

Lesley chewed a fingernail. "D'you think it might have been a burglary gone wrong? Maybe somebody thought the house was empty, didn't expect Susannah to be in bed?"

"What about the man, though?" Dennis asked. "He wasn't in bed."

"We need to work out what the pair of them were doing before it happened. Were they both in the bedroom when she was attacked? Did he come in while it was happening?"

"There's a chance he attacked her," Dennis said. "Maybe he stabbed her, she defended herself."

Lesley looked at him. "No. She didn't move after she was stabbed. The bed's too clean."

"Maybe it was the other way around. She attacked him, he pushed her onto the bed, retaliated."

"It feels too staged. Someone else was in that room. We just need to find out who."

"None of it makes sense," Dennis said.

"You're right there," Lesley replied. "Let's stop speculating, wait until Fiona Brightside gets here."

"Who?"

"The new pathologist. Whittaker's off sick."

Dennis frowned. "Poor man."

Lesley nodded.

Lesley had noticed that Whittaker seemed unwell, but said nothing. Whittaker wasn't the kind of man who would appreciate concern for his well-being. But now she felt guilty.

She sighed.

"Come on," she said. "We've got a witness to interview."

CHAPTER FIVE

Ines stood in the front garden, trying not to imagine the neighbours staring out of their windows at her.

The two policemen who'd arrived after she'd called 999 had told her to get out of the house and stay out. Contaminating a crime scene, she imagined.

But had she already done that?

And besides, her fingerprints and DNA would be all over the house. She spent more time in it than Susannah did.

But she wasn't about to disobey them. With Susannah dead, she would soon be out of a job. And without a job, she would be sent home.

To her mother's pity, her father's disapproval, and her brother Tomas's *I told you so*. She'd been determined to make this job work. To claw her way up to something better, one job at a time.

She brushed her hands up and down her arms, shivering. They could at least let her sit in one of their cars. She wondered if she was being treated like this because of her accent. The policeman who'd spoken to her had smiled, but he'd been businesslike. She was a witness, or an obstruction.

A suspect, maybe.

The tall blonde woman who'd hurried in half an hour earlier emerged with an older man in a grey tweed jacket that made Ines think of her grandfather. The two of them approached her. The man was smiling, the woman not.

"Ines Perez?" the woman asked.

"Yes."

Now the woman smiled, and held out her hand. Ines took it.

"I'm DCI Clarke, Senior Investigating Officer. Was it you who called 999?"

"Yes."

"You found them?"

"Yes."

"Can you tell me their names, please?"

The man got a notepad out of his inside pocket.

"My boss, Susannah Ramsay. I don't know who he is."

The woman arched an eyebrow. "No idea?"

"No. Sorry."

"Boyfriend? Husband? Colleague?"

Ines shook her head. "I don't recognise him."

"How close did you get?"

"I... I approached the bed. When I saw she was dead, I left. Called the police."

The detective nodded.

"What about him?" asked the man.

"Sorry?"

"Was he dead when you found them?"

"Yes." Ines shivered.

The woman reached out and touched her arm lightly. "Let's sit in my car."

Ines nodded her thanks. "Please."

The pair led her to a long, dark car parked on the double yellow lines outside the house. The man opened the front door and Ines pulled back.

"You want me to sit in driver seat?"

The man frowned.

"No," the woman said. "We drive on the left, remember. That's the passenger seat." She was standing on the other side of the car, looking at Ines across the roof.

Ines slid inside, her mind racing. Were they about to take her away, arrest her?

She didn't know how these things worked.

The woman was already in the driver's seat. The man heaved himself into the back and closed the door.

Ines placed her hands in her lap, twirling her fingers together. Her nails needed cutting, one of them was hanging off. She heard a cough in the backseat and turned to see the man shuffling to get comfortable.

"You're the housekeeper?" the woman asked.

"Yes."

"Nice house," said the man.

Ines knew he was referring to the opulence of it, but still she felt pride.

"Thank you."

"But it's not yours," the man said.

Ines smiled. "No. I clean it. I look after it."

"Right." He wrote in his book.

Ines sometimes liked to imagine the house was hers, that she was tending to her own property. Susannah was here so rarely, it was easy to feel that way. But last night had been the first time she'd brought someone home.

She'd picked the wrong night.

"So," the woman said, "can you take us through what happened?"

Susannah swallowed. She closed her eyes and turned to face forward.

"I went out last night, in Bournemouth. I got home around half past ten. Susannah left in the morning, for her chalet in Verbier."

"Except she didn't," said the man.

"What time did you think she'd left?" the woman asked.

"Morning. I was out. Shopping. She said she didn't need me, wanted me to replenish the wine cellar. There's a place in—"

"Tell us what happened when you got home."

Ines nodded, her throat tight. "I went straight upstairs. I stopped, to check Susannah's room. It's beautiful, in the moonlight."

"You go in there a lot?" the man asked. The woman frowned.

"I go in to clean, and to change the sheets. I changed them earlier yesterday."

"And when you went in there, what did you see?" the woman asked.

Ines swallowed. "A shape, on the bed. I was expecting it to be smooth. I turned on the light, and saw them."

"Did you touch them?" the woman asked.

"No."

"How close did you get?" The man, this time. Ines felt like she was under interrogation.

"Do I need a lawyer?" she asked, realising that she should have asked this before getting in the car.

"Do you think you need a lawyer?" the man asked.

The woman turned to him, frowning. "You're not under arrest. We haven't cautioned you. All this is, is us asking you some questions. If you'd like a lawyer, you have the right to one. But we won't take much longer."

Ines took a breath. "OK." She could do this.

"How close did you get?" the man repeated.

"My foot brushed..." She swallowed. "My foot touched the man. Sorry."

The man smiled. "It's OK. At least we know."

"I assume we'll find your fingerprints and DNA all over the house?" the woman asked.

"I live there. I work there."

The woman nodded. "And you're sure you don't know who the man is?"

"Sorry."

"Did you see anyone else come to the house yesterday? Maybe after you thought Susannah had left?"

Ines shook her head.

"You didn't?"

"No."

"And you were alone when you came home?"

Ines stared ahead, her eyes sore. "Yes."

"OK. Can you tell me about your employment here? How long have you worked for Ms Ramsay? How did you get the job?"

"I've been here for fifteen months. I came here from Spain before the rules changed. Susannah got me a visa. She worked for an international company with offices in Spain, that helped apparently. She kept me on, she's a good boss. As long as I keep her house clean and cook her meals. The two of us lead very separate lives."

"So you didn't see much of Susannah?" the woman asked.

Ines shook her head. "She's here maybe once or twice a month, the rest of the time she's in London."

"Where in London?"

"I'm sorry, I don't know."

The man wrote in his notebook.

"Do you know the name of Susannah's employers?" he asked.

"Sorry."

"We can find that out," the woman said.

Ines nodded. She wished she knew more, but she preferred not to ask questions of her employers. In her experience, they didn't like it.

"When was the last time you saw your employer before you found her last night?" the woman asked.

Ines looked down at her hands. That fingernail was almost coming off now, she'd been tugging at it so much.

"Two weeks ago," she said.

"Two weeks?" the man asked. "You work here full time and you only saw her two weeks ago?"

Ines turned and nodded to him. "She has been in the house for the last three days, but I haven't seen her. She gets up early, she goes out. I hear her moving around the house, but she doesn't like me to come out of my room."

"So she kept you prisoner?" the female detective asked.

"No, not prisoner," Ines said. "She's a good employer, we just stayed separate."

The two detectives exchanged looks.

"And you say you were alone when you found her?"

"Yes," Ines replied, her voice firm.

"Did you ever bring anybody into the house? Did people know you work here?"

"No," Ines said. "It is not appropriate for someone like me."

"In what way not appropriate?" the man asked.

"I could never have a house like this myself. And I feel uncomfortable with telling people I'm a servant."

"Is that how you think of yourself?" the woman asked. "A servant?"

Ines shrugged.

"Where will you be if we need to speak to you again?"

"I do not know, it depends when they let me back into the house. I have nowhere else to go."

"Can we put her in a hotel, boss?" the man asked.

The woman looked into Ines's eyes as if trying to size her up. Ines blinked back at her, her breathing shallow. She wondered what Vali was doing now, whether he'd told anybody what he'd seen. She needed to speak to him. She had questions of her own.

"We can find somewhere for her," the woman said. "We'll look after you, Ines, don't worry."

CHAPTER SIX

———

Dr Brightside arrived as Lesley was re-entering the house. She'd told Dennis to get back to the office and kick off the formal investigation.

"DCI Clarke, good to see you again." The pathologist put out a hand and Lesley shook it.

"Have you been briefed?"

"Two victims, one man, one woman. I gather you don't have an ID for the man yet."

"Any identifying marks you can find will help with that."

"Of course. Up here?" Fiona gestured up the stairs.

"Master bedroom, straight on at the top."

The doctor smiled and hurried up the stairs. She was a short, stocky woman but she moved fast. At the top, she paused to confer with Gail then approached the bodies. She stopped just short of them.

Lesley almost stumbled into her. "What is it?"

"Just paying my respects." The pathologist had her eyes lowered.

Lesley remembered this from a post-mortem she'd

observed: Dr Brightside liked to show reverence to the dead before she touched them.

Lesley jabbed her fingernail into her thigh while she waited. They needed to get an ID on the man, and quickly. The killer could still be at large.

"Ready?"

Fiona turned to her. "Ready." She stepped forward and bent over Susannah's body.

She pointed to the wound at the centre of the woman's chest. "Deep stab wound immediately below the sternum, angled up and right, approximately forty degrees. Clearly a knife..." she bent over further, "... and not serrated. The fabric of her dressing gown has a clean cut. The blade had been sharpened. No practice wounds, either the male victim was stabbed first or the killer was confident."

Gail came forward, holding up an evidence bag. "Consistent with this?"

Fiona took it from her. Inside was the kitchen knife that Gavin had found. "Sabatier. Heavy, sharp. Examine it for residue, see if you can identify the type of steel used to sharpen it."

Gail smiled and nodded. Lesley wondered if she was comparing Dr Brightside to Henry Whittaker.

Fiona shuffled to one side. "Has she been moved?"

"Not an inch," said Gail. She looked at Gavin, who nodded.

Fiona squatted to bring her head level with the bed. She was at its bottom corner, away from the man's body. "No sign of other injuries from this angle. Have you taken enough photos?"

"You can move her, if that's what you're asking," Gail said.

"Good." Fiona walked around the bed and stood on the other side. She reached across and placed her outstretched arms beneath the body. She rolled it a little.

"No immediate evidence of other injuries. She's heavier than she looks. Good muscle tone."

"Maybe she worked out," said Gavin. "There's a gym along the corridor."

"She was rarely here, according to the housekeeper," Lesley added. "What about him?"

Fiona glanced at her then moved round to crouch next to the man's body, her feet on protective plates. "Defensive wounds, he fought back." She pointed. "The killer had a swipe at his face."

"Time of death?"

Fiona looked up at Lesley. "Sometime in the last twelve to sixteen hours, judging by the progress of rigor mortis and the temperature of the room." She looked round. "Can someone find out if this room would have been cooler overnight?"

"Gav?" said Gail.

"On it." He left the room, in search of the heating system.

The pathologist stood up.

"Any theories?" asked Lesley.

She shook her head. "It's not suicide, if that's what you're wondering. The angle of her wound, it's too awkward for her to have done it herself."

"Could one of them have stabbed the other?"

"I'm not sure. There's a chance she went for him, he received fatal wounds but was still sufficiently mobile to stab her before going down himself."

"But?"

Fiona smiled. "Who said there was a but?"

"Your tone," Lesley told her. "You don't believe that's what happened."

"No. He's not tall, and she was fit. But she's slender, and would have struggled to overpower him. There are no wounds on her body that might fit with him defending himself against her. And the way she's been laid out..."

"D'you think that was done after she died?"

"That would be the logical conclusion, but based on the blood pattern..."

"There's arterial spray on the side of the bed, the bedside table and the wall," said Gail. "But the angle means it's his blood. Her blood seems to have stayed on the bed."

Fiona nodded. "She didn't move after she was stabbed. Which means she was either asleep, or drugged." She turned to Lesley. "I think he came in while it was happening, went for her attacker."

"Collateral damage," said Lesley.

"An unlucky hero." Dr Brightside looked down at the man's corpse, her eyes sad. "What was their relationship?"

"We don't know. He's unidentified right now."

"Nothing in his pockets?"

"They're empty," said Gail.

Lesley sighed. "Which means one of two things."

"The killer emptied his pockets," Gail said.

"Possibly," Lesley replied. "But the other option is that he didn't want anyone knowing who he was."

CHAPTER SEVEN

THE HOTEL ROOM that the police had found for Ines was cramped and dingy. It was nothing like her room in Susannah's house. She imagined this place wasn't for holidaymakers, but for those with nowhere better to live.

The duvet had pale stains. There were crumbs on the floor and damp rose up the wall behind the bed.

Ines wrinkled her nose. She could find somewhere better than this. Susannah gave her access to a household budget, generous funds for food and other necessities.

Was it right to use it for accommodation? If Susannah hadn't been killed, Ines wouldn't be in this situation. She deserved to be somewhere nice. Somewhere she could recover from the trauma of what she'd seen.

She lowered herself to the bed, then thought better of it and stood back up. There was a sink in the corner, grey marks around the plug hole, and the tap dripping.

A shudder ran down her back. There was no way she was staying here.

In Spain she'd lived in a small but comfortable house

near the coast with her parents. When she'd come here, she'd started out sharing a one-bedroomed flat with another girl. But then she'd started working for Susannah. It hadn't taken long to get used to that house.

She picked her bag up off the floor and made for the door. As she reached for the handle there was a knock.

"Who is it?" she called out.

"It's me."

She swallowed and opened the door.

"Vali," she breathed.

He closed the door behind him and pulled her into his arms. She let him hold her for a moment, glad of the contact, then pushed him away.

"I lied for you," she told him.

He smiled and stroked her cheek.

"Thanks, sweetheart."

"Don't thank me," she said. "Lying to the police is a crime. What if they find evidence that you were there?"

"They won't," he said. "It was the first time I'd been there. All we did was walk up the stairs and find them."

She shook her head. "We went in the living room first, I showed you around the kitchen."

"I stood in the doorway," he replied. "There's no way..."

"You don't know how it works. Haven't you seen *CSI*?"

He laughed. "That crap? None of that is realistic. This is Dorset, not Los Angeles." He tugged at her arm. "It'll be fine. Come here."

He wrapped his fingers around the back of her neck and pulled her towards him. She let him kiss her then pulled away.

"I don't feel comfortable with it," she said. "I'm sure that if you tell them you were with me, that will make it easier when they do discover..."

His face hardened. "They're not going to discover."

"Why shouldn't they? You're a student, there's no reason you shouldn't be there. I worked there, there's nothing wrong with me bringing friends home."

"You're sure?" he asked. "A woman like that really would have been happy with me in her house?"

"Why wouldn't she?" She remembered her nerves as they'd entered the house. The gardener.

He laughed. "I'm a poor kid from Romania, Ines. Women like Susannah Ramsay don't want the likes of me sleeping in their plush beds. I'm fine as a garden boy or a driver. But as a guest? No chance."

"Susannah's dead," Ines said. "Why should she care? We just should let the police know."

He put a hand on her chest. "No, Ines. Please."

She stared back into his eyes then dropped her gaze.

"I've lied to them now. I just won't say anything else."

"Not even if they ask you?"

"I won't give them a direct response."

He nodded. "That should throw them off the scent."

She pulled back.

"What scent? Why is it you don't want them to know you were there?"

"I've told you, sweetheart," he said. "I'm a Romanian kid on a student visa that's about to run out. I don't want the police putting me anywhere near a murder scene."

She felt her heart chill. "Did you know Susannah? Had you met her before?"

"Me, meet *her*? You've got to be kidding. Ines, stop worrying. You're being paranoid. Some bastard came in and stabbed your boss, they'll find some DNA or fingerprints and they'll work out who it is. It'll be all cleared up within twenty-four hours, don't worry."

He cupped her face in his hands.

"It'll all be fine, believe me."

Ines wished she shared his confidence.

"Anyway," she said. "I'm not staying here."

He looked past her around the room. "What's wrong with it?"

"It's filthy!"

He shrugged. "I've slept in worse."

"Well, I'm not about to."

She grabbed his hand and picked up her bag.

"Come on," she told him. "Let's go to your place."

CHAPTER EIGHT

"Right," Lesley said. "Let's see where we are."

She stood in her office at Dorset Police HQ, surveying the board. It was almost empty, just a few crime scene photos at the top.

"I've got photos, boss," Tina said.

"Go on."

Tina walked to the board and stuck up a photo of Susannah Ramsay. She also placed one of Ines Perez, the housekeeper.

"What about the male victim?" Lesley asked. "Any sign of an ID on him yet?"

"Not yet," said Dennis.

"Can't the housekeeper help with that?" Tina asked.

"She'd never met him before," Dennis replied. "Doesn't know him from Adam."

"OK."

Lesley frowned. "We need to go through Susannah's social media accounts, emails, texts. He'll turn up."

"I can do that," Mike said. "Gail's team have brought in her laptop and phone."

"Thanks. Then there's CCTV, a property like that would have a doorbell camera at the very least."

"There were cameras on the front of the house," Dennis said. "I made a note of the security company's name."

"Good. Tina, can you take that off the sarge and make contact? We want recordings from yesterday morning through to the time when Susannah and the male victim were found."

"No problem, boss," said Tina.

"Have we got a time of death?" Mike asked.

Lesley looked at her watch. An hour had passed since she'd been standing in Susannah Ramsay's bedroom with Gail and the pathologist. "Between thirteen and seventeen hours. So somewhere between six and ten last night."

"The housekeeper found them at half past ten," Dennis added.

Lesley nodded. "Which means their attacker had time to leave, given that she saw no sign of anyone in the house. Tina, ask for camera footage from three pm onwards. There's a chance the killer got in earlier on."

"Boss."

Lesley's phone rang: Gail.

"Good timing," she said as she answered. "How are you getting on?"

"Still analysing the trajectory of blood spatter," Gail said. "The male victim was stabbed multiple times, arterial spray radiating from the area around where he fell. We've confirmed that none of the spatter on the wall or the side of the bed is from Susannah, but we have found her blood smeared on the doorframe and the wall downstairs. It was wiped, but there are traces."

"So her killer got her blood on him, transferred it to surfaces and tried to remove the evidence."

"There's no discarded clothing. Whoever killed her would have been wearing clothing that was heavily blood-stained."

"Do you still think she was asleep or drugged?"

There was the sound of muffled voices down the line. "DCI Clarke, Fiona Brightside here."

"Fiona. What do you think?"

"I've been looking at her pupils and changes to skin colour, and I think she was drugged. Hang on."

"We've got you on speaker," Gail said. "We've found a glass in the bathroom which may have traces of whatever she was given in it."

"Good. I want to know as soon as you have any identifying forensics from that, too. Prints, DNA."

"Of course."

"Was the man drugged too?"

"Not as far as I can tell," said Fiona. "We're moving them both in the next half hour or so, I'll know more when I'm able to run blood tests."

"Anything elsewhere in the house?"

"We're still working on that. I've got a team dusting the place right now."

"Good," Lesley said. "Let me know if you get anything else. Boots, fibres."

"You don't have to tell me how to do my job, you know," Gail said.

"Sorry." Lesley hung up and turned to her team. "You all get that?"

"Do we think the dead man drugged Susannah?" Mike asked.

Lesley shook her head. "The arrangement of the crime scene doesn't fit with that. Also the blood on the doorframe and wall. He was lying on the bedroom floor dead, so he couldn't have left those marks."

"They could have been taking recreational drugs..." suggested Dennis.

"That's a possibility. Let's wait till we have more from Forensics and Pathology. Meanwhile, we need to know who he is. And I want CCTV and witness statements. Was anyone seen in the area last night?"

"I'll talk to Uniform," said Dennis. "I know they've been doing house to house."

Lesley looked at him. "Get back over there, yes? I would come with you, only I need to go and see Carpenter."

"What about, boss?"

"None of your business."

He flushed. "Sorry. I didn't mean to..."

Lesley laughed. "It's alright, Dennis. It's not about any of you, in case that was what you were wondering."

Tina stifled a smile.

"OK," Lesley said. "We'll reconvene in a few hours, see where we are. Keep me updated in the meantime. First priority is to identify our second victim though."

"Yes, boss," said Mike.

He and Tina hurried out the room. Lesley noticed that Tina flinched as Mike made contact with her arm.

She grabbed her jacket and flung it over her shoulders. She pinched her cheeks; she wanted to look awake for Carpenter.

As she passed Tina's desk, the PC turned in her chair. "Boss..."

"What is it?" Lesley asked. "You got an ID?"

Tina shook her head. "It's not that. I think you're going to want to see this."

CHAPTER NINE

LESLEY STOOD behind Tina's chair, watching her screen. Tina had the BBC website open, local news.

Lesley looked up at the clock. "Is this a scheduled bulletin?"

"No," Tina replied. "Breaking news."

"What have they interrupted?" Lesley asked.

"Some antiques thing," Mike said. He rose from his seat and stood next to Lesley, his fingers on the back of Tina's chair. Lesley noticed the tip of his thumb graze Tina's skin.

A banner appeared at the bottom of the screen, moving from left to right. "Local reporter missing."

"Shit," said Lesley. She put her hand to her forehead.

"Should we know about this?" Mike asked.

"What's going on?" Dennis emerged from Lesley's office, where he'd been taking notes from the board.

Lesley turned to him. "Sadie Dawes. She's officially missing."

"I thought she was in Malta."

Lesley shook her head. "She never came home. She never went in the first place, I guess."

"So how come...?"

Lesley shrugged. "Matt Crippins said she'd boarded that flight, that he knew for sure she was on holiday. Now he's backtracking on that. He reckons nobody's seen her for a week."

"But what about...?"

Lesley held up a hand. "Shh."

A young male reporter appeared onscreen. He stood on the clifftop north of Swanage, not far from Old Harry Rocks.

"That's where..." said Mike.

Lesley nodded.

It was the exact spot in which DCI Mackie had died.

"What the blazes?" said Dennis.

Lesley clenched her fist and placed it on the back of Tina's chair. Mike moved his fingers away.

"I need to speak to Carpenter," she said.

"Wait," said Tina.

The reporter was speaking. Lesley listened, her heart thundering in her ears.

"Sadie Dawes was last seen by a colleague on this clifftop just over a week ago. She told him that she was returning here for a meeting the next day. However, she didn't say who that meeting was with."

Zoe, thought Lesley. Zoe had seen Sadie up there with a man. Then Sadie had texted Zoe and arranged a meeting. A meeting Sadie hadn't shown up to.

"The BBC is working with local police to find out what's happened to Sadie. Did she come to these cliffs? Did something happen to her here? If anyone watching has any evidence, we urge you to call this number."

The rolling banner at the bottom of the screen was replaced by a phone number.

"Shit," Lesley said. How much did Carpenter know about this? And why hadn't Matt Crippins told her they were going to put this on TV?

"Why is he saying that?" Mike asked. "She could be anywhere. Who's to say it's got anything to do with that cliff?"

Lesley raised a finger. "Wait."

She held her breath, waiting for them to say who had last seen Sadie on that cliff.

"Sadie's colleagues," the reporter continued, "believe that this meeting is linked to her disappearance. No one has seen her for over a week. In that time, she hasn't reported to work, and it appears she missed a scheduled holiday. If Sadie was killed or abducted in the performance of her job as a journalist, we want to make sure that whoever is responsible is punished."

He looked into the camera.

"We know that Dorset Police are just as concerned."

Lesley felt her jaw hang open. "Was that a threat?"

She brought her fist up. "I need to see Carpenter, right now."

CHAPTER TEN

SUPERINTENDENT CARPENTER THREW OPEN his door.

"Lesley," he snapped. "What the hell's going on?"

She glanced sideways, up and down the corridor.

"Sir," she said. "Don't you think this would be better done in your office?"

He pursed his lips, looking into her eyes. "Come on in, then."

She followed him, pushing her shoulders back. *Don't let him rattle you.*

He strode to the desk, and turned as he rounded it, his fist firm on the surface.

"Why wasn't a missing persons case opened a week ago?" he asked her. "Have you seen what they're saying on the television?"

He pointed at his laptop, which was open on the coffee table in the opposite corner of the room.

"I just watched it," she said. "I had no idea that they were going to—"

He thumped the desk. "I don't care what you thought the

BBC were going to do. The reality is a woman went missing a week ago, you knew about it and you didn't start a missing persons investigation."

"With respect, Sir," she said. "You spoke to her editor at the BBC. He assured you that she'd gone on holiday, or so you told me. He believed that she'd got on her flight to Malta."

"So how the fuck did he believe that when she didn't go to Malta in the first place?"

"That's one of the things we're going to have to determine, Sir."

"One of the things?" he said. "I've got Susannah Ramsay dead in her bed with some unidentified young man, and now I've got a missing BBC reporter. Do you know that Susannah is friends with Godfrey Plumley?"

"I'm sorry, Sir. I don't know who Godfrey Plumley is."

He slapped his forehead. "The local MP, for God's sake. You're a DCI in the Major Crime Investigations Team, you should know things like that."

She stared back at him, saying nothing. Lesley believed it was her job to know how to solve a crime, how to find evidence, how to manage a team. Schmoozing with politicians was above her pay grade, thank God, and that was why she had no intention of moving further up the ranks.

"And what about the person she was supposed to be meeting?" he asked.

Lesley swallowed the bile in her throat. "Sadie had arranged to meet DI Finch."

"Your mate from the West Midlands. Yes?"

"It was Sadie's idea, she—"

"Christ on a bike, DCI Clarke. You talk to your mate DI Finch, find out every little scrap of what she knows about

Sadie's movements that day. I'll be speaking to her commanding officer. And I assure you, it won't be an enjoyable conversation."

"I'm sorry, Sir. Do you want me to switch resources from the Susannah Ramsay case?"

"No I bloody well don't. Manage it, Lesley. Find Sadie Dawes, find Susannah Ramsay's killer."

"I'll assign half of my team to the Sadie Dawes case immediately. I'll make sure that they're dedicated to it and that they're working on tracking her down as soon as possible."

"And what about your DI Finch?" he thundered.

"She's gone back to the West Midlands, she'll have nothing to do with it."

"Make sure she stays there, yes?"

"Sir."

"Get out of my sight."

"Sir," she said. "Can I ask if anyone from the BBC has been in contact with you?"

"You're really asking me that, after—?"

"One of their reporters has gone missing. Zoe saw her with a man the day before she went missing. We have to consider that someone from the BBC is involved."

"Great. That'll do us the world of good, going up against the press."

"It's a case, Sir. We have to follow where the evidence takes us, however difficult that may be politically."

"Don't talk to me about politics. You don't even know who the local MP is."

Lesley took a step back, regretting her words. "I want to talk to Matt Crippins again," she said. "I want to know why he insisted that Sadie was on holiday, when she wasn't. He told us she'd boarded her flight. There's a chance that—"

He waved a hand. "Just do what you need to do, Lesley. But tell me if you're going to land Dorset Police in the shit again, please?"

"Of course."

His face reddened. "That was a joke. I don't expect you to land us in the shit at all."

"Of course."

"And tread carefully around Crippins. He's just lost one of his best reporters."

"With respect, I wouldn't say Sadie Dawes was anybody's best reporter."

"The woman is missing!" Carpenter shouted. "She could be dead for all we know. How can you possibly disparage her reporting skills now?"

"I'm not going to lie about the woman. She was a nuisance." Carpenter glared at her and she looked down.

Lesley couldn't understand why people felt it necessary to talk about the missing or dead as if they'd been saints. Sadie Dawes had been nothing but a hindrance. She'd found her way onto Brownsea Island when they were in the middle of a murder investigation. She'd videoed an attempted killing and been arrested for her interference.

But now, Lesley had to think of her as a victim. She had to forget how she'd felt about Sadie's implied threats that she would go public with what she knew about DCI Mackie.

Now, she needed to track Sadie down. She also needed to find out what Sadie's colleagues knew about Mackie.

She couldn't get Dennis on this one, he'd been too close to Mackie. The man had been his mentor, and she'd kept him out of her investigation into Mackie's death.

"Sir," she said. "I'll head up the Dawes case. I'll put DS Frampton on the Ramsay case. We'll have a strategy meeting right away and we'll ensure we've got resources allocated appropriately."

"There's only four of you since Johnny Chiles left," he said. "And one of you isn't even CID."

"Tina Abbott's taken the CID exam. I think we should take her out of uniform in the meantime."

"You think she's going to pass?"

"It's highly likely, Sir. She's had plenty of experience in my team and she's a diligent worker."

"Good," he said. "It's not enough, though. I'll need to assign you somebody else from a local CID team."

"That works for me, Sir," she said. "We've been short-staffed since we lost Johnny."

He raised an eyebrow. "It was you who asked for Johnny to be transferred to the Met."

"It was right for him at the time, Sir," she said. "I stand by that request."

He grunted. "Very well. I'll see what I can do. Keep me in the loop though, yes?"

"Yes, Sir."

CHAPTER ELEVEN

GAIL YAWNED.

It was late afternoon, and she'd been doing detailed work at her desk for two hours. Normally, she'd send Gav and Brett back to the lab for this kind of job, but she wanted to give them more experience at the crime scene itself. The three of them had worked together for four years now, and they made a good team. But she recognised her own tendency to give them the grunt work. And besides, her son had kept her up late last night and she was happier sitting in a chair.

She stifled a yawn with the back of her hand and peered at the screen. She'd found four distinct sets of prints in the bedroom. Some them had been in blood, some sweat.

Two had come from the victims. She could rule those out straight away. The third had been from Ines, the house-keeper. That one had been on the doorframe. There'd been others on the bedside table, but just sweat prints, nothing in blood.

They'd also taken Ines's shoes and looked for a match

between those and any footprints around the room. There'd been nothing: the carpet was clean. Ines said she'd approached the bed: had she cleaned up afterwards?

The fourth set of fingerprints, however, was harder to explain. They had come from the bedroom door handle. It didn't belong to anybody on record as working for Susannah. It also didn't match any of the elimination prints they kept on file for members of the investigating and CSI teams.

Either those prints had been put there by somebody visiting Susannah's bedroom before the crime had taken place, or they'd been left by the killer.

She watched the screen as images of fingerprints whirled past. It always made her eyes swim and she knew that looking at the screen as the computer attempted to find a match wouldn't make the process any more accurate. But she'd learned to do this manually decades ago. She'd pored over images looking for specific elements of a fingerprint: arches, loops and whorls.

At last, the computer stopped: a match.

Gail sat up straighter in her chair. She peered into the screen and brought up the file.

It was a young Romanian man, a student at Bournemouth University. Vali Florescu.

She scanned his file. He had no link to Susannah, no association with her house or her businesses. He was a student who had only come to this country three months earlier.

She picked up her phone. As far as she could tell, Vali Florescu had no reason to be in Susannah's house. Lesley would want to know about this.

CHAPTER TWELVE

LESLEY JERKED her head at Dennis as she passed his desk. "I need to speak to you."

"Everything OK, boss?"

"It will be."

He exchanged glances with Mike and stood up, following her into her office.

She sat behind her desk and gestured for him to take one of the seats opposite. She leaned back in her chair for a moment, pausing to take a breath.

Today had been one of those days where she'd wondered if she was about to make the right decision. She'd talked to Elsa about staying in Dorset long term, about moving in with her and applying for a permanent position. But today she was wondering whether she might be better off back in the West Midlands.

She closed her eyes. She didn't even know who her commanding officer would be now, if she went back. Her old boss was lost to witness protection and he'd been replaced by a newcomer.

She balled her fist in her lap and gritted her teeth.

"Right," she said to Dennis. "We've got a team of four and two high profile cases to deal with."

"Tell me what I can do."

"You and I are going to have to split up. I'll take Sadie Dawes, you take Susannah Ramsay and her friend."

"You sure about that?"

"Yes. Both of them are becoming political."

He nodded.

Lesley leaned forwards. She placed her hands on the desk and spread out her fingers. She'd only just stopped wearing the wedding ring that Terry had given her twenty years ago, and had a white patch on her finger. On the middle finger of her right hand she wore a ring that Elsa had given her. It was sapphire: simple, modern.

She smiled. Staying down here was the right move.

"So the BBC are careering around the place, telling everybody about what may or may not have happened to Sadie Dawes. They know that she was on the cliffs outside Swanage before she died, and I believe they know why."

"Why was that, boss?" Dennis asked.

Lesley closed her eyes.

"She was meeting a friend of mine."

Dennis frowned.

"I don't understand."

"DI Zoe Finch," she said. "You met her. I asked her to come down and deal with some allegations that Sadie was making. I wanted to keep it out of the team, it was too sensitive."

"How so?"

She took another breath.

"It was about DCI Mackie, Dennis. I have no idea

whether there's anything concrete to go on, but now the fact that Sadie has disappeared... Well, I don't know what to think, but we need to get to the bottom of that first and then we can deal with what happened to Mackie. There's a chance the two incidents might be related."

Dennis had stiffened in his chair.

"Mackie committed suicide, boss. He was suicidal, depressed, couldn't deal with retirement."

Lesley eyed him across the desk.

"Do you really believe that? Mackie booked himself on a cruise. He had a happy marriage, a wife who was looking forward to spending more time with him. Why would he kill himself?"

"There was no evidence of foul play."

She shook her head.

"Gail showed me the crime scene. It doesn't fit with suicide."

She clenched a fist in mid-air.

"Anyway, you're not working this case. I want you heading up the Susannah Ramsay investigation. That's going to be just as sensitive, turns out the woman's friends with the local MP."

"Godfrey Plumley?" Dennis asked.

"So you know who he is too?"

"Why wouldn't I?" said Dennis. "I voted for him."

Lesley bristled. She couldn't imagine voting for a man with a name like Godfrey Plumley. But she didn't pay much attention to politics.

"You're in charge, this is your investigation," she told him. "Carpenter's going to give us another member of the team and you can have Tina too."

"I'd rather have Mike."

"You're having Tina and the new person. I think that's fair. I'll take Mike."

Dennis clenched his jaw. "Very well."

"I take it you don't need instruction, you were in on the briefing."

"Yes, boss." He stood up.

"Good." Lesley forced her muscles to relax. Outside, Tina rose from her desk. She knocked on the door of Lesley's office, her expression agitated.

Lesley waved for her to come in. "What's happened? Have you got an ID for the man yet?"

"No, boss," Tina replied. "I just had a call from Gail."

"And?"

"She's got a match for those prints, the ones that don't belong to the housekeeper or the two victims."

Dennis turned in his chair.

"Who?"

Tina looked at him.

"A Romanian student, name of Vali Florescu."

"OK." Lesley stood up. She looked at Dennis. It was his case now.

She sat down.

"Dennis," she said. "You know what to do."

CHAPTER THIRTEEN

VALI LIVED in a student flat in Boscombe. Ines was impressed: the building was bright and modern, with spacious communal spaces downstairs, and Vali's room was clean and light, if spartan. Three other students lived in the flat, but today they were all out.

"It's nice," she told him.

He smiled. "You can sit down, you know."

The only place to sit was on Vali's bed. Ines hesitated before she sat down. She'd been planning on taking him to her room at Susannah's house; she didn't know why she should feel uncomfortable here. Maybe it was the prospect of his flatmates returning home. Maybe it was the image of her boss that kept flashing in front of her eyes.

"Are you alright?" Vali asked her. "You've gone very pale."

"I'm still... I can't..." She swallowed. "Can I have a glass of water, please?"

"Of course."

He hurried out of the room and returned with a Star

Wars mug. "Sorry, no clean glasses. The water's OK, though."

She took a sip, then another. She made herself lean back against the bare wall.

"I keep remembering it too," he said. He was sitting on a hard chair at the built-in desk, angled towards her.

She closed her eyes. "It's never going to leave my mind."

What was she going to do, now Susannah was dead?

Susannah had been a good boss, not interfering with Ines's life or her work. As long as the house was clean and Ines was barely noticeable, her boss was happy. Ines had grown up with four younger siblings and had learned to clean up after them. Cleaning up after a single, wealthy woman who didn't even live in the house most of the time was easy.

"How long can I stay here?" she asked him.

"As long as you need. They don't mind us having guests. Do you need to tell the police you're not in that bedsit anymore?"

She nodded her head. "That can wait."

He turned away and looked out of the window. She wondered if he was regretting ever having met her.

"Sit with me," she said. "I need a hug."

He smiled and moved to the bed. He shuffled up and put his arm around her shoulders. She leaned into him. Vali was slim and probably weighed less than she did. But he had a hidden strength that she found attractive.

"I'm glad you're with me," she said, "but I do wish you'd let me tell the police about you being there."

She felt his body stiffen.

"Please, Ines. Not that again."

There was a muffled knocking sound. Ines straightened. Vali's breathing had picked up.

"Who's that?" she asked. "One of your flatmates?"

He shook his head. "No one's due back yet."

She shrugged. "Maybe one of them came home early."

He frowned and stood up. The knock came again.

"It's the outer door," Vali told her. "Wait here."

"Don't answer it," she said.

"I have to. It'll be fine."

"Whoever it is, they can wait."

Vali opened the bedroom door. The knocking came again, louder. Ines shivered. She didn't want to talk to anyone. Not even Vali's friends. Especially not Vali's friends.

She stood up and watched Vali cross the narrow hallway and go to the door.

"Who is it?"

"Police."

"Shit," Vali muttered.

Ines drew in a breath. She hadn't told them she was here. Not yet. "Why...?"

He looked back at her, his eyes wide.

"Answer it," she told him. "They'll break the door down if you don't."

Vali opened the door. Two men stood outside: one in uniform, the other not. Ines remembered the one in his own clothes from earlier. He'd been in the back seat of the car.

"Vali Florescu?" the man asked.

Vali nodded. "That's me."

"We need to talk to you."

"Am I under arrest?"

"We need you to come to the station for questioning."

"So I'm not under arrest?"

"Don't be funny with us, lad. Cooperate, and I won't arrest you. But if you give me trouble..."

"It's OK, I'll come with you." Vali looked back at Ines. She stepped back into the bedroom and grabbed his jacket. She walked straight back out and thrust it into his hand.

The police detective looked past Vali, at her. "What are you doing here?"

"Vali's my friend. He..."

The man looked back at Vali. "Were you with her, when she found the bodies?"

Vali met the man's gaze. "Yes."

The man looked back at Ines. "You told us you were alone."

Ines said nothing. She still didn't know why Vali hadn't wanted her to tell them. But now they knew.

The man sighed. "You leave me no choice."

"Sorry," she whispered. "I'll go back to that hotel. It was—"

He nodded at his colleague, who put a hand on her arm.

"Vali Florescu, Ines Perez, I'm arresting you both for conspiracy to pervert the course of justice."

CHAPTER FOURTEEN

DETECTIVE INSPECTOR ZOE FINCH parked her beloved green Mini outside her terraced house in Birmingham. She'd been back from Dorset for just over a week, back at work for the same amount of time. But Lesley's case still preyed on her mind.

She'd seen the reports: a Dorset journalist had gone missing. She knew that journalist was Sadie Dawes, the woman she'd been supposed to meet on the clifftop at Swanage just over a week ago. It was Zoe who'd reported Sadie's disappearance to Lesley. But then Lesley had spoken to Sadie's boss who'd told her the journalist was on holiday. They'd been told to drop it.

But now, it seemed Sadie hadn't returned from her holiday. Where had she been for the past week?

And did it have anything to do with Zoe finding the woman's scarf not far from where they'd been due to meet?

Zoe had been assigned a fraud case, the kind of job that her team found dull as a puddle. But it appealed to the document nerd in Zoe. She loved sifting through files, finding evidence hidden in text and numbers. She was hoping for a breakthrough in this one soon.

She closed the car door and shrugged her shoulders, trying to shake out tension. The house would be empty; Nicholas was at university and her lodger Sacha had graduated. She hadn't taken the time to advertise for a new lodger for this academic year, and was missing having young people around.

She opened the front door to find her cat waiting on the doormat. Miaowing. Zoe gathered her up and tickled her between the ears.

"You waiting for me, Yoda? You want some biccies?"

Yoda miaowed again in response.

Zoe heard the sound of an engine from behind her. She turned to see the road devoid of movement. This street was lined with terraced houses and parking was difficult, but most of the households didn't have cars, and the ones that did rarely used them. The university was only a five-minute walk away.

She took a long breath and placed Yoda back down on the mat.

"Come on, then."

She caught movement out of the corner of her eye and turned again. The street was quiet. Was she imagining things?

She stood in the doorway, staring out at the street, controlling her breathing.

"Hello?" she said.

Nothing.

She scanned the front gardens of the neighbouring houses. They were separated by low hedges or walls, nothing big enough to hide behind. The house next door, occupied by

students who treated her like their mum, had no barrier sepa-
rating it from hers. On the other side, two low hedges separated her house from the next one and the one after it.

She squinted. Somebody was behind the hedge two
doors up.

"Hello?" she called out. "Are you OK?"

No answer.

She was being paranoid. That hedge was low, nobody
could fit behind it.

Stop being daft, she told herself.

She looked down at Yoda, who was rubbing against
her leg.

"Your mum's going doolally. I really need to get a lodger."

"Miaow."

Zoe smiled.

She scooted the cat into the house with her foot and
closed the door behind her, resisting the urge to peer out as
she did so. She needed to stop being so melodramatic.

CHAPTER FIFTEEN

Ines glanced at the solicitor she'd been assigned as the two detectives entered the room. The man, the one who'd arrested her, frowned as he sat. The woman gave Ines a faint smile and took the chair next to him. The man was about the same age as her dad, wearing a brown tweed jacket and a crumpled expression. The woman wore a navy suit and was trying not to yawn. Ines had been here for almost two hours and it was getting late. She wondered where Vali was.

Ines's solicitor, Ms Thomson, reached out and gave her hand a squeeze. Ines gave her a tight smile in return. She'd never had contact with the police before, not at home in Spain, not here in the UK. She was scared.

She swallowed as they arranged themselves opposite her. She ran her hands down her skirt, determined not to let them shake. She realised she was slouching. Talking silently to herself, she forced herself to sit up straight.

"Don't worry, Ines. You haven't done anything wrong." That's what the solicitor had said to her before they'd come in. Leanne Thomson, her name was, only a few years older

than Ines by the look of her. Her suit had a stain on the lapel
and her shoes were scuffed. She'd been sent by the housekeeping company, but she didn't look like she used their
services.

The male detective cleared his throat.

"For the benefit of the tape, I'm Detective Sergeant
Frampton. I'll be leading this interview."

He looked at his colleague.

"Police Constable Abbott," she said.

Ines knew that police constables in this country wore
uniforms. This woman was wearing a suit, a cheap one, but a
suit nonetheless. Had she misheard, or were they just short of
staff?

"Leanne Thomson, Ines's lawyer," the lawyer said after
clearing her throat. The male detective looked her up and
down.

"Ines Perez," said Ines, relieved that her voice didn't
break on the words.

"Thank you." The sergeant nodded at her. "We want to
ask you some questions about Sunday night, and also about
the statement that you made to me and my colleague DCI
Clarke afterwards. When we spoke to you outside your
former employer's home."

Ines gritted her teeth.

Why had she lied? Why had she listened to Vali, and not
told them the truth? Lying to the police could get you thrown
in prison. It was the same in Spain, it would be here. Even if
they didn't put her in jail, she'd be sent back to Spain. The
humiliation of going back to her family and telling them
she'd been kicked out by the police. What would her
mum say?

"Can you run us through the events of Sunday night?"

the man asked. "Tell us what happened from when you met Vali Florescu?"

Ines pulled in a breath. "I met him in a pub in Bournemouth, we'd arranged to see each other for a drink."

"Were you planning on going back to the house afterwards?"

"Not until later on. Vali didn't know that Susannah was away, she'd only gone that morning." She paused. "That's what I thought."

Ines felt her shoulders slump. Had Susannah been killed before she'd had a chance to leave for Verbier, or had she changed her plans?

"Where was this pub?" the man asked.

"Richmond Hill," replied Ines.

"Was it busy?"

"Yes."

"Will people have remembered seeing you there, do you think?"

She shrugged. "Vali bought drinks, we only had one." She felt her cheeks flush. "We don't have a lot of money, you see. We're good at making it stretch out for the evening."

The female constable smiled at her. "Don't worry. Just tell us what happened."

The man shifted in his chair.

"I met him at eight. We had a drink. We were there for..." Ines tried to remember. "An hour and a half, maybe an hour and three quarters," she continued. "We went outside. We went for a walk through the park, to see the illuminations. They are one of my favourite things about Bournemouth. Sorry."

"That's alright," the man said. "You just tell us what you remember, any information might be relevant."

She looked at him, her chest tight. "Yes."

"So what time did you leave the pub?" he asked her.

"About half past nine. Maybe a little later."

"And how long was your walk?" the woman asked.

"It was cold, so not long. Ten, fifteen minutes maybe?"

"Where did you walk to?" said the man.

"Just through the gardens, towards the beach and back again."

He nodded. The female police officer was making notes, barely looking at Ines as she wrote.

"At what time did you decide to go over to the house?" he asked.

"Like I said, it was cold. We were walking, chatting." She paused, feeling her cheeks warm. "Kissing. I thought it might be a good idea to take Vali back to the house."

"Had you planned to do that before you met up with him that evening?" the man asked.

"No. Well, maybe. No."

The woman looked up and gave her a smile. "It's OK, you're allowed to take a boy back to your house."

Ines looked at her. *Not when you work for Susannah Ramsay*, she thought. She could only imagine how her boss would have reacted if she had found Vali there.

"Did you take a taxi?" the man asked.

"The bus."

"Which bus?"

"The Breezer. Number 50," Ines replied. "It goes over the ferry to Swanage."

"We know it. Where did you get off?"

"At the roundabout where the road splits for the ferry."

The woman looked up. "You didn't go to the stop nearest the house?"

"No."

"Why not?" asked the man.

She glanced at her solicitor, who nodded.

"I wanted to check no lights were on. Just in case."

"You thought Ms Ramsay might have been at home?"

"No. But I wanted to be sure."

He frowned and pushed his glasses up his nose. "And you walked straight to the house?"

"Yes."

"Did anybody else get off the bus at the same time as you?"

"No, the bus was quiet."

"How many people were there on the bus?" the female officer asked.

Ines blinked at her. "Four or five, maybe? We sat upstairs at the front, for the views."

"Do you think people will remember you?" said the man.

"I don't know," Ines replied. "Nothing happened that would make them remember us."

They didn't believe her. She couldn't give them proof that she'd been in the pub or on the bus. And she'd lied...

While she'd been out at that pub, somebody had been in the house, murdering Susannah. What would have happened if she'd come home earlier, if she hadn't gone out? If she hadn't been with Vali?

She shivered and glanced at her lawyer, who was gazing at her phone. Was the woman going to speak?

Ines cleared her throat. "Umm..."

The lawyer looked up. "Are you OK?"

Ines shook her head.

The lawyer turned to the detectives. "We need a short break. My client is clearly finding this difficult."

"We can take a break in a moment," the man replied. "Tell me which route you took to get to the house from the bus stop. The road, or the beach?"

Ines waited, but the lawyer said nothing.

"The road, or the beach?" the detective repeated.

"Banks Road," she said. "It only took five minutes, if that."

"And which entrance did you use to enter the house?"

"The front door. I have all the keys."

"Which rooms did you go into?"

Ines closed her eyes, remembering. She could see the moonlight on the furniture as she'd walked through the house with Vali.

"We went into the living room first. I wanted to show him the house." She felt embarrassed. "My job is to look after that house. I sometimes feel almost like it's mine. I care for it, cared for it, like it was my own."

She wouldn't be doing that anymore.

Or would she have to clean up the blood? Would she get the chance?

She felt her stomach dip.

"I showed Vali the downstairs and then I took him upstairs." Ines's voice was shaking. The rest of the story, she'd told them. Vali had done nothing, he'd just been there with her.

Ines nudged her lawyer, who flinched then looked up.

"My client is young and it's late," she said. "She needs a break. Give us five minutes and then we can reconvene."

Ines sighed with relief as the male detective switched off the recording machine.

CHAPTER SIXTEEN

DCI MACKIE HAD LIVED in a squat red brick bungalow on the edge of Lychett Minster. Lesley rang the doorbell and surveyed the tidy front garden while she waited for the man's widow to appear.

A few moments later, a smiling woman opened the door. "You must be DCI Clarke."

Lesley frowned. "How do you know?"

"Dennis Frampton described you to me."

"Am I that easily recognisable?"

The woman laughed.

"Sorry, I'm probably being a bit rude, aren't I? Come in."

Lesley followed the woman in. The hallway was narrow, leading into a cosy living room at the back of the house.

"I presume this is about Tim?" Mrs Mackie asked.

"Indirectly," Lesley said. "I'm working on a missing persons case."

Mrs Mackie frowned. "Who? Not one of his team?"

Lesley smiled. This woman's husband had died after retiring from the police force, and still she was worried about the team he had headed up. She wondered how well she'd known Dennis, and what her relationship had been with Johnny and Mike.

"Take a seat." Mrs Mackie checked her watch. "I was about to pour myself a glass of wine, if you'd like one..."

"No thanks." Lesley raised an eyebrow. "Still on duty."

"At seven o'clock at night? You all work too hard. How about a coffee?"

"Perfect. White with one sugar, please."

Lesley didn't dare drink wine, not having eaten since a snatched bowl of cornflakes at Elsa's that morning. Her blood sugar was dropping and she could feel irritability kicking in.

She rummaged in her bag, hoping she'd left a snack in there yesterday. She needed to get herself organised.

Empty. She sighed and walked to the window. The house looked out over fields, but all she could see was the back garden. A security light came on, illuminating a fox which stopped in its tracks and turned to look at the house. Lesley watched as it edged slowly away and disappeared into the shadows.

She turned as Mrs Mackie came back into the room, carrying a tray with two mugs and a tin of biscuits. Lesley felt her shoulders relax.

"I decided it was a bit antisocial to be drinking when you're on the coffee." She opened the tin and placed it on the coffee table. "Help yourself."

"If you don't mind?"

"I wouldn't have brought them in if I didn't want you to have one, would I? Tim was rubbish at eating when he was working, came home starving every night." She smiled, then her eyes glazed over. She balled her fist and brought it to her mouth, then sniffed and looked at Lesley. "Please. I like feeding people. Reminds me of when the kids were still at home."

"Thanks." Lesley took the armchair nearest her. She leaned over and grabbed three biscuits, then dunked the first into her coffee.

Mrs Mackie sat on the sofa and took the other mug.

Lesley nibbled on the rich tea biscuit that she'd just pulled out of her mug.

"You and DCI Mackie had children?"

"Yes. And please, I'm Gwen and he was Tim. I know that's what Dennis called him."

"Really?"

"They were good friends. I'm surprised you're here, to be honest, instead of him."

"I'm the senior member of the team."

"And you worry Dennis would find this too difficult. I understand." Gwen slurped her tea. "Oh hang it, I need a drink. Wait a moment."

She rose and left the room. After a moment she returned with a glass of red wine. She sipped it and closed her eyes.

"That's better." She caught Lesley watching her. "I'm not some sort of alcoholic, don't worry. But some days, well some days are harder than others."

"And today was one of those days."

Gwen nodded and took another sip.

"Any specific reason?" Lesley asked.

"No. It just hits you occasionally, that's all." She put down her glass. "Now, I'm sure you have a home to get back to and a husband waiting for you, so why don't I let you ask me whatever it is you came for?"

Lesley considered correcting the woman, then decided it wasn't relevant that she had a girlfriend and not a husband.

Terry was still legally her husband anyway, at least for a few more weeks.

"How old are your children?" she asked.

"David's thirty-six, he works in London. Sheena's thirty-four, she has a job in a care home in Poole, and then Bobby, he's the little one, only twenty-eight."

Lesley smiled. *Only twenty-eight.* Her own daughter Sharon was sixteen, she couldn't imagine her at twenty-eight.

"So," she said, "this missing persons case."

Gwen leaned forward in her chair. "Sorry, yes. You wanted to ask me about it. Was it something Tim was working on?"

"Did a woman called Sadie Dawes come and see you just over a week ago?" Lesley asked.

Gwen nodded, a frown knotting her brow.

"Young woman, a reporter. Blonde, skinny. A bit brash for me. She was asking about Tim."

"What sort of questions was she asking?" Lesley said.

Gwen's body language had changed. Her muscles were taut and her mouth thin.

"I'm not sure I should..."

Lesley gave her the most reassuring smile she could manage.

"I'm new to the team," she said. "I've been looking into DCI M— Tim's death, wondering if he really killed himself." She cocked her head. "I gather Sadie was thinking much the same thing."

Gwen blinked back at her. "You mean you agree with me?"

Lesley said nothing. Zoe had told her about Gwen Mackie's theory, but she'd wondered if it was simply wishful thinking.

"I don't believe he killed himself." Gwen took another gulp of the wine. "Tim was happy, he'd booked that cruise. We were looking forward to his retirement. I couldn't wait to spend more time with him."

Lesley wondered whether she and Elsa would be like that one day. She allowed herself a small smile.

"So, you don't think your husband committed suicide?"

Gwen placed her hands between her knees and squeezed her legs together.

"It just wasn't like him. He attended three suicides while he was on the force, and each one of them cut him up. He thought it was horrendous that people would leave that kind of trauma behind for somebody else to deal with." She looked into Lesley's eyes. "Tim would never have done something like that."

Lesley took another sip of her coffee. It would keep her awake, but right now, that was what she needed.

"Was there anything else to make you doubt the coroner's verdict?" she asked. "Other than your husband's mood?"

Gwen looked down, her face dark. "The coroner's report."

"Yes?" Lesley leaned towards her.

"I believe... I believe that pressure was applied."

"What makes you think that?" Lesley asked.

Glenn swallowed. "Superintendent Carpenter. The coroner was a friend of his." She looked up. "Freemasons."

Lesley had to work to stop her jaw from dropping open.

The Freemasons had been an influence in West Midlands Police Force around the time she'd begun her career. She'd assumed that kind of thing was history.

"Anthony Carpenter is a Freemason?" she asked.

Gwen nodded, her eyes bright.

"That's what Tim told me."

"How did your husband know?" Lesley asked. "Was *he*?"

"No, never. That wasn't his kind of thing. Tim didn't like those sort of clubs, funny handshakes, trousers over the knee, nursery rhymes, all that kind of thing. He thought it was just little boys playing dress-up." She hesitated. "Very powerful little boys."

"So, who was the coroner?" Lesley asked.

"Frank Howarth," Gwen replied. "He was a friend of your superintendent's."

"Is he still working as a coroner?"

Gwen shrugged. "I don't know, sorry."

Lesley would be able to find that out.

"I'm sorry, Gwen. But do you have concrete grounds to believe that Howarth deliberately tampered with or falsified the report on your husband's death?"

Gwen pursed her lips.

"Not concrete, no. But I know what they're like, those masons. They pull together when something bad happens, they protect each other."

"You think that Superintendent Carpenter needed protecting?"

Gwen hunched into herself.

This couldn't be easy for her. Or was there something she wasn't prepared to say?

"Was there anyone else in the force who might have been involved in this? Any of Tim's colleagues?"

Gwen looked away. "No." She blinked. "No, just Carpenter."

Lesley narrowed her eyes. There was something else, she was sure of it. Something Gwen wasn't saying.

"Anything you tell me will be confidential," she said.

"I know." Gwen licked her lips. She was shaking. "I could be wrong," she said. "It's just conjecture. But..." She looked into Lesley's face. "... I'm positive Tim didn't do that to himself. I believe somebody pushed my husband off that cliff. And your boss wanted to hide the fact."

CHAPTER SEVENTEEN

LESLEY'S NERVES were on edge as she drove home. She flinched when her phone rang, then relaxed when she saw the name onscreen: Sharon.

"Hi, love. How's things?"

"Hi, Mum. Dramatic."

"Dramatic how? What's happened?"

"It's OK. You don't need to worry. I'm fine."

No matter how many times Sharon told Lesley not to worry, she always did. Despite Sharon's fortnightly trips to Dorset, the fact that she was normally a hundred and seventy miles away in Birmingham meant that Lesley could never fully relax.

"What's happened?" she asked.

"It's Dad."

Lesley felt her body slump. "What's he done now?"

"He hasn't *done* anything. His girlfriend's dumped him."

"Julieta's dumped him?"

"She moved all of her stuff out yesterday, took the brat with her too."

The brat was the woman's little boy. He'd irritated Sharon at first, but she'd grown fond of him.

"I'm sorry, sweetheart."

"House feels quiet. Dad's been working long hours."

I bet he has, Lesley thought. Both of them had worked long hours when they'd been together, their way of avoiding each other.

"Do you want me to come up?" she asked.

"You're busy. What are you working on now?"

"A murder in Sandbanks. Do you remember that posh area I showed you?"

"Millionaire's row. Who was the victim?"

"A millionaire, believe it or not."

Sharon laughed. "Sorry. It's not funny, is it?"

"Not really," Lesley said. "But if we can't see the funny side sometimes, we'd go mad, wouldn't we?"

"Guess so. Anyway, I just wanted to tell you what was happening in case Dad calls you."

"That's OK, love."

Lesley hesitated at a roundabout, trying to remember where she was going.

"Chat to me while I drive home, tell me what you've been doing. How's sixth form going?"

"It's fine, Mum. It's boring. I don't want to talk about it."

"OK. So what happened with your dad and Julieta?"

"That trip to Spain they had last month, when I was down with you. I don't think her family approved of him."

Lesley identified the turn she needed and glanced in the rear-view mirror. A car was behind her, its headlights bright. *Alright, be patient.*

"In what way didn't they approve of him?" she asked.

"I don't know," Sharon replied. "But things seem to have

gone downhill from there. They were having arguments, Sammy was crying."

"Poor kid. Where's she living now? Will you keep in touch with her?"

Lesley felt weird encouraging her daughter to stay in contact with the woman who'd attempted to replace her. But once she'd got over her resentment at Julieta's affair with Terry, Lesley had learned to like her. And her son had been good for Sharon.

"Not sure, Mum," Sharon said. "Feels disloyal to you."

"You're not disloyal, love. If you want to spend time with her or her son, you do that. Don't worry about me."

"I do though, Mum. I worry that you're OK down there in Dorset."

"I'm fine." Lesley swallowed. "Have you changed your mind about me staying down here?"

"No. No, in fact I wanted to talk to you about that."

"OK." Lesley turned onto the A3049 towards Bournemouth.

"It's OK," Sharon continued. "We can talk about it at the weekend. I'll get the train straight after school on Friday, yeah?"

"Looking forward to it," Lesley said. "I'll see you then."

"Yeah. Thanks, Mum."

"No problem, Sharon. You look after yourself, call me if you need to chat. It doesn't matter what case I'm working, I'm always here."

"OK."

"Love you." Lesley hung up, her chest tight.

CHAPTER EIGHTEEN

As Lesley was getting out of her car the next morning, she noticed Mike pull up not far away. She paused near the doors to Police HQ, waiting for him to catch up.

Mike got out of the driver's side of his car, closed the door, then stood by the car staring into space. Lesley watched him, wondering what he was thinking about.

The passenger door opened and Tina got out. Lesley watched as she spoke to Mike across the car, both of them facing away from the building.

Lesley took a step backwards.

She'd been observing the two of them together over the past week or two, and this wasn't a surprise. Still, it could cause problems further down the line.

She approached them.

"Morning, both."

Tina turned, her face red. Lesley smiled.

"It's alright, Tina. I wasn't born yesterday."

Tina reddened even further.

"Boss," she said.

Lesley gestured for the two of them to follow her inside.

"Tina, how's the Ramsay case progressing? Any ID on the second victim yet?"

"Not yet, boss. We've got two suspects, though. One's the housekeeper."

"I heard about that. You've interviewed them?"

"Her, yes. We're interviewing him first thing, we had to wait for a solicitor."

"Make sure you get what you can within the twenty-four-hour window."

"Boss."

They reached the door to the building. Lesley held it open and waited for the two constables to enter. Tina went first, sharing a glance with Mike as she did so. Lesley suppressed a smile.

"I know I'm working this missing person case with Mike," she said, "but I expect you and Dennis to keep me updated."

"Of course, boss," Tina replied.

"When will you know the results of the detective's exam?"

"Friday."

"Good luck." Lesley crossed her fingers. "I'm rooting for you."

The lift doors opened. Tina and Mike hung back, waiting for Lesley to enter first. They stood in silence as the lift ascended, the air thick with tension.

The doors opened. Lesley extended a hand to keep them from closing, and turned to her colleagues.

"I've got no problem with the two of you having a relationship. It's not as if you're the first. But all I can say is that if things don't work out, I need you to be professional. I won't have two of my team falling out."

"I think that's a little premature," said Mike.

Lesley raised an eyebrow. "Is it? Good." She let go of the doors and led the two of them to the office. She could sense them itching to speak to each other.

As they approached, she could see Dennis already sitting at his desk. Lesley pushed open the door. Tina's jaw tightened and Mike clenched his fists.

Lesley looked at the DS. No, she wasn't about to tell him.

She gave Tina a wink and walked through to her office, feeling the tension dissipate as she moved further away.

CHAPTER NINETEEN

DENNIS SAT with Tina beside him at the interview table, looking across at Vali Florescu. The young man hadn't had his own solicitor, so they'd been forced to wait overnight for the duty solicitor. She was rifling through her notes, looking down at the table. Vali was staring into his lap, where his hands were balled in fists.

"So," Dennis began, the formalities out of the way, "tell us about your relationship with Ines Perez."

Vali shuffled in his chair but didn't look up.

"She's just a girl I know. I met her in a bar in Bournemouth about five weeks ago."

"Is she your girlfriend?" Tina asked.

Dennis flinched. He'd told Tina not to ask questions. She hadn't passed the detective's exam yet.

Vali looked across at Tina.

"I suppose she is, yes."

His English was heavily accented, but his grammar was impeccable.

"What are you studying?" Dennis asked.

"Architecture," Vali replied, "and English." He looked into Dennis's eyes. "Of course."

Dennis nodded.

"How long have you been at Bournemouth University?"

A shrug.

"Since September, beginning of this academic year. I came over from Romania in August, tried to find myself a job." His gaze hardened. "But nobody would employ me. Stupid Romanian boy with a nasty accent and background that your people don't like."

Dennis bristled. It wasn't his fault that Vali had experienced discrimination.

"Tell me about what happened on Sunday night," he said.

Vali turned to look at his solicitor, who nodded. He turned back to Dennis.

"I was with Ines," he said. "She brought me back to the house, we wanted to spend time together, hang out. You know the kind of thing."

He gave Dennis a conspiratorial look. Dennis felt his lip curl.

"What time did you arrive at the house?" he asked.

Another shrug.

"Ten, ten-thirty."

"Did you check the time?"

Vali held out his wrist. "I don't have a watch. See?"

"How do you get to your lectures on time?" Tina asked.

"I use my phone."

Dennis sighed.

"OK, so did you check the time on your phone when you arrived at Ms Ramsay's house?"

Vali shook his head and smiled. "No. I was distracted. Ines has that effect on me."

Dennis felt a muscle in his face twitch.

"Tell me what happened after you entered the house."

Vali nodded.

"We went into the living room, she wanted to show me. She looks after the place, she was proud. It's big, huge. I was impressed."

"Did Ines take you to her bedroom?" Tina asked.

Vali looked at her.

"Not straight away."

"Where did you go next?" Dennis asked.

"We left the living room, went upstairs. Ines wanted to take me to her room. She said it had beautiful views. The sea, the trees."

Dennis swallowed. The bedrooms did indeed have beautiful views. The view inside the master bedroom right now wasn't quite so beautiful.

"So that was the first room you went into upstairs?" he asked.

"We went into her mistresses' bedroom. It was the first."

"Why?"

"I wanted to see." He shrugged. "I don't know why."

"Was the door to the room open when you reached the top of the stairs?"

"No. I opened it."

"Not Ines?"

"She didn't want to go in. I shouldn't have done that. It was her house."

"Not her house," Dennis corrected.

"Where are you going with this?" the solicitor asked.

"We found your client's prints on the door handle," Dennis said.

"And now you know why." She looked at Dennis. "My client isn't denying being in the property."

"No. But his girlfriend did lie about it." Dennis looked at Vali. "Did you ask her to lie for you?"

"I didn't ask her to lie. I just asked her not to mention me."

The solicitor tensed.

"Why?" asked Dennis.

"Because I know what you are like. I was arrested eight weeks ago, marijuana, personal use. You gave me a caution. But I know that you assume a man like me shouldn't be in house with two dead bodies."

"We're just trying to get to the truth," Dennis said.

"My client has already admitted to being in the building. There's a perfectly legitimate reason for his prints being on the handle."

"So you'd never been in that house before?" Dennis asked, ignoring the solicitor.

"Never."

Dennis tapped his pen on the table. "Very well. So you opened the door. At what point did you notice the bodies?"

Vali's face darkened.

"Not immediately, it was dark. There was some light shining into the bedroom, but there are trees at the back. Privacy, Ines tells me. We walked in and then we saw them."

"Describe to me what happened."

"There was a shape on the bed. We couldn't see clearly, it was too dark. We turned on the light, and then we saw her. A woman on the bed. Man on the floor, young man. Asian.

Ines said she did not know him. I think he was the mistress's boyfriend, maybe?"

"Possibly," Dennis replied. They still didn't know. "What did you do then?"

"I wanted to check on Susannah, to feel if she had pulse. Ines said not to. Sensible not to leave prints, not to *contaminate the evidence.*" Vali raised his hands in mock quotation marks. "She's right. I watch *CSI*, I know how it works."

Dennis looked at the young man. He was too calm, too confident. He didn't seem distressed by what he'd seen, or by the situation he found himself in.

"How did you feel when you saw those bodies?" he asked.

"Surprise. Shock. Ines was upset. I feel sympathy for her, but I did not know Susannah and her friend. It's difficult to feel sad for them."

He leaned forward.

"I come from a country where lots of people died. Brutal government, parents separated from children. When you live through that, you become hard."

Tina shifted in her chair.

"So why didn't you come forward?" Dennis asked. "Why didn't Ines tell us that she wasn't alone when she found the bodies?"

Vali lifted his chin.

"It is not Ines's fault, is my fault. All of it."

"How?" Dennis asked.

"I asked her not to tell."

"Why did you do that? Surely you would know that we would eventually find out you'd been there."

"I hoped you wouldn't. I am a Romanian student, I have

temporary visa. I have historical problems with the authorities in my country."

"What kind of problems?" Tina asked.

"I criticised them in my blog, they don't like that."

Dennis frowned.

"I don't see what your situation in Romania has to do with lying to the police about being at a crime scene?"

The man shrugged.

"I do not want to go back to Romania, I want to stay here after I finish my studies. Being involved with police would not help."

Dennis looked at him. *Being involved with police* was an understatement. Right now, this man was the number one suspect in a double murder enquiry.

"How do you explain your fingerprints being on the bedside table near the bed?"

"I don't know. I don't remember everything."

"Did you step in the blood?" Tina asked.

A firm shake of the head.

"No, I was careful. I checked. Ines did not step in blood either."

"Good," Dennis said.

The young man was right, the blood hadn't been disturbed. Dennis looked back at him.

"Had you ever been to the house before that evening?"

"Never. Ines did not want me there when mistress was there. You can understand why."

"Enlighten me."

"She was worried she would lose her job, of course. What else?"

"So had you ever had contact with Susannah Ramsay before the night when you found her dead?"

"No, nothing. Ines only told me her name that night."

"And does her name mean anything to you?"

"No, she's just anonymous rich English woman like so many others. We have people like her in Romania. Not so many, but worse."

Dennis gritted his teeth. All they had was this man's fingerprints at the crime scene, and now he was admitting to having been there. But he'd lied. Or at least, he'd persuaded his girlfriend to lie for him.

The lawyer lifted her head.

"You've got no grounds to detain my client," she said. "He's freely admitting that he was at the house on the night of the murder."

"He lied," Dennis replied.

"No, he didn't," she said. "His girlfriend lied for him. I suggest you speak to her instead."

CHAPTER TWENTY

MIKE GAZED around the studios as he was led through to see Matt Crippins, Sadie's producer. On TV this place looked spacious and open, but in real life it was small, cramped and dingy. Without the studio lights and the wide camera angle, he could see that in the flesh, it was a third its apparent size.

Not that Mike watched TV news: this was the twenty-first century after all. But when he went round to his mum's house, she always had it on in the background. BBC night and day, like a constant friend.

The young assistant ushered him through to a tiny office filled with paperwork, and with screens lining one of the walls. Matt Crippins sat at a desk facing that wall. It was strewn with documents, equipment that Mike didn't recognise, and cups of tea that looked like they might explode if Crippins tried to drink from them. The young woman closed the door with a friendly smile. Matt Crippins turned in his chair. His smile dropped when he recognised Mike.

"You're here about Sadie?"

"I want to know more about her movements in the days before she disappeared."

"Of course."

Matt looked back at his desk. He frowned and then swept some paperwork to one side.

"I'll sit on the desk, you take my chair."

"Is there anywhere better we can talk?" Mike asked.

"I'd take you down to the canteen, but..." Matt shook his head. "It's very public."

He rubbed an eye. It was red.

"How are your team reacting to her disappearance?" Mike asked.

A shrug.

"Not good. We're hoping she'll turn up sometime. Maybe she's gone undercover."

"Was that like Sadie?"

Matt gave Mike a look.

"You know what she's like. Tenacious. Persistent. But she's always squared it with me before she's gone off the radar."

"Even when she hired a boat and came over to Brownsea Island in the middle of a murder investigation?" Mike asked.

Matt pursed his lips.

"Yes, as a matter of fact," he said. "I approved her investigating further, your lot were hiding details of that case from us. But the boat was her idea. These things cost money, you know."

Mike resisted the urge to ask about the BBC interfering with a police investigation. This, he knew, really wasn't the time or place. Matt heaved himself onto the desk and pushed the chair towards Mike. Mike reluctantly took it, finding himself a good foot lower than the other man.

"Can you tell me what she was working on before she disappeared?"

"She was following the threatened strike at the glassworks in Beaminster."

"What did that involve?"

"It was a straightforward one. Camping out outside the place waiting for somebody to come out, trying to get a quote. She would have been one of a few reporters there."

"Did she have an advantage because she was BBC?"

Matt smiled. "Sadie never had an advantage because of who she worked for, or where she worked. She had an advantage because she was Sadie, and she didn't take no for an answer. She got us the goods alright."

"So, she was booked on a holiday to Malta last week," Mike said, "And you thought she'd gone?"

Matt reddened. "I spoke to the airline, they told me she was on the plane. I've since discovered that was wrong."

"How can they get that kind of thing wrong?"

"Computer glitch."

"Which airline was it?"

"FastJet."

"From where?"

"Bristol."

"And they told you it was a computer glitch?"

A shrug.

Mike frowned. For an airline, knowing who was on which flight was an obsession. It was basic security.

"So, before she was due to go on holiday, did she have any meetings lined up? Anybody unsavoury she was due to meet?"

Matt laughed. "Which kind of unsavoury?"

"You tell me."

"OK. So, there was a trade union official at the glass-works, and two of the directors there. Local residents' association in Christchurch, complaining about changes to the waste disposal plant."

"Is there anything else in Sadie's life that might have put her at risk?" Mike asked. "Personal life, boyfriend, ex-boyfriend? Anybody she'd fallen out with?"

"Sadie doesn't have a personal life," Matt replied. "She lives for the job. I'm not aware of her ever having had a boyfriend."

Mike made a note. No official boyfriend didn't mean there hadn't been encounters that might have put her at risk.

"Who are her friends, people on the staff here I might talk to?"

"She doesn't really socialise, but yeah, you can talk to them. I'll get you a list of names."

"Thanks," said Mike.

Matt leaned forwards and down, bringing his face closer to Mike's.

"You find her for me, will you? Find our Sadie."

CHAPTER TWENTY-ONE

LESLEY KNEW this was a call she should have made a few days ago.

She waited as it rang out, and then a familiar Scottish voice answered.

"Petra," she began. "Did you get those files I sent you?"

"Well, hello to you, too. We're no' doing the niceties these days?"

Lesley clenched her jaw. "Sorry, Petra. How are you?"

"I'm just dandy, thank you. And how are you?"

"Fine. Busy."

Dr Petra McBride, psychologist and criminal profiler, laughed. A long, deep-throated laugh that sounded as if it had taken years to perfect.

"I guessed as much. And yes, I got those files. You'll be wanting to know if I've looked at them too, I imagine."

"Well, yes."

Petra had been challenging when she'd been down here helping them on the Paul Watson case. It seemed that over the phone, she was no easier.

"So, this suicide note of DCI Mackie's," Petra said. "Good name by the way. What was a man with a solid name like that doing working in Dorset?"

"No idea," replied Lesley.

"Fair enough. Anyhow, this suicide note, you've had graphologists look at it?"

"That's what the CSIs tell me."

"And they confirmed it was his writing?"

"They did."

"Did they compare the line quality and the pen pressure?"

"I read the report," Lesley said. "I can't remember the details, but I know that Gail was happy with it."

"Gail's your crime scene manager?"

"She is."

"Is she good?"

"Very good," Lesley replied.

It was Gail who had alerted Lesley to her own suspicions around DCI Mackie's death in the first place.

"So," she continued, "is there anything in the suicide note that gives you a clue as to his state of mind before his death?"

"Well, it is a suicide note after all," said Petra. "So there's not a huge amount to work with."

"No?"

"Are you sure he wrote it?"

"The graphologists," Lesley replied. "Yes, we are sure."

"That's not what I meant. Are you sure he *composed* it?"

"What do you mean, composed?"

"It's in his handwriting, but somebody else might have told him what to write."

"You think that's possible?"

"I wouldnae like to say, but if I had some more samples of his writing, I might be able to hazard a guess from his style."

"Just a guess?"

"Ach, that's a figure of speech. I don't do guesses. What d'you think I am, some sort of quack?"

Lesley left that question unanswered. "You can tell who somebody is from their writing style?"

Another of those deep laughs.

"We're clever, us psychologists, you know. We know how the human brain works."

"Sorry," said Lesley. "Of course you do."

Petra laughed. "It's OK, I'm used to people treating me like some sort of magician."

Lesley smiled. "What kind of writing do you need? I probably have access to case files that he made notes on."

"Nah, that's not good enough. I need personal writing. Letters, diaries, more natural writing."

"I'll see what I can do. Would you like to take a look at anything I do find?"

"Are you payin' me?"

Lesley swallowed. "This investigation is unofficial."

Another laugh. "I get it. Consider it a favour. I like you. Just as long as you don't ask me down there, I've got a trip planned."

"Anywhere nice?" Lesley asked.

"You could say that. New York. I'm meeting some— sorry, you don't need to know about my personal life."

"No." Lesley was intrigued, but knew better than to pry. "I'll see what I can find and send it to you."

"OK. Good luck with that team of yours."

Lesley frowned. Did she need luck?

"Thanks," she replied, uneasy.

CHAPTER TWENTY-TWO

"So, what did you think, Sarge?" Tina asked as Dennis pushed open the door to the office.

He shrugged. "Well, he certainly had a reason to be in the house."

"But he didn't tell us."

"No."

Dennis peeled off his jacket and placed it carefully over the back of his chair. He put a hand on it. His shoulders felt tight.

The chairs in the interview room were low and uncomfortable. The older he got, the more he felt it.

He turned to Tina. "I want to know why he felt the need to make his girlfriend lie to us about him being in that house. I want to know why Ines agreed to it. Were they in it together, or did he have to convince her?"

"Are you going to talk to her again?"

"We need to get more background first. I want to know more about the pair of them. What reason would they have to lie?"

Tina nodded.

"Cup of tea?" she asked. "Two sugars?"

"Please."

Tina grabbed her own mug, then took Dennis's. As she did so, the door to the office opened and a young man walked in. He wore a thin smile and a dark blue suit. His hair was immaculately arranged: blond, thick but short.

"Can I help you?" Dennis asked.

The man smiled. "I think you're expecting me."

Dennis glanced at Tina. "Er, sorry?"

"DC Brown. I've been assigned to your team." The man put out a hand. Dennis looked down then shook it. The man's handshake was firm.

DC Brown smiled again. "Call me Stanley."

"You're our extra body," Tina said. "Good."

The man's eyebrows rose. "More than just a body, I hope." He grinned at Tina.

Dennis swallowed his irritation and looked at the mugs Tina was holding.

"I'm DS Frampton. Do you want a drink?" he asked the DC.

Stanley gave Tina a smile, his eyes sparkling. "Black coffee, please. No sugar."

Tina nodded. "I'll find you a mug."

Stanley laughed. "Make it a nice one, yeah? No coffee stains."

"I'll do my best," Tina replied, her body language stiff. She left the room, casting a frown back at the newcomer as she did so.

Stanley looked at Dennis. "So, where do I sit?"

Dennis pointed at Johnny Chiles's desk. "You'll be there."

"What do you want me doing?"

"We're working a double murder enquiry," Dennis said. "Your job is to identify one of the victims."

Stanley rubbed his hands together.

"Sounds like fun, I'm in."

Dennis tensed. Murder enquiries weren't fun, and this man had no choice about whether he was 'in'.

Tina returned with two mugs. "Black coffee, no sugar." She placed a mug with a picture of a pink cat on Stanley's desk. "Two sugars for you, Sarge." She placed his down. "I'll be right back with my own."

"Thanks," Dennis said.

DC Brown picked up his mug, seemingly oblivious to the cat picture. "Thanks, love."

Tina's smile dropped. "Call me Tina. Or PC Abbott."

"PC?"

"I've just taken the detective's exam. Due to hear in a couple of days."

"Ah, good. Well, good luck to you."

Tina said nothing, instead leaving the room.

The newcomer approached Johnny's old chair. He stroked the arm then sat down, shuffling to make himself comfortable. He carried a smart briefcase, which he placed carefully on the desk then snapped open. He took out a notepad and some pens and arranged them on the desk.

"Right," he said. "Point me in the right direction, and I'll identify your victim."

CHAPTER TWENTY-THREE

Ines was in another interview room. They weren't taking her back to a cell, which was something. They'd even returned her mobile to her.

But they weren't letting her go yet. She wasn't sure why.

She sat on the metal chair, staring at the patch of mould climbing up the wall opposite her. She shivered. How long before she was allowed back into the house? Would she ever be allowed back? Would she have to go home now, or would the agency find her another job? She picked up her phone and shifted it from hand to hand.

She knew she should call Bernard, her boss at the agency, ask to be placed with a new employer. But she couldn't face talking about it yet. The image of Susannah spreadeagled on the bed, blood pooling on her chest, crashed into her thoughts every time she closed her eyes. She wondered if she'd ever be able to sleep again.

Her phone rang. She flinched and dropped it on the floor.

She cursed and picked it up. A call from Spain. Ines felt her stomach dip.

"Mamá," she said, trying to sound calm.

"Ines, *querida*, how are you? I haven't heard from you."

"I'm fine, Mamá. You don't need to worry so much."

"Don't be silly. I'm your mother, of course I worry. That woman you work for... Is she kind to you? Does she treat you well?"

Ines drew in a breath.

"She's great, mum. She's hardly ever here, I get the house to myself." She forced a smile. "It's like I'm a millionaire waltzing around in my own beautiful home."

Her mum tutted. "Don't get too used to it, sweetheart. That woman could kick you out any day. I know what they're like, people like her, I worked for them myself when I was in Madrid. You keep your nose clean, keep away from her as much as you can, don't draw attention to yourself."

"It's not like that, Mamá."

A grunt. "You can always come home, you know, if things don't work out."

Ines clenched her teeth. She gripped the side of the chair.

"I'm fine. I've got a great job, I'm living in a beautiful house. You should see it, it's gorgeous."

"Maybe I'll come and visit?"

Ines felt her skin run cold.

"Not yet, Mamá. I'm too busy. Work, yeah?"

Her mother chuckled.

"You're always too busy for me. When are you going to come home for a visit?"

"Soon, I promise."

"We miss you, your Papá too."

Ines closed her eyes. She had a sudden yearning for home. She thought about getting on the next plane and letting them look after her. But going back meant failure. In her village, there were no jobs for young women. And she'd defied her mum to come here.

"I promise, Mamá. I'll come home soon. It's not too long till Christmas."

"It's weeks away. Call me next week, yes? You missed our regular call on Sunday."

"Yes, Mamá." Ines hung up. She realised she was shaking.

CHAPTER TWENTY-FOUR

DENNIS MADE the call before he got into his car. His beige Vauxhall Astra was equipped with hands-free, but he still didn't feel comfortable activating it. Not even when he was stationary in the car park.

"Bournemouth police station, can I help you?"

"I need to speak to DS Bannerman," Dennis said.

He'd had a voicemail message. He hoped it would solve the missing part of the jigsaw.

"Who's calling, please?"

"DS Frampton, Major Crime Investigations Team. He called me about five minutes ago."

"One moment."

He pulled out of the Dorset Police HQ car park as the on-hold music came on. He was already driving towards Bournemouth police station. He preferred to do these things face to face.

"Dennis," came the voice at the end of the line.

"Christopher. How's things?"

"Oh, not too bad. Plodding away." A chuckle. "Pun

intended, of course. But seriously, things are more exciting here than you fancy lot in MCIT might expect."

Dennis clenched his teeth. He and Christopher Bannerman went back a long way. They'd trained together as new CID members. Chris liked to show off; Dennis just wanted to get the job done.

"I hear you've had a woman come into your station about my case," he said.

"You guys work fast, don't you?"

Oh, shut up, Dennis thought.

"Tell me about the woman, please."

A pause.

"OK, if that's how you're going to play it."

Dennis glanced in the rear-view mirror as he turned onto the A35. He wasn't *playing* anything. He just wanted to do his job.

"She's reported her husband as missing, yes?" he asked.

"Yup," came the reply. "Came in about an hour ago."

An hour ago. So why had he only got the call now?

"She says her husband's been missing since Saturday night?"

"That's right."

Saturday night was twenty-four hours before the bodies had been found. So if this was him, where had he been in the meantime?

"What's his name?" Dennis asked. "Description?"

"Ashok Verma. Twenty-eight years old, IC3. Brown skin, brown hair, as you'd expect. He was wearing a grey suit when she last saw him."

Dennis thought back to the crime scene photos. The second victim had been Asian, but then, so were thousands of men. But he had been wearing a grey suit.

"Any distinguishing features?" he asked.

"A birthmark."

"Where?" Dennis didn't remember any birthmark from the photos or from being at the crime scene.

"On his back, low down. Took one of our female PCs about half an hour to get it out of his wife she was so embarrassed. You'd think the poor woman wasn't allowed to look at her husband's arse."

Dennis bristled. "Where is she now?"

"We're supplying her with cups of tea, hanging onto her until you guys drag your sorry backsides over here."

Dennis indicated to turn right into Bournemouth, his heart rate rising. The psychiatrist had told him to avoid stress. As if he could do that in this job. And dealing with Chris Bannerman ramped up the anxiety by about three hundred per cent.

"I'm twenty minutes from your station," he said. "I'd like an interview room reserved so I can talk to this woman. Somewhere she won't feel threatened."

"No problem, Dennis," replied Bannerman.

"Thanks."

Dennis hung up and squinted ahead, trying to focus on the road.

CHAPTER TWENTY-FIVE

THE NEW DC, Stanley, leaned across the desks.

"What's your name again?" he asked.

Tina looked at him. "Tina."

"No, your proper name. The one you give the public."

She frowned. "PC Abbott, but you don't have to call me that."

He smiled and leaned back in his chair. "Nice to meet you, PC Abbott."

"Do you expect me to call you DC Brown?"

"We don't know each other yet."

"Fair enough." She returned to her work. She was writing up the details of the phone conversation she'd had with Vali Florescu's tutor at Bournemouth University. The man was a model student, never in trouble. The tutor had known nothing about the drugs.

"Frampton, he the boss then?"

Tina looked up from her computer. "DS Frampton. Yes. On this case, at least."

"He fair?" DC Brown asked.

"Very fair," she replied. "But the sarge isn't really the boss, it's DCI Clarke. She heads up our team."

"Major Crime Investigations Team," DC Brown said. "Long-winded title."

"It does what it says on the tin."

He raised his eyebrows. "I suppose you could put it like that."

"Anyway," she said, "we've got work to do."

"Hmm," he replied. "Our second victim seems pretty elusive. Can't find anyone matching him on the system."

Tina gripped the edge of her desk. Was he going to need hand-holding?

"Which team did you say you worked in before?" she asked.

"Dorchester CID."

"You work any murder cases?"

"Yes, I'm not completely green, you know."

"Good. Well if you're not getting anywhere with the ID, maybe you can help me with this CCTV. I've got footage from four different properties to go through."

"Of course." He reached out a hand.

"I'm not going to give it to you. It's on the system."

"I knew that."

Tina resisted a laugh. "Good."

She turned back to her work. *Get on with it*, she thought. *Stop chit-chatting*. There'd be plenty of time to get to know each other when they had to go out and interview witnesses.

CHAPTER TWENTY-SIX

LESLEY WATCHED as Mike got out of his car and approached hers. They were in a pub car park just outside Corfe Castle. Rain beat against the windscreen and the car park was empty. It was November, half term had been and gone and no grockles to be seen. In the summer, this pub would be heaving, but today it was eerily quiet.

She heard a crash and looked round to see a fox jumping off a bin. She smiled. Dorset must be so much nicer for the wildlife out of season.

The passenger door opened and Mike dived inside, spraying water towards her as he did so. Lesley grimaced and batted some off her sleeve.

"It's horrible out there," he said, then caught her expression. "Sorry, boss. Bit of rain never stopped an investigation, eh?"

Lesley had dealt with more than *a bit of rain* since she'd been here.

She popped the last of the Lion bar she'd been eating into

her mouth and crumpled up the wrapper. She chucked it into the back seat of the car. Lesley needed to stop using the back seat as a bin, she never emptied it when she got home like she intended. On a day like today, all she could do when she got back to Elsa's flat was hurry into the warmth.

"How'd you get on with the BBC?" she asked him.

He shrugged.

"I talked to Matt Crippins and a couple of Sadie's colleagues. Didn't get much of interest. Sadie was working on an industrial dispute, but she was pretty much her own boss by the sound of things."

"An industrial dispute? Where?"

"Glass works in Beaminster. Nothing dodgy, if that's what you're thinking."

"Anything else?"

Lesley hadn't told Matt about her meeting with Gwen Mackie. She felt uneasy about dragging him into that until she knew for sure it was connected to Sadie's disappearance.

Mike looked out through the rain. "The thing is, boss... senior reporters down here are part of a network. They all know each other. Politicians, businessmen, senior police, councillors, BBC guys. If Matt Crippins knew about anything like that, I don't think he'd tell me."

"All guys?" Lesley asked.

He turned to her. "All guys. White guys."

She sighed. "That pisses you off."

"Of course it does."

Mike had never spoken about this before.

"You want to challenge the status quo?" she asked.

"I'd have thought that was more your place." He cleared his throat. "If you don't mind me saying."

"I don't. But don't do yourself down. You're young, but

you're bright. No reason you shouldn't be part of that network in a few years' time."

He snorted.

"Of course, that would mean going for my job, as part of your climb up the greasy pole."

"I'm a DC, boss. I don't think..."

Lesley tapped the steering wheel. "It's alright, Mike. I'm joking. I won't be here for ever, it's good that you have ambition. Was Matt Crippins still sure Sadie's missing, or did he think she might have taken herself off on a case?"

"He didn't know."

"What about her colleagues?" Lesley asked. "Anyone able to tell you who Sadie had been talking to?"

"Sorry, boss."

"Bloody journalists," Lesley said. "Why can't they keep a diary like us coppers?"

"Beats me."

"Had she got herself into trouble on a case before?" Lesley asked. "Any dealings with organised crime?"

"Organised crime? D'you think they've got a hand in this?"

"Just putting ideas out there," she told him.

Outside the car, two people ran past. Lesley watched as they dived into a car on the other side of the carpark.

Should she share her suspicions about Carpenter with Mike?

No. She needed more concrete information. She didn't want him getting into trouble.

"OK," she said. "See if you can find anyone else Sadie might have spoken to. Friends, ex-boyfriends, family. Someone must be able to tell us something."

"Apparently she didn't have any boyfriends, and not

many friends. But I'll keep looking, boss." Mike opened the passenger door and darted back to his car.

CHAPTER TWENTY-SEVEN

Tina yawned. She'd been up late the night before, and was regretting it. She'd tried calling the new DC Stan, but had only earned herself a dirty look. She was still trying to work him out. The smart suit, the neat hair, and the attitude.

He frowned into his screen and cocked his head.

"Have you got something?" she asked.

He looked at her. "Shouldn't you be working on your own videos?"

Tina bristled. "I just noticed your body language, that's all. Let me know if there's anything I can help with."

He gave her a look. She knew what was behind that look: *I don't need help from a PC.* But she'd been in this team, and on this case, for longer than him.

"So?" she said.

He leaned back and stretched his hands above his head, twisting his wrists and making them crack. Tina tried not to wince audibly.

"It's the CCTV," he said.

"From the house?"

He shook his head.

"Opposite."

"I thought there wasn't a good enough view?"

"There's a good enough view of the road. I've got a car parked on the double yellows, man getting out, going towards the property."

"OK."

Tina stood up, rounded her desk and positioned herself behind Stanley.

"That car there?" she pointed at his screen.

"It's not as if there are loads of them."

Tina tightened her jaw.

"Watch," he said.

He rewound the video for a few minutes, then hit play.

Tina watched over Stanley's shoulder, careful not to touch the back of his chair. She saw the car pull up and a man get out of the driver's side. He peered up and down the road then rounded the car and walked towards the gated entrance to Susannah Ramsay's house. After a few moments peering through the gate, he tried it. It didn't move. He looked up and down the road again and then walked back towards the camera.

"He's crossing the road," Tina said.

"Wait," replied Stanley.

The man was only just visible in the frame, his head at the bottom of the screen. He stopped, facing Susannah's house. After a few moments, his head rose a little, as if he was standing on something.

"What's he got?" Tina asked.

"Damned if I know," Stanley replied.

"Maybe he's on tiptoe?"

Stanley peered into the screen. "You behave like that on

a road like that, people are going to notice. I suggest someone speaks to those neighbours."

She looked at him. "No reason why we can't do it."

He grunted. "The sarge has asked us to look at CCTV evidence."

"I think you'll find the sarge appreciates initiative," she told him.

"We should check first," Stan said. "Shall I call the DCI?"

"No," replied Tina. "The sarge."

Stanley was still running the video. Tina looked at his screen. "What was that?"

"Nothing else to see," he said.

"Rewind it a minute, please?"

Stanley screwed up his nose and rewound the video to the point where the man's head had risen in the frame. After a few moments of looking towards the house, his head bobbed back down again and he walked across the road. He went to his car. He held the door handle and watched the house.

"What's he doing?" Tina asked.

"Getting the lay of the land, I imagine."

Onscreen, the man moved away from his car.

"There's a cut-through along from there," Tina said. "Leads to the beach. He's going that way. But why has he stopped there?"

Stanley swivelled in his chair, turning to look at her.

"What are you getting at?"

"If you wanted to watch that house, you'd walk along the beach, or you'd take a subtle stroll along the road. You wouldn't drive your car up, park right outside and then wander around the street looking at it."

"Somebody did."

"What if it's a distraction?" Tina said. "Do we have video from the beach, same time?"

She checked the time stamp on the video: four forty-six pm. Still daylight, just.

Stanley raised an eyebrow. "You're the one collating the CCTV."

"So I am." Tina returned to her desk and found the relevant email. "Here. You take this one. It's landing in your inbox right now."

CHAPTER TWENTY-EIGHT

PRISHA VERMA WAS A TALL, slim woman with dark hair scraped back from her face. Her skin was sallow and her eyes ringed with dark shadows. If her husband had been missing since Saturday, Dennis imagined she hadn't slept much in the nights between. He entered the room and gave her the most reassuring smile he could muster.

"Mrs Verma," he began. "Thank you for coming in. My name is DS Frampton. Do you mind if I ask you a few questions about your husband?"

She nodded. "I've already spoken to your colleague. Do you know where he is?"

Dennis swallowed. "How much did DS Bannerman tell you?"

The woman shrugged. "He told me he needed to contact a colleague. I assume that's you?"

"I'm working on an enquiry which we think may involve your husband."

"What kind of enquiry?"

"Please," he replied. "Let me check a few things first."

She stared back at him. "He's dead, isn't he?" she said. "You found him?"

Her voice had become shrill.

Dennis put a hand on the table and lowered himself into the chair, not breaking eye contact.

"Please," he tried again. "Can you describe your husband?"

"I can do more than that." She pulled a phone out of the pocket of her jacket. "I've got photos of him, hundreds of them."

Dennis felt the muscles in his cheek tighten. He hated doing this.

She pushed the phone across the desk. Her fingers were long and slim, her nails painted purple.

Dennis took the phone. It was already open on the Photos app, the screen full of photographs of this woman with a man. The two of them were in their mid-twenties, the man short with dark hair that curled around his ears. He had well-defined cheeks, and a smattering of acne on his chin.

Slowly, Dennis brought his own phone out of his pocket. He scrolled to a photo of the unidentified victim. This one had been taken by the pathologist after the body had been cleaned up. It was the best he had.

"I'm going to show you a photograph that you might find disturbing," he said. "But I need you to tell me if this is your husband."

She blinked at him. "I've already shown you. Surely you can identify him."

"I'm sorry, madam," he said. "But I'd appreciate it if you could confirm...."

She shrank back in her chair.

"OK," she whispered.

Dennis brought up the photo. He put the phone on the desk and turned it towards her, his eyes on her face. Her expression shifted from dread, to puzzlement, to shock.

A tear dropped onto the desk.

"That's him."

"My colleague said that your husband had a birthmark," Dennis said.

Mrs Verma stared back at him, her jaw clenched. She nodded. "It was intimate."

She moved her own hand down her back, as if to indicate where it was.

Dennis nodded.

"We'll check," he told her. "Can you tell me what shape the birthmark was in?"

"A kidney bean," she said. "It was like a kidney bean."

She pushed Dennis's phone back across the table, and he took a moment to compare the photo on it with the ones she'd shown him from her own phone.

"What's your husband's full name?" he asked.

"Ash," she said. "Ashok Verma. Where was he when you found him?"

CHAPTER TWENTY-NINE

AFTER SIX RINGS, Lesley was close to hanging up. She sighed and pulled her phone away from her ear.

"Hello?"

Yes. She put the phone back to her ear.

"Zoe, it's me."

"Lesley. Everything OK?"

"No," she replied.

"What's happened? Is it Sadie Dawes?"

Lesley leaned her head back to look up at the ceiling. She was alone in Elsa's flat. She knew she should have gone back to the office, but given the sensitive nature of the leads she was following, she preferred not to invite questions. At some point, she was going to have to tell Mike what Sadie had been working on.

"She didn't come back from Malta," she told Zoe.

"I can't say I'm surprised."

Lesley shook her head. "Matt Crippins got it wrong. Her producer. He said the airline had a computer error."

"Really? He said he'd checked. She boarded the plane."

"Well, she didn't. She hasn't been seen since you spotted her on the clifftop a week ago on Saturday."

Lesley leaned over, staring down at the carpet. Elsa had good taste in rugs. This one was white with a black geometric pattern, soft and fluffy under her feet.

"Do you want me to come back down?" Zoe asked.

"I don't think that's a good idea right now. My super's sniffing around. He's taken me off a double murder case to find Sadie."

"I saw that," Zoe said. "Wealthy woman, and her unidentified boyfriend."

"Dennis is running the case."

"Didn't you say he was having mental health problems?"

"He'll be fine. If anybody knows how to compartmentalise, it's Dennis."

"Still," said Zoe, "tell me if you need help, yeah?"

"I've got Mike working it with me."

"Does he know about Mackie?" Zoe asked.

Lesley closed her eyes. "Not yet, but I'm going to have to tell him."

"Good luck with that."

"It's fine," Lesley said. "I can cope with Mike."

"So..." Zoe said. "Your secondment is up in a month. Have you decided what you're going to do?"

Lesley stood and walked to the window. This flat was three streets back from the sea. If she opened the window in the summer, she could hear the waves crashing on the beach, but the view was of the back of other buildings.

If she returned to Birmingham, she'd need to find a house. Rebuild her life, reinstate herself with her old team. None of it she relished, but then there was her daughter Sharon to think about. She hadn't seen her for a couple of weeks and was planning to devote this weekend to her. If her caseload allowed it.

"Sorry, am I putting pressure on you?" Zoe asked. "Are you OK?"

"I'm fine," Lesley replied. "Too far inside my own head."

"But you haven't decided yet?"

She thought she had, but...

"No," she said.

If Lesley wanted to stay on in Dorset, she would need to apply for a permanent DCI posting. She had no idea what the competition would be, and what Carpenter's attitude was. Would he want her to stay, after everything that had happened?

"Keep my seat warm for me, will you?" she told Zoe.

Zoe laughed. "Frank's keeping it plenty warm with his ample backside."

Lesley allowed herself a smile. She knew Acting DCI Frank Dawson would be enjoying the chance to lord it over the rest of the team. If she went back, she would be his boss again. Would he give her trouble?

She swallowed.

"Tell me about Sadie's scarf," she said to Zoe. "Where exactly did you find it?"

"On the clifftop, near where Mackie died. I took photos before I picked it up."

"Good," Lesley replied. "Send them to me. I need all the evidence I can get."

CHAPTER THIRTY

DENNIS ENTERED the office and looked over his diminutive team. Tina stood behind Stanley, both of them focused on his computer screen.

Dennis yawned and stretched his arms, and immediately regretted it. His muscles ached today and he felt heavy. The police psychiatrist had put him on antidepressants, and the side effects were kicking in. He eyed the DCI's office. No sign of her. Could he take over in there?

No.

"OK, everybody," he said. "Pull your chairs out, we'll try and sit in a circle."

Tina frowned at him.

"What d'you mean, Sarge?"

"I mean exactly what I say, Tina."

"Sorry, I didn't mean to—"

"It's alright," he told her. "Ignore me."

She looked back at her screen, her expression uneasy.

Dennis had found Tina irritating when she'd joined the team. She'd been young and keen, inexperienced but eager.

He hadn't been sure she'd be up to the job. But now she was about to become a fully-fledged DC and would be a permanent fixture. He'd come to realise he was looking forward to that.

And now Tina wasn't the new kid. Now, it was DC Brown. With his smart suit and superior attitude, Dennis was wondering how much he would contribute.

"Certainly, Sarge," said Brown.

The DC pulled his chair away from his desk into the space near the doors. He smiled and placed his hands in his lap, waiting. Dennis pulled his own chair over and Tina followed. The three of them sat in a circle, approximately a metre between each of their chairs. Tina had her hands in her lap, and was tugging at her fingernails.

Dennis realised he felt stupid. "Let's go back to the desks."

"Should we go in the DCI's office?" Tina suggested.

"No, she might get back any minute. She'll need it for the Sadie Dawes case."

"What about the board?"

Dennis looked towards the office. Tina had a point, the board was in there. Would they be using it for the Dawes case or the Ramsay one?

"OK," he said. The board already had photos of the Ramsay crime scene.

He heaved himself up from his chair, pushed it back towards his desk and made for the DCI's office.

"Let's get this over with."

The two constables followed him. The board didn't have much more on it since the last time he'd checked.

Dennis walked to it and jabbed his forefinger into the man's photo.

"So now we know who he is," he said. "Ashok Verma. We still need to know how he met Susannah Ramsay."

"He was in her bedroom," said Stanley. "So they were more than friends."

"He worked for a Quantity Surveyor," Dennis added. "Not exactly the same circles as her."

"Maybe they met online," suggested Stanley.

"I've gone through Susannah's social media profiles looking for any trace of him," Tina said. "Nothing so far."

"What about dating apps?" DC Brown suggested. "She might have met him through one of those."

"Good idea," Dennis said. "Thanks, DC Brown."

"We can call you Stanley, can't we?" said Tina.

"You can."

The new DC was in his early forties with a crisp blue suit, immaculate hair and the kind of face you wouldn't remember if you passed him in the street ten times. He didn't look like a Stanley.

"Very well, Stanley," Dennis said. "Tina, you look at the dating apps. Stanley, you've been on the CCTV. Have you got anything?"

"Yes, Sarge, both of us have. This just came up." Stanley opened the laptop he'd brought in with him. It was open on a video of the beach.

"Cameras mounted in the trees outside the back of Susannah's house," he said. "This one has a view of the beach northward and this one to the south."

Stanley leaned over his laptop and pressed a key. Dennis watched as the video unfolded. People strolling along the beach, the sun low behind the houses.

"What time was this?" Dennis asked.

"Five o'clock, Sunday afternoon."

"OK," Dennis said. "Anything in particular I should be looking at?"

"Not yet. D'you want me to speed it up?"

"Please."

Stanley fast-forwarded the video. The people on the beach sped up. Dogs running, bounding through the surf. Trees swaying at an unnatural pace.

After a short while, Stanley pressed another key and the video slowed. He pointed at the screen.

"It's this guy."

Tina took two steps towards Stanley and Dennis and leaned over to get a better look.

"He's wearing a heavy coat," she said.

"They always do, don't they?" replied Stanley.

Dennis grunted. "So what's he doing?"

"Wait a moment and you'll see."

They watched as the figure in the video approached the camera. He was well below it, only the top of his flat cap visible, and the upturned collar of his winter coat.

"Is this chap about to do something?" Dennis asked. "Or are we going to be here all day?"

Stanley exchanged glances with Tina. "Here." He nodded at the screen.

The man onscreen approached the gate to Susannah's back garden, towards the bottom right of the shot. He put a hand on it and tugged. Not repeatedly, not heavily, not in a manner that might draw attention. But just enough to check if it was locked. Clearly it was.

The man looked up and down the beach. He walked along the fence to another gate and did the same thing.

"You think he's trying to find a way in?" Tina asked.

"He could be," Stanley said.

"Have we got CCTV round the front?" Dennis asked.

Stanley nodded. "There was someone acting suspiciously. That's why we checked the back. Not sure it's the same person, though. No hat."

"Well then," Dennis said. 'That's your next job. Find any footage from other angles. I want this man's movements from the point at which he leaves this shot."

As he said that, the man did just that. He walked out of shot, looking sideways out to sea as if trying to appear casual. He disappeared in the direction of the headland, which would take him around the side of Susannah's property.

"Get me that man's route around the property and see if he managed to get in, OK?"

"Yes, Sarge," said Stanley.

CHAPTER THIRTY-ONE

"DC Legg, can I help you?" Mike was in his car, heading home for the day.

"It's Matt Crippins. Sadie Dawes's boss."

"Matt. What can I help you with?" Mike felt his heart rate pick up. "Have you heard from her?"

"Sorry, no. I've been asking around. People you might want to talk to."

"Go on," Mike replied.

"There might be a flatmate, I think."

"What's the flatmate's name?"

"Guy Toomey."

"Are you sure?" asked Mike. Uniform and CSI had been to Sadie's flat. They hadn't said anything about a flatmate.

"I don't think she was supposed to sublet, he would have made himself scarce when she was reported missing."

"So where will I find him?"

"Sorry. Only place I know of is her flat."

Mike sighed. "Anybody else I should speak to? What about her family?"

"Her parents live in Yorkshire, I think. I don't imagine they'll be much use to you."

"She might have gone up there," Mike said. "Surely you have details of her next of kin, emergency contacts, something like that?"

"I'll check," Matt replied. "Don't you lot have that sort of information?"

Uniform had gone through Sadie's flat looking for an address book or diary. Her laptop and phone – the places she'd be expected to keep that sort of information – were nowhere to be seen.

"Just send me what you can, please," Mike said.

"Will do."

"And if you think of anything else..."

"I'll call you as soon as I get it."

"By the way," Mike asked. "How did you get my mobile number?"

The man laughed. "I'm a journalist."

Mike hung up, the skin on the back of his neck prickling.

Mike dialled the DCI: voicemail.

"Boss, it's Mike. Matt Crippins has given me a possible lead, Sadie's flatmate. I'm going to go around there now in case he's come back."

Half an hour later, he was pulling up outside of a row of shops in Upper Parkstone. Sadie's flat was above a pizza takeaway. He pressed the buzzer and stepped back to peer up at the first-floor windows. There was a light on.

The intercom crackled. "Who is it?"

"I'm Detective Constable Legg. I'm investigating Sadie Dawes's disappearance. Are you Guy Toomey?"

"Shit. You haven't spoken to the landlord, have you?"

"I don't care about her subletting, if that's what you're worrying about. Are you going to let me in?"

"Sorry, yeah. Come on up."

The door buzzed and Mike pushed it open. He stepped over a pile of post and climbed a narrow flight of stairs. He could smell stale curry mixed with disinfectant. At the top of the stairs was a single door, which opened as he arrived at it. A short, skinny man with spiky brown hair stood in front of him. He scratched his head and yawned.

"Sorry mate, only just woke up."

Mike frowned. It was past 7:00pm.

"I work nights," the man explained. "Porter at Poole hospital."

"Ah. Sorry to disturb you."

"That's OK, I was expecting you lot to come back some time."

"This is Sadie's flat?" Mike asked.

"She rents a room to me. I've been going through her stuff, seeing if she left anything that might tell me where she's gone. I can't find anything, but you might be able to do a better job."

"Our crime scene people have already been here. I'm not surprised you didn't find anything."

"Ah." Another scratch of the head. "Makes sense."

"So, which is her room?" Mike asked.

Guy pointed in the direction of a closed door.

"That one."

Mike reached into his pocket for gloves, then remembered that he no longer needed them. He put his hand on the door handle.

"What state is it in?" he asked.

"Pretty neat. That was Sadie, she kept her stuff tidy. Helped her brain function, she said."

"Don't talk about her in the past tense," Mike said. "She's gone missing, that's all."

Guy reddened. "Yeah, you're right. Sorry." He bowed his head.

Mike opened the door and looked inside. Sure enough, the room was tidy. The bed had been made, the duvet stretched smooth across it. On a dressing table, bottles of cosmetics and hair products were lined up in height order. A pile of notebooks sat on the bedside table. Shoes were arranged under the window and the curtains were open. Either this was a room that was habitually tidied, or one that had been left by somebody who knew she was going away for a while.

"Did Sadie talk about going anywhere?" he asked.

"Nothing, mate. Sorry. D'you want a coffee?"

"Please."

That would get the man out of his hair while he looked around the room. Mike stepped inside and surveyed the walls. The pictures were bland: wallpaper art, the kind of thing his mum liked. Apart from the clothes and the cosmetics, there was little evidence of the woman who lived here. The notebooks were blank. If there was anything to be found, Gail and her team would have it by now.

He headed into the kitchen, where Guy had poured two mugs of instant coffee. The kitchen was less tidy: coffee stains on the worktop, rubbish spilling out of the bin. He handed one to Mike. "Sugar?"

"No thanks." Mike took a sip. It was bitter. "So, when did you last see her?"

"About ten days ago. Week ago last Friday, yeah."

"And did she say anything about going anywhere?"

"She booked a holiday to Malta, that's where I thought she was. Then I get a call from her office asking if she's coming into work, that was yesterday morning. I'd just assumed she'd stayed in Malta for a bit longer."

"Did she give you contact details for Malta?"

"Sorry, mate. We're not that close."

"What was she working on before she disappeared?"

Guy cocked his head. "You don't know?"

"Why would I?" Mike asked.

"I'd just assumed you lot would all know what she was doing."

"Why?" Mike asked, again.

"She was investigating the death of one of yours. Some DCI."

"Which DCI?"

"Can't remember the name. Some Scottish guy, threw himself off a cliff. Sadie reckoned he was murdered. Some sort of revenge killing."

Mike clutched his mug tighter. "What do you mean, revenge killing?"

"Sorry, I didn't always listen to what Sadie was on about. She had all sorts of ideas. But yeah, I can remember his name now. Mackie, DCI Mackie. I remember her talking about it when it happened. She did the piece to camera up on the clifftop where he was killed. In fact, she told me she was going there last weekend. I presume you've sent someone up there, haven't you?"

Mike looked at Guy. His brain had ground to a halt.

Sadie was investigating Mackie's death?

Why?

CHAPTER THIRTY-TWO

DENNIS STOOD in front of the board in the DCI's office, his hands planted in his pockets. It was still dedicated to the Susannah Ramsay case. The Sadie Dawes case, the one that the DCI was working, hadn't yet grabbed itself a space on the board, and maybe it never would. Dennis wondered how much Lesley had told Mike about why Sadie might have gone missing. The woman had been investigating the death of DCI Mackie. She'd spoken to Dennis and he'd told her to get lost.

The door opened and he turned to see Tina coming in with the new DC. Dennis gave DC Brown – Stanley – a nod, which was returned. The man seemed like a positive addition to the team. He was matter of fact and straightforward, didn't waste time on pleasantries. Or on trying to chat Tina up, unlike Mike. Dennis had noticed the two of them coming in together, and he didn't approve. It could only lead to trouble.

"Right, both of you," he began. "Let's review what we've got."

He turned back to the board.

Tina approached and pinned up another photo, a CCTV still.

"What's this from?" Dennis asked.

"The CCTV from the beach," Tina said. "We checked the footage from a neighbouring house, too. The man who was trying the gate at the back came round the side. He went through a gate there."

"Broke in?"

"It didn't take him long," said Stanley. "Either he had a key, or he knew what he was doing."

Dennis frowned. "How do you know it was the same man?"

Stanley pointed at the picture. "His hat."

The man was wearing a flat cap, similar to one Dennis owned himself.

"Nothing distinctive about that," Dennis said.

"The man's young," Stanley replied. "In his twenties, thirties maybe. The way he walks, there's a spring in his step. Not many young men wear flat caps."

Dennis turned to him. "One of those hipsters? Don't they wear flat caps?"

Tina stifled a snort. Dennis gave her a look.

"I know, Tina," he said. "You don't expect an old fogey like me to have heard of hipsters, let alone know that they like to wear flat caps."

She looked back at him, her mouth twisting. "Sorry, Sarge."

"So have we got more photos?"

"Yes." Tina pinned up two more photos. Dennis leaned in to look.

It might have been the same man, but he couldn't be

certain. A flat cap and the shape of a coat weren't much to go on in a murder enquiry.

"And there's this." Stanley placed a laptop on the desk and ran a video. It showed the man in the cap pushing open the house's side gate and disappearing inside.

"Does he go into the building?"

"We can't see that," said Tina. "But a minute and ten seconds later, this happens."

Stanley pressed a key and the screen went black.

"What's that?" Dennis asked.

"CCTV deactivated," said Stanley. "It stays off for good after that."

"Just at the front?"

"Front and back."

Dennis shook his head. "Do we have footage from any other houses covering that angle?"

"Not for the time period after this, no," said Tina.

"We don't have Ines Perez and Vali Florescu arriving?"

"Sorry," replied Tina.

"Hmm," Dennis said. "See if we can get any of this enhanced." He stepped towards the board. There was a portrait of Ashok Verma on there now, one his wife had supplied. "And have you looked for Ashok Verma on the system?"

"No record of him on HOLMES," said Tina.

"What about his car? Has it turned up yet?"

"Uniform found it in a car park in..." Tina checked her notepad. "Branksome. Early this morning. Someone reported some kids trying to break into it."

"What's it doing in Branksome?"

"Maybe he met Susannah there," she replied, "then they took her car."

"Or a taxi," suggested Dennis. "Both of them had alcohol in their systems."

Tina and Stanley nodded.

Dennis took a breath. "See what Verma left in his car. His phone, for one. A laptop. We need to know how he and Susannah knew each other. And we have to consider the possibility that he might have been the target, not her."

"D'you think so, Sarge?" asked Stanley. "With the way she was positioned..."

Dennis knew enough from their last case to not trust the positioning of a body. It might be significant, but it could equally be designed to throw them off the scent. "That might not be relevant, Stanley."

"OK." The DC stood still, staring at Dennis.

"OK, then," Dennis said. He didn't like being stared at like that. "Just because the DCI isn't here, doesn't mean we're going to stand around all day."

"Sorry, Sarge." Tina stood up.

Dennis grunted. He made a shooing motion with his hand. "Get me anything you can on Ashok Verma. And keep digging into Susannah Ramsay's business dealings."

"Boss." Tina opened the door.

Stanley followed her, giving Dennis a wary look as he did so. Dennis wondered if he was reporting back to his home station.

Dennis clenched his fist inside his pocket. He walked to the board, his footsteps heavy. At last he heard the door close. He let his body slump, his eyes closed. Maybe he needed to book an appointment with the police psychiatrist.

CHAPTER THIRTY-THREE

DENNIS WAS LEAVING the building as Lesley climbed out of her car. She watched him hurry towards his own car. His body language was flustered, his face red. The hair that he normally combed across the top of his head was loose, flopping in front of his eyes.

What had happened?

She approached him. "Dennis, everything OK?"

He stopped and stared at her, as if she'd brought him out of a trance.

"Boss."

She frowned. "What's happened? Is it the case?"

"It's nothing, boss. Frustrated, that's all. We're not making the progress I'd like."

He looked at her for a moment, as if about to say something else. He clamped his lips shut.

"Dennis," she said. "Are you sure you're OK?"

He pulled his shoulders back. "I'm fine, I just..."

His gaze slid up the front of the building to the broad windows of Lesley's office.

"I need to get back up there, I shouldn't have…"

"You shouldn't have what?" Lesley asked.

"Leave me to manage it myself," he snapped, his mood suddenly changing.

Lesley didn't like this. She'd left Dennis in charge of a tricky case and now he was losing his temper. She'd never seen him like this.

"Dennis, have you spoken to the police psychiatrist?"

He blinked at her. "Not yet."

"And you will?"

"If I need to, I will."

"I think you need to."

He shook his head. "You don't need to worry about me."

Lesley gritted her teeth.

Dennis was the kind of man who would push problems under the carpet, focus on the job, ignore the impact it had on him.

"If I think you're having problems," she told him, "I will make sure you get that appointment."

"You don't need to do that."

She nodded. "Let's hope so. So, brief me on the case."

He shivered. "Should we go inside? It's chilly out here."

Lesley was wearing a blue wool coat, her favourite. She'd managed to avoid getting mud on it so far. Dennis, on the other hand, was in his tweed jacket, the same one he wore year round. She wondered if he'd only just noticed the cold.

"Of course," she said. "Come on."

They entered the building and headed for the stairs up to their office.

"What have you got so far?" she asked as they walked.

"Not much. Ines Perez I don't think we'll be able to

charge. We know she's lied to us, but CPS say it's not enough to charge her."

"What about her boyfriend?" Lesley asked. "The Romanian kid?"

"He's still in custody, we need to speak to him again. But now we've got a man on CCTV going inside the property."

"You know who he is?"

"Not yet."

"Have you IDed the second victim yet?"

He stopped walking. "Sorry, yes. I should have told you that."

Lesley dug her fingernail into her thumb inside her pocket. Dennis's mind was elsewhere. She'd need to keep a closer eye on him.

"Who is he, then?" she asked.

"Ashok Verma," he said. "His wife went into a local station this morning, reported him missing. She confirmed ID from a photograph."

"What was his connection to Susannah Ramsay?"

They were at the top of the stairs, standing in the hallway.

"We don't know yet," Dennis said. "Tina and Stanley are looking into it. His car was found in Branksome."

"Stanley?"

"DC Brown. The new chap."

"How's he settling in?"

"Fine."

"Good. You need to find the connection between this Verma and Susannah Ramsay. It'll help you understand their movements on Sunday night, and whether they were both the intended victims, or one was just in the wrong place at the wrong time."

'She must have been the intended victim. It was her house."

"Not necessarily."

"We've got a man going in via the side gate, earlier on. And then the CCTV cuts out completely."

"What time did Susannah and Ashok come back to the house?"

"We don't know. The housekeeper says Susannah left before lunchtime, heading for a holiday supposedly. She didn't see her, but the house was empty by then."

"So at some point between lunchtime and ten pm, she came back with Ashok Verma."

"Yes, boss."

"And you don't have CCTV showing that."

'No."

"Which means they arrived after the man you've seen."

Dennis's eyes flickered. "Yes. That makes sense."

"Nothing from door to door?"

"Nothing, boss. Not that kind of road."

"No." Lesley glanced at the doors to the office. "Keep me informed, then. Tell me if you find anything more on the man on the CCTV."

"Boss." He hesitated. "What about your case? Sadie Dawes?"

She shook her head. "Not much progress, yet. But don't worry, we're on it."

"You spoke to Gwen Mackie?"

"Did you know the woman well?"

His face clouded. "Not very."

Lesley pulled Dennis into a corner. Carpenter's office was at the other end of this corridor, and she didn't want him hearing.

"Gwen suspected a cover up," she said. "Do you know anything about that?"

Dennis blinked back at her, his back against the wall.

"I don't know what you're talking about."

"What was Carpenter like, when Mackie died?"

"What do you mean?"

"How did he react? Was he shocked? Business-like? Upset?"

Dennis frowned. "I don't remember." He bit his bottom lip. "I don't see what it has to do with Sadie's disappearance."

"If she discovered something, then someone could be trying to keep her quiet."

"DCI Mackie killed himself. He left a note."

Lesley looked away from him. She felt like punching the wall.

"I think that's still open to debate," she said.

"Not according to the coroner."

"Hmm." She pulled away. "Just keep me up to date on the Sandbanks case, won't you?"

He nodded. "And you will inform me on the Sadie Dawes case?"

"If I need to," she replied. She watched as Dennis walked away. He hadn't seemed surprised when she'd asked about Carpenter. She probably shouldn't have said anything. But if he wasn't surprised by the question, then why?

CHAPTER THIRTY-FOUR

As Lesley parked her car outside the office the next morning, she spotted Mike ahead of her. He was hurrying, out of breath. He looked annoyed.

She got out of her car, moving fast to get to him before he entered the building, and called out his name.

He flinched, then stopped, He turned around, his fists clenching and unclenching.

Lesley approached him. "Everything OK, Mike?"

"I need to speak to you." He glanced towards the building. "Not in the office."

"Let's go to my car."

She led him across the car park to her car, wondering what this was about.

Mike got in the passenger seat beside her, his body language stiff.

Lesley turned to him. "What's happened? Tell me it's a breakthrough."

He shook his head, facing forwards. "I spoke to Sadie Dawes's flatmate."

"I didn't know she had a flatmate."

Mike turned to her. "I tried to call you about it, but you weren't picking up. I figured you'd rather I got on with it."

She nodded. "Thanks for showing initiative. Did he give you anything useful?"

Mike swallowed. He turned again to face forward.

"He told me what Sadie was working on."

Lesley felt her muscles relax. So that was what this was about.

"DCI Mackie," she muttered.

Mike nodded, his jaw clenched.

"I should have told you," she said.

Another nod.

Lesley put out a hand and then withdrew it before making contact.

"It was sensitive," she told him. "The super could be involved."

"What about the sarge?" He turned to her. "Does he know?"

"He knows Sadie was looking into Mackie's death, but that's it. He doesn't know any more than you do now. Probably less. I've been doing this on my own." She took a breath. "Sadie approached me."

"When?"

"The week before she disappeared. When we were working the Paul Watson case."

Mike blinked. "So that's why you had that detective from the West Midlands down here."

"Yes."

He frowned. He knew as well as she did what kind of trouble that could get her into. But it hadn't. Why?

Lesley sighed. "OK, Mike. This is sensitive. You weren't

as close to Mackie as Dennis and Johnny were, so I hope I can trust you with this."

"You could have trusted me two weeks ago."

"It's been longer than two weeks."

"How long?"

"Since July. Gail took me onto the cliffs above where he was found. She made it clear he couldn't have committed suicide."

Mike nodded, saying nothing.

"After my conversation with Gail, I started doing some digging," she said. "I found out that Mackie was happy in retirement. There was no depression, no hint of suicidal thoughts. The note..."

"The graphologist said the note was in his handwriting," Mike said.

Lesley nodded. "I've had it checked out."

"Which means someone forced him to write it?"

"Possibly," she agreed. "The question is, who?"

He leaned towards her. "Any hypotheses?"

"No."

Lesley leaned back. She didn't like not having any working hypotheses for who had killed Mackie. Had it been an arrestee, out of prison and angry with him? Or something more sinister?

Her mind went back to the case she'd worked on just before leaving Birmingham. Organised crime. Police corruption. Surely that wasn't what she was looking at here?

"I don't know," she said. "But Mike, the focus right now is on finding Sadie Dawes. We can worry about Mackie after that."

"You think whoever killed Mackie has got her?"

"I don't know what I think. She could have gone into

hiding. I think she had information, she'd uncovered something that we don't know yet."

"And did your DI Finch know about all this?"

"I'm sorry, Mike," Lesley said. "I brought her in because she didn't know Mackie. At the beginning, when I was just getting to know the team, I had no idea where people's loyalties lay. I didn't know who I could trust."

"You can trust me."

"I've learned that. No more secrets."

He put a hand on her arm. She turned to him, trying to make herself relax.

"Really," he said. "You mean that?"

She straightened. "Mike, I'm still your DCI."

He withdrew his hand. "You lied to me. I stood there talking to Sadie Dawes's flatmate and I felt like an idiot. He knew more about what's been going on than I did, than any of us did. Even you."

"I know," she said. "And that's something we need to rectify."

CHAPTER THIRTY-FIVE

TINA LEANED back in her chair, watching Stanley at his computer. The office was quiet, the only sound Stanley's fingers travelling across his keyboard. She checked the clock over the door: half past nine.

"Where is everybody?" she asked.

Stanley shrugged. "None of my business. I'm just getting on with my job." He looked at her across the desk. "You should be, too."

Tina stood up and stretched her arms out in front of her.

"I don't like this. Normally, the boss comes in and we have a review of where we are at the beginning of the day."

He shrugged. "She's working a different case, isn't she? The sarge is in charge, his MO is different."

Tina grunted. She sat back down in her chair. She had phone calls to make, Susannah's colleagues in London. She needed to get on with it, and maybe she'd have some news by the time the sarge got in.

Stanley frowned. "Here," he said, "we've got the phone records back."

"Whose phone records?" Tina asked.

"Vali Florescu and Ines Perez, they both came in overnight."

"Why don't you throw one of them over to me and we can take one each?"

He nodded. "You have Ines, I'll take Vali."

"Thanks."

She opened up her email and picked up the message Stanley had forwarded. It was data from Ines's phone on the night of the murder. Triangulation of the phone masts gave them a map of her various locations.

She opened up the attached image. It was a plan of the streets around Bournemouth and Poole, with markers showing where Ines had been. Tina clicked on each of them to bring up a label, telling her the time at which Ines had been at each point.

Her pattern was clear. She'd spent the morning in the house, then gone out in the afternoon. It looked like she'd gone shopping in Bournemouth. Then back to the house, half an hour there and returning to Bournemouth at around 7:00pm. She'd spent the evening in Bournemouth moving between three different spots, all pubs as far as Tina could tell. And then, at 10:00pm, she'd returned to Sandbanks, following the road down past Branksome Chine. It chimed with what Ines had told them about getting the bus back with Vali.

"This fits with her story," Tina said. "She wasn't in the house for long, then she was out till she came back and found the bodies."

Stanley looked at her over the desk. "Vali's is similar. He was on campus at Bournemouth University all day, and then it looks like he went into town in the evening. Does this match up with Ines's?"

Tina read out the three locations where Ines had been in the evening.

Stanley nodded. "The same three pubs. The two of them were out together. And then I've got them travelling back to Sandbanks at ten o'clock."

"Me too," Tina said.

He looked at her across the desks. "They're not lying to us," he said. "At least not about where they were. They were both in Bournemouth at the time of the murders."

Tina nodded. "They didn't kill Susannah and Ashok."

CHAPTER THIRTY-SIX

MAYFAIR HOUSEKEEPING SERVICES occupied an office above a row of shops in Dorchester. Outside were two small hatchbacks bearing the company logo: blue on a yellow background. Dennis pressed the buzzer and stood back to look up at the first-floor windows.

"Who is it?"

He took a step towards the intercom. "DS Frampton, Dorset Police. I need to speak to the manager."

"Oh." A pause. "You'd better come in, then."

The intercom buzzed and he pushed the door open. Another door led off to one side, into a shop, and another one ahead of him. *Mayfair Housekeeping Services* had been etched into the glass. He pushed it open and climbed the stairs beyond.

At the top, a young woman sat behind a desk. She wore a shirt with the company logo on it. The shirt looked as if it had been starched and thoroughly ironed. Dennis approved. His own shirts were always immaculate.

He approached the desk, ID in his hand. "Is the manager in? Bernard Timms, is that correct?"

"He is." The woman was well-spoken, subtly made-up. Dennis wondered how many walk-ins they had, or if she was just the telephone voice of the company. "Just go through there please."

She gestured towards a door, which opened as Dennis looked up. A man emerged, hand outstretched. He was in his late fifties, with brown hair that looked as if it had been dyed. He too wore a freshly ironed shirt, only his didn't sport a logo.

"Mr Timms?" Dennis asked.

"That's me. You'll be wanting to talk to me about the Ramsay murder, I imagine. Terrible business, tragic." He stood back and gestured for Dennis to enter his office.

The office was small and starkly furnished, but clean. Dennis took a chair opposite the desk and Timms sat opposite him.

"Are you aware that we have one of your employees in custody?" Dennis asked.

Timms's face darkened. "Ines Perez. I arranged a lawyer for her. How is she?"

Dennis ignored the question. "How long has Ines been working for Susannah Ramsay?"

Timms glanced at the computer on his desk. "Fifteen months. She came here from Spain last summer and went straight to work for Susannah. We've had no complaints. Her supervisor checks in on the house every fortnight and has been happy with her work."

"And was Ms Ramsay happy with her?"

"Well, we received no complaints. I can't tell you much more, but I'm assuming that means she was happy."

"What kind of salary does Ines receive?"

"You think she might have wanted to supplement her income by stealing from Ms Ramsay?"

"We don't think anything. Her salary?"

"Good, for the industry. We pay them fifty per cent above minimum wage. Most cleaning companies stick to the minimum. But our clients expect more, so we ensure our girls are well compensated."

"And how much would Ms Ramsay have been paying your company for Ines's services?"

"Enough for us to cover our overheads and taxes and pay our other employees, if that's what you're wondering." He leaned his chin on his fist. "I don't see why that's relevant."

"Just getting background." Tina had already made a call to the company pretending to be a potential customer, and he knew what their rates were. He'd just wanted to know how open Bernard Timms would be about it. "Would you describe Ines as trustworthy?"

"Well, I would have done before all this happened..." Timms sucked his teeth. "We have a strict policy that we don't send girls into houses without thoroughly vetting them. We run all the relevant background checks before we hire them, and make sure they're updated every year." He sniffed. "Can't get them all right, I suppose."

"Were you surprised when Ines was arrested?"

"Not really."

"No?"

Timms shifted in his seat. "Well, she found the bodies, didn't she? I watch enough crime programmes to know how it works."

Dennis wanted to roll his eyes. If he had a pound for

every witness who believed they were an expert on police procedure because they watched *CSI*...

"Ms Ramsay had someone with her when she died, a second victim."

A muscle flickered under Timms's left eye. "Did she?"

"His name was Ashok Verma. Ash, to his friends. Does that mean anything to you?"

Timms held Dennis's gaze. "Nothing."

"You're sure you haven't heard the name before?"

Timms smiled. "Never heard of the man. We only had one client at that property, Ms Ramsay was the only person present at the original client interview."

Dennis made a note in his pad. "Have you had any contact with Ines, since we arrested her?"

Timms drew in a breath. "No. It's... well, we are very embarrassed by the whole affair."

I bet you are. Dennis took out his card. "If you think of anything that might be pertinent, please call this number."

"Of course. The sooner we can get this all sorted, the sooner my business can get back on track. I hope you're able to build a solid case against Ines."

"You think she did it?"

"Well, you've arrested her, haven't you? I assume you people know what you're doing. I just regret taking the girl on in the first place."

CHAPTER THIRTY-SEVEN

GAIL WAS in the bedroom of the Sandbanks house when Lesley entered. She looked up and stretched as she spotted Lesley.

"I thought you were working the Sadie Dawes case," she said.

Lesley nodded. "That's what I wanted to talk to you about."

Gail yawned and scratched her cheek. "Let's go outside."

She led Lesley through the house, down into the open-plan living room at the back and out of the sliding doors.

"Have you covered all this?" Lesley asked.

"Brett and a couple of the other guys did the whole house. We've still got the bedroom to finish, but we should easily be done by the end of today. That housekeeper can come back."

"She's in custody, I thought."

Gail shook her head. "I just spoke to Tina. Phone records show her and her boyfriend in Bournemouth at the time of the murders."

Lesley felt her heart sink. "So there's no suspect right now?"

"Not that I know of. Unless Dennis isn't saying something. Have you spoken to him recently?"

"I've been a bit preoccupied," Lesley replied. "He doesn't need hand-holding."

"He's been biting the heads off the team," Gail told her. "And apparently he hasn't shown up to the office yet today."

Lesley checked her watch. "That's not like him."

"He could be off working on a lead somewhere, but you'd expect him to check in."

Lesley nodded. "I'll speak to him. Find out what's going on."

Gail leaned against one of the tall trees that separated Susannah's house from the beach. "What did you need me for?"

"Sadie had a meeting with a detective from the West Midlands up on the clifftop. The day she went missing."

"Why?"

"Her name's DI Finch," Lesley replied. "I asked her to do some initial investigating for me. She may have spooked Sadie."

"Whose idea was the meeting?"

"Sadie's."

"But they didn't actually meet?"

Lesley shook her head. "Zoe – DI Finch – found Sadie's scarf on the clifftop. She thought Sadie was missing, but her producer said she'd gone on holiday."

"We've already checked the scarf. There are hairs on it that match Sadie's from the hairbrush we got from her flat. Nothing else suspicious."

"I don't think it just fell off."

"You think something happened to her up on the clifftop? Do we need to establish a crime scene?"

"It was eleven days ago," Lesley said. "I'm not sure how much use it would be."

"Still..."

"OK. When you're done here, can you and your team head over there, see if there's anything to be found?"

"Of course. Do you want me to look for similarities to Mackie's death?"

Lesley looked at her friend. "Please."

"No problem." Gail looked out to sea then back at Lesley. "I may have something that'll help you. If you think Mackie's death and Sadie's disappearance are linked."

"Oh?"

"It's at the forensics lab. You got time for a trip to Dorchester, when I'm done here?"

CHAPTER THIRTY-EIGHT

TINA PUSHED BACK from her desk, looking at Stanley.

"We need to tell the sarge about this."

Stanley nodded. He was wearing another smart suit today, this one light grey. "We do. But where is he?"

Tina shrugged. It wasn't like the sarge not to be in early. She looked up at the clock. Ten past ten.

"I'll call his mobile," she said.

She dialled: voicemail.

"Sarge, it's Tina. We've got the phone triangulation evidence. Ines and Vali were nowhere near the house when the murders took place. Call me when you get this, please."

She hung up.

"Still can't track him down?" Stanley asked.

"No."

"Their custody extension runs out in just under an hour."

"I know." Tina pushed her chair back and walked to the window. From here she had a view of the car park. DS

Frampton's Astra was down there, towards the fence that separated the car park from the road.

She'd noticed that the sarge had developed a habit of parking as far away from the building as he could. It gave him a little bit of extra exercise, he said. Tina thought it was daft.

"His car's there."

"Maybe he's on his way up."

She nodded. "I'm worried about him."

Stanley raised his hands in a shrug. "I hardly know the guy."

"He's like a rock," Tina said, "A rock covered in barnacles. Most predictable person I know. He comes in at eight forty-five every morning, hangs his coat up, gets a cup of tea, sits down, pushes his specs up his nose, sniffs a few times and gets to work."

Stanley laughed. "You've been monitoring his habits to that level of detail?"

She tapped her nose. "CID exams, remember. Doesn't do any harm to practice."

"I'm sure he'll be in soon. Maybe he's got a meeting or something. Maybe he's conferring with the DCI."

Tina turned back to the window. There was no sign of the DCI's car.

"She's not here," she said. "So where is *he*?"

"Do you want to go looking for him?"

Tina frowned. "No. If he's got something he needs to be doing that doesn't involve us, I don't want to interfere."

"Fair enough." Stanley went back to his computer. "He'll be here soon, you can update him."

Tina sat at her desk, her mind racing.

She was worried about the sarge. Maybe she *should* go looking for him?

CHAPTER THIRTY-NINE

Dennis sat in the high-backed chair, clutching his knees. The psychiatrist sat opposite him in a similar chair. The chairs were covered in a practical fabric, the kind of thing you could easily wipe down. Dennis wondered how often that was necessary.

His throat felt tight, his chest taut. Dennis wasn't the kind of man who liked to talk about his feelings. Pam had a way of seeing into his mind, of knowing what was going on in his head without having to ask.

Pam was a genius. He wondered if this man sitting opposite him was half as clever as his wife.

The man leaned back in his chair, trying to project an air of calm and comfort, probably in the hope that Dennis would do the same. Dennis didn't shift from his hunched position.

"So, DS Frampton," the psychiatrist began.

Dennis tightened his jaw. At least the man was calling him by his title. He'd been dreading the prospect of walking in here and being addressed as Dennis, the kind of touchy-feely familiarity that these so-called professionals had. The psychiatrist he'd seen in Bournemouth had been respectful and polite. He'd been expecting this man, employed by the police, to be some kind of hippie.

"You referred yourself," the doctor continued.

Dennis nodded.

"But I did also get a note from your commanding officer."

Dennis blinked.

He wanted to ask which commanding officer. He knew that Carpenter had found out about him seeing the private psychiatrist, but it was the DCI who he'd spoken to about his problems. If speaking was what you'd call it.

He nodded and cleared his throat.

"DCI Clarke's concerned about you," the psychiatrist said. "She said you took some time off sick. You told her you had the flu when you didn't."

"That was a one off," Dennis replied. "I'm never normally sick."

The doctor looked down at his notes.

"You took holiday leave when you had an injury earlier this year."

"I struggle to use all my leave. It seemed a logical thing to do."

"Does logic drive all of your decisions?"

Dennis looked back at the psychiatrist.

"I'm a police detective. Of course I use logic. That's how we solve cases."

A raised eyebrow. "Never with your gut instinct? The accumulated wisdom of years of experience?"

"The accumulated wisdom of years of experience means that we know when not to follow our feelings. We follow the evidence. That's what the DCI does, that's what I do."

"And are you logical when dealing with your colleagues?"

"Entirely. I treat them fairly. If they work hard and they're respectful, they get the same from me."

"Do you think any of them might have noticed a change in you recently?"

"Definitely not."

The psychiatrist nodded and made a note in his pad.

What was he writing? Would Dennis get to see his file after this was finished?

And how long would this last? How many times would he have to come here?

He was beginning to regret referring himself. But then, he'd recognised stress in himself yesterday, when he'd snapped at the team. And for once, he didn't want to confide in Pam.

He missed Johnny Chiles. With Johnny, he didn't have to pretend to be something he wasn't. Years of working together meant they could trust each other.

"I'll need to get some thoughts from your colleagues," the psychiatrist told him. "Just to get some background."

"I thought this was confidential?"

"Oh, it is. I'll be talking to your DCI, and I'll ask her to have the conversations. Don't worry, your team won't know anything about this."

Dennis pursed his lips.

It wouldn't be long before people worked out where he'd been. Dennis Frampton losing his marbles. How humiliating was that?

"How long is this going to last?" he asked.

"We have an hour today. I normally pencil people in for blocks of four sessions, so that means three more hours after today. Today is about getting to know you, finding out what's bothering you, what's been causing you strain."

Dennis opened his mouth, about to say nothing was causing him strain.

But that wasn't true, was it? There was the new DCI, losing Johnny, and, of course, the death of Mackie.

He preferred not to think about that. Was he going to have to talk about Mackie to this man?

He straightened in his chair and rubbed his eyes. His palms were sweaty. He glanced at the clock above the psychiatrist's head. Only ten minutes had passed. This was torture.

"Very well," he said. "Let's get it over with."

CHAPTER FORTY

LESLEY FOLLOWED Gail into the evidence store. This room was in the basement of Gail's offices in Dorchester and Lesley hadn't been here before. Normally, Gail brought evidence to HQ at Winfrith or had it ready in her offices upstairs when Lesley needed to access it.

She picked her way through the narrow space between filing cabinets and piled-up boxes. The room was gloomy, lit by a flickering fluorescent bulb overhead.

"This way," Gail said.

She led Lesley to the back of the room. The shelves here were lined with boxes, all of them catalogued: crime number, name of the responsible CSI. Gail ran her fingertips along the boxes, muttering under her breath.

Gail's hand stopped on a box and she pulled it down. Her own name was written on it.

"This is the one," she said.

She gestured for Lesley to return to the entrance, where there was a table. Gail placed the box on top and opened the lid. The box didn't appear to contain much: a waterproof jacket, a pair of boots and a woolly hat. All labelled up inside evidence bags. Gail pulled out the jacket to reveal two more bags. One held a sheet of paper and the other a mobile phone.

Lesley reached for the bag containing the sheet of paper.

"This was Mackie's suicide note?" she asked.

Gail nodded, her eyes on Lesley's face.

Lesley scanned the note. It was in scrawled handwriting in blue ink on lined A4 paper. There was something sad about such everyday paper being used for a suicide note. The ink, however, seemed less ordinary.

"Fountain pen?" she asked.

Gail nodded.

She rummaged in the box and brought out another bag containing a pen. "We got this from his home."

"The note was analysed?" Lesley asked.

"We got a graphologist in, it was definitely his writing."

"What about the content of the note? Did you get an expert to look at the language he used?"

Gail frowned.

"I suggested it, but the SIO said it wasn't worth the expense. The coroner had already delivered his verdict by the time I thought of it."

"Who was the SIO?"

"They brought in a guy from the Hampshire force. DCI Jacobi."

Lesley nodded, staring at the note. "Do you mind if I take this?"

"Sorry," Gail replied. "You're not part of the investigating team, I can't let it out of this room. You can take photos."

Lesley placed it flat on the table. She smoothed it out and

fired off two photos with her phone. One of the front, the other of the back.

"Has the phone got power?"

Gail pulled out the bag containing the mobile phone.

"Gwen Mackie gave us this after the coroner's report, so it wasn't used as evidence at the time."

"How long after?"

"A while. Around the time you started here."

"Have you looked at it?"

Gwen shook her head. "Your Corfe Castle case was kicking off at the time, we were stacked out."

"So this is Mackie's mobile phone," Lesley said, "and nobody's gone through it?"

"Nope."

Lesley took the phone from Gail.

"Please tell me I can get it out of the bag."

"In this room, yes. Put gloves on, obviously."

"Obviously," Lesley said, snapping on a pair of gloves.

She drew the phone out of the bag and pressed the on switch. It was dead.

"Don't suppose there's a charger in there?" she asked.

Gail shook her head. "I can get you one, though. We keep all types of chargers upstairs."

"OK." Lesley slid the phone back into the bag. "Let's do that. I want to see who Mackie was talking to before he died."

CHAPTER FORTY-ONE

INES LEANED against the cold wall of the police cell. They'd
told her that they could only keep her for twenty-four hours,
but then they'd extended it by another twelve while they'd
gone through more evidence. She wondered if they were
going to keep extending it, every twelve hours. She had no
idea how the police worked here, or what her rights were.

They'd mentioned a conspiracy but hadn't said much
else that made sense. Her English was good, but it didn't
cover legal terms. Her solicitor had tried to explain, but her
words had been a blur. She should have accepted the trans-
lator they'd offered her yesterday.

She pulled her knees up to her chest and wrapped her
arms around them, determined not to cry. She wondered
where Vali was. Had the police been right, thinking he had
something to do with Susannah's murder? Surely not. She'd
been with him all evening in Bournemouth, moving between
ever-noisier pubs. He'd been just as shocked as she had when
they'd found Susannah and the man. If he'd known that

Susannah was dead in that bedroom, he would surely never have gone in there.

Leaning her head back, Ines looked up at the ceiling. This room was freshly painted; she knew the sharp smell. It made her eyes water.

There was a bang on the door and the hatch in its centre opened. She couldn't see who was behind it, but she pulled herself in tighter anyway. The door opened and a uniformed officer came in, followed by a man in a blue suit.

"Ines Perez," he said. "You're free to go."

Ines felt the tension leave her shoulders.

"You're not charging me?"

"No."

"Why?"

"Records from your mobile phone show you were nowhere near the house at the time Susannah died."

Ines nodded.

"What about the perverting...?" She didn't remember the rest.

"Not enough to charge you."

Thank God for GPS. So now they believed her.

She stood up and brushed herself down.

"What about Vali?" she asked.

The man nodded. His eyes were sharp. "Him too, we're letting him go."

Ines closed her eyes momentarily.

"Where is he?"

"He's already left."

She felt a jolt of shock. "Gone, already?"

"Sorry."

She swallowed. Vali wanted nothing to do with her now.

If it hadn't been for her, and her job, he would never have been arrested.

But then, if he hadn't asked her to lie...

Would she have to go back to that awful bedsit?

"Can I go back to the house now?" she asked.

He frowned. "I'm not sure, I'll find out."

The uniformed officer stepped forward.

"If you want to wait in our reception area while we sort out a place for you to go, you can."

Ines didn't like the idea of staying in the police station; she couldn't help worrying that if she was there, they might arrest her again.

"Where's my solicitor?" she asked.

"You don't need her. We're not pressing any charges."

With Vali gone, the only person who could help her was her solicitor. Although – there was the housekeeping agency, as well. How would they treat her, after what had happened?

She swallowed. She had to trust these men.

"I'll wait in the reception area," she said.

She looked at the detective.

"Tell me when I can go back to the house, please."

CHAPTER FORTY-TWO

LESLEY SAT down at the table, Mackie's mobile in her hand. Gail had provided her with a compatible charger and it had taken ten minutes to get it up to five per cent.

"You want me to hang around?" Gail asked.

"Not unless you feel the need to."

"I've got plenty to keep me busy."

"It's fine. I'll come and see you when I'm done."

Gail glanced at the phone. "Good luck."

"Thanks. Don't tell anyone about this, will you?"

Gail chewed her fingernail. "OK. Don't go doing anything silly like taking it out of here, please."

"I won't."

"I mean it, Lesley. It's my name that's on that box."

Lesley looked up at her. "I promise."

"Thanks." Gail turned and left the room.

Lesley switched the phone on. She waited for it to boot up, wondering if any notifications would kick in.

The phone was quiet.

Where to start?

The call log.

She scrolled through the list of calls. They were all unassigned numbers, no names listed. She went to the address book. Empty. Mackie didn't keep a record of names and numbers, it seemed. Should she be suspicious, or was he just old school?

She went back to the list of callers. There had been plenty of calls in and out, some numbers repeated multiple times. She made a note of them in her pad. She'd call the most commonly used numbers later, see if they were registered on her own phone.

She opened up voicemail and waited a moment while the introductory message kicked in. There were no new voicemails but three that had been saved.

Two were from Gwen Mackie. The first was breezy.

"Hi, love. I've made lasagne for dinner. See you later."

The message had been left on the day of Mackie's death.

The second message was left two hours later. It was agitated.

"Tim, where are you? Your dinner's gone cold. Call me, please?"

Lesley felt a lump form in her throat. She imagined what would have been going through Gwen Mackie's mind while she waited for her husband to come home.

How long after she left that message had she phoned the police? How long had it been before they'd given her the news?

Lesley hit the button to listen to the final message.

She recognised the voice. It was Dennis.

"Boss, I waited at the car park, like we agreed. Where are you? Is everything OK?"

CHAPTER FORTY-THREE

INES ALLOWED the uniformed policeman to usher her into the house. He handed over the key and gave her a friendly nod. She tried to smile in return.

"Good," he said. "You going to be OK?"

She nodded. "Thanks."

He gave her another thin smile, then hurried back to his car which was parked on the double yellow lines outside Susannah's house.

Ines closed the front door and leaned against it. She looked through into the living room and shivered. She slipped off her shoes – habit – and padded through, her feet cold on the marble floor.

The living room was just as it had been when she'd been here with Vali on Sunday. If anything, it was cleaner. The surfaces gleamed, the worktops were tidy. The only difference was that the flowers that had been delivered last Friday had wilted. Petals littered the floor beneath the coffee table. She would have to fix that.

Ines's mind felt foggy. Coming back here after what she'd

seen, not to mention what she'd been accused of, filled her with confusion. She went to the sliding doors at the back and put her hand against the glass. Outside, it was raining, gusts of wind making the trees in the garden sway. She swallowed and balled her fist against the glass.

She turned and leaned against the window, looking back towards the hallway. She'd have to go up there eventually; she might as well get it over with.

After a deep breath, she strode out of the living room and towards the stairs. Not allowing herself to pause for even a second, she carried on up the stairs, her movements swift.

At the top, the doors to all the bedrooms were closed. She eyed her own. Had the police been in there?

Probably; they'd arrested her after all. They'd have been looking for evidence. She felt her skin go cold.

She took the few steps towards the doors to Susannah's bedroom and stopped in front of them. She reached out for the door handle. They'd said something about fingerprints on this handle. There was dust on it, grey and fine, like icing sugar. Ines rubbed her fingers together to try and clean it off.

Go on, she told herself. *You can do this.*

Even if she wasn't going to clean the room herself, she'd have to arrange for somebody to do it. Could she make someone do that?

Maybe one of the other girls from the agency would take pity on her. Ines hadn't exactly made friends there.

But she couldn't expect another cleaner to go in there if she didn't have the nerve to do it herself.

She pushed down the door handle, cleared her throat and opened the door.

Inside, the room was empty. The bed had been stripped,

the mattress bare. The curtains had been removed and the carpet was clean apart from a dull patch next to the bed.

Ines felt her breath catch in her throat. That was where the man had been.

She moved towards the bed, her breathing ragged. There was a stain at its centre, pale and brown.

Ines threw her hand to her mouth, pushing back the rising nausea.

The memory flashed in front of her. Susannah's face as she lay there on the bed, posed.

Ines squeezed back tears. She turned back to the door and slammed it shut behind her.

She'd done it. She wouldn't have to go in there again.

She sank to the floor, panting.

There was no way she could sleep in this house. What if Susannah's killer came back? What if they were watching the house, right now?

Ines turned towards her own bedroom. She would pack a bag and go to Vali's flat. She could only hope, after everything that had happened, that he'd let her stay.

CHAPTER FORTY-FOUR

LESLEY WALKED THROUGH HER OFFICE, nodding at Tina and the new DC.

"Everything OK here?" she asked.

The new guy stood up and smoothed down his trousers. He held out a hand, which she ignored.

"DC Stanley Green, Ma'am. I've been brought onto the team to help with the Susannah Ramsay case."

"Good for you," she replied. "Any developments?"

"We've managed to ascertain that Vali Florescu and Ines Perez were nowhere near the house at the time that Susannah was killed. And the sarge has spoken to Ashok Verma's wife."

Lesley frowned. "Poor woman. Is he interviewing her?"

Tina looked uneasy. "That was yesterday, boss."

The door opened and Dennis entered. He stopped as he spotted Lesley.

"Boss," he said. "I wasn't expecting to see you here."

Lesley raised her eyebrows. "I think your team have been looking for you."

"Yes, boss."

He approached the desks, giving Tina and Stanley wary looks.

"You've been trying to get hold of me, Tina. I picked up your voicemail. Good work."

"Ines and Vali have been released," Stanley said.

Dennis's shoulders fell.

"Who did that?"

"I did." Stanley's voice was clipped. "The twelve-hour extension was up. I had to speak to the custody sergeant."

"It was the right thing to do," Lesley told him. "If you have proof they weren't involved in the murder, it's only fair to let them go."

Tina nodded. She cast Dennis an uneasy glance.

Lesley stepped towards the DS. "Everything OK, Dennis?"

The door opened again and Mike entered.

"Afternoon, all," he said.

Tina looked up at the clock. "It's half past eleven."

Mike shrugged, then frowned. "What's happened?"

"Nothing has happened," Lesley said. "I'll leave you to it," she told Dennis. "Let me know if you need anything from me, yes?"

She thought of what she'd heard on Mackie's phone. She wasn't about to address that in front of the rest of the team, or even in this building.

"It would be good if we could catch up later," she told him.

"Yes, boss," he replied, pushing back a stray lock of hair.

Lesley nodded. "Mike?"

"Boss."

She jerked her head towards her office and he followed her to it.

CHAPTER FORTY-FIVE

LESLEY CLOSED the door to her office. Mike leaned against it, looking at the board.

"What's going on out there?" she asked him.

"No idea."

"Hmm. Let's hope they sort it out, whatever it is."

She eyed him. "So," she said. "Are you going to be civil to me today?"

He met her gaze. "Now that I know what's really going on with this case, yes."

Lesley bit back a laugh. She had to admire Mike's balls. But she wasn't about to tell him what she'd just discovered on Mackie's phone.

She rounded her desk. The board was full of the Susannah Ramsay case. Nothing about Sadie Dawes, that was all in her head.

"So where are we?" she asked him.

"Nowhere," he said. "As far as I know, all we have is that Sadie Dawes was investigating DCI Mackie's death."

He flicked his gaze out to the outer office and then back

to her. She balled her fist on the desk. Yes, she'd lied to him. But that didn't excuse insubordination.

He turned back to her. "We have to consider the possibility that she either fell or was pushed off the clifftop, then was taken by the currents. Before DI Finch found her scarf. Did she see anything else?"

Lesley sat down. It was good to be in her own chair. She'd have to make sure Dennis didn't take over possession of it the way he had the board. "The day before, she was on the cliffs with a man. Zoe didn't recognise him."

"Did she provide a description?"

Lesley leaned back. "I'd appreciate you not taking that tone."

Mike's shoulders slumped. "Sorry, boss."

She grunted. "The man was tall, wearing a hat, coat and scarf. Bundled up against the weather."

"Black? White? Facial hair?"

"White, no facial hair." She raised an eyebrow. "Like ninety per cent of the men in Dorset I'd imagine."

Mike approached the board. "It looks like they've ground to a halt on the Susannah Ramsay case too."

"You don't need to worry about that," Lesley said. "Focus on this one. The sooner we can find Sadie Dawes, the sooner we can get back to helping Dennis with his case."

"Helping?"

Lesley shook her head.

"Dennis is SIO. If I need to assist him, I will."

Mike looked at her, as if not quite believing her. "And we haven't got anything else? No forensics, no sightings of Sadie?"

"Nothing," Lesley told him. "She turned her phone off on the Saturday afternoon, it hasn't been turned on since."

She closed her eyes. She needed to stop thinking about what she'd heard on Mackie's phone. It had nothing to do with Sadie. Or did it?

"Look," she said to him. "Until we get anything else concrete on Sadie, I want you to help Dennis with the Susannah Ramsay case."

Mike put his hand on the desk. "Why?"

"Because there's no point in us running around in circles on a case where we've got no evidence."

"But what if Sadie's in danger?"

Lesley cocked her head. She thought about Sadie's behaviour on Brownsea Island, where she'd almost wrecked an investigation. "This is Sadie Dawes we're talking about. She knows how to handle herself."

"Still," Mike said, "what about the man that Zoe saw her on the cliff with?"

"I don't think that man's got anything to do with it. My guess is that Sadie's going to turn up safe and sound and she'll have the scoop of the century."

"Mackie's death?"

She nodded. A shiver ran down her back. "Possibly. She's going to make fools of us all, I can feel it in my water."

"It won't be the first time she's done that."

"Exactly." Lesley stood up. "Now, let's get the rest of the team in here. I want to know what they've been doing."

CHAPTER FORTY-SIX

LESLEY STOOD up from her desk and moved to the far end of the room, as far away as she could get. Dennis entered and she nodded at him, indicating for him to take her place.

He gave her a questioning look.

"This is your case," she told him. "Pretend I'm not here."

He gritted his teeth as he sat down and the rest of the team filed in. She knew how hard he'd find it to ignore her, but this was the best way to find out what progress they'd made on the Susannah Ramsay case.

She looked down, surveying her fingernails in the hope that by breaking eye contact, she might relieve the tension.

Dennis cleared his throat.

"Very well," he said, looking at the board. "What do we have?"

He glanced at Lesley and then stood up, walking around the desk to stand beside the board with his back to her.

Lesley smiled. Mike gave her an amused look that she ignored.

"Vali and Ines have been released," Tina said. "Mobile

phone data puts them miles away from the house at the time of death."

"And we've got a time of death?" Dennis asked.

"Yes," Stanley said. "The pathologist called in earlier. The full report is in your inbox, Sarge."

"Good work," Dennis said. "So now we don't have Vali and Ines as suspects, who do we have?"

"No one," said Stanley.

"No." Dennis out a hand on the board. "Come on, people. We can do better than this. Where should we be digging? What's likely to give us useful information?"

"The second victim," Tina replied. "Ashok Verma."

"Yes," Dennis said. "We need to know more about him. Who was he, why was he with Susannah? There's a chance he could have been the intended target."

"You think, Sarge?" asked Mike. "With the way the bodies were left?"

"It does look like he got caught up in the crossfire," said Stanley. He blushed. "Not literally. But looking at the way the bodies were left, it looks like her murder was more ritualised and deliberate."

"Maybe he disturbed the killer," Tina added.

"Maybe," said Dennis. "Or maybe the killer left her like that deliberately to throw us off our game. Either way, there's no point in speculating about what happened unless we know more about the victims. Knowing who the victims were can help us identify who might have wanted to hurt them. We need to talk to Ashok Verma's family. His work colleagues. Find out if he owed money, if he'd been in trouble with the law. I assume someone has looked him up?"

"Yes, Sarge," answered Tina. "No sign of him on the system."

"So that's a dead end. What about Susannah? Do we have any more on her?"

Lesley smiled. It was good to see Dennis directing an investigation like this. The cloud that had been hanging over him seem to have lifted, if only temporarily.

She caught him looking at her and averted her gaze. Was this a performance? Was he trying to prove something to her?

"We've been focused on Vali Florescu and Ines Perez so far," Dennis continued, after leaving a brief pause. "We need to widen our frame of reference."

"There's the CCTV," said Stanley. "The man who entered the property."

"Good," said Dennis. "We need to identify him. Get back on the forensics."

"I can do that," said Mike.

"I thought you were working with the DCI?"

"You need the resource more than I do right now," Lesley said.

Dennis looked at her. "Fair enough."

"But I reserve the right to take him back if there's a development in the Sadie Dawes case."

"Of course." Dennis looked around the team. "So Mike's on forensics. Stanley and Tina, follow up with Ashok's workplace. I'll talk to his wife." He looked at Lesley. "That alright with you?"

"It's your case." She gave him a nod, trying not to think of the conversation they were going to have later, and left the room.

CHAPTER FORTY-SEVEN

Ashok Verma had lived in a squat bungalow in Mudeford, near Christchurch. Dennis straightened his jacket as he knocked on the door. His wife answered, her eyes red-rimmed.

"Hello, Mrs Verma," he said. "I'm DS Frampton." He held up his ID. "We met yesterday, at Christchurch police station."

"I could hardly forget. You're here to ask questions, aren't you?"

"I'm sorry," he replied. "I know this isn't easy for you."

She sniffed. "One of your colleagues is already here."

"Oh. Who might that be?" Had somebody beaten him to it?

"PC Hughes," she said. "He calls himself a family something officer, he said he's here to look after me."

"Ah," Dennis said, relieved. "Yes, PC Hughes is here to shoulder some of the burden for you. He'll take phone calls, help you with some of the day-to-day things. Make life a bit easier, hopefully."

She shrugged. "I have my mother for that. I suppose I'd better let you in, though."

She stood back and let Dennis pass.

On the left was a small kitchen. An elderly woman dressed in a green sari stood at the sink. She turned to nod at him.

"Good afternoon, officer," she said.

"Good afternoon," he replied. "Do you live with Mrs Verma?"

"I do," she replied. "I have a room in the loft." She winked. "Bet you didn't think I could make it up to the loft, did you?"

He returned the smile. "I'm not judging, madam."

She chuckled and turned back to the sink. Mrs Verma was behind Dennis, her breathing heavy.

"Where's PC Hughes?" Dennis asked her.

"He's in the garden. With my two boys."

Dennis nodded. "You just have the two children?"

"Yes." She sniffed.

"Do you mind if we talk somewhere in private?" Dennis asked.

"Of course," she said. "I've been expecting..." her voice trailed off. "Will you be OK, Mummy?"

"Yes, darling." The elderly woman squeezed past Dennis and gave her daughter a kiss on the forehead. They clutched hands for a moment. Dennis shuffled between his feet, feeling superfluous.

Ashok's wife turned and led Dennis into a living room at the back of the house. It had been extended, walls knocked through to create a large open-plan space. A huge cream leather sofa sat in the centre and a TV hung on one wall. Next to him was a dining table made of heavy wood.

Through the patio doors at the back, Dennis could see PC Hughes playing with two small boys. They kicked the football back and forth, not speaking. PC Hughes pretended to chase the younger boy for it and feigned a missed tackle, allowing the boy to kick the ball between the two jackets serving as goal posts. Dennis allowed himself a smile. Football wasn't in the FLO's job description, but here, it was helping.

"PC Hughes is a good officer," he said, nodding in the direction of the garden. "If you need anything from him, or from the police in general, just tell him."

She sniffed and drew a handkerchief from a pocket. She blew her nose.

"I suppose so. It won't bring Ash back, though."

"I'm sorry for your loss," Dennis said.

She frowned. "You're not here to give me sympathy, you're here to ask me questions about Ash. Aren't you?"

"The more we know about a victim, the easier it is to identify who might have wanted to hurt them."

"Hurt them." She eyed him. "Kill him. I know where he was, you know. I know what he was doing."

Dennis frowned. "Should we sit down?"

"I suppose so."

She shuffled towards the sofa and sat at one end. Dennis took a matching armchair opposite it. There was a thud behind him as the ball hit the patio door. Dennis turned to see PC Hughes raise a hand in apology then run away with it, chasing one of the boys. He turned back to Mrs Verma.

"I'd be grateful if you could tell me where you believe your husband was on Sunday."

Her jaw tightened. "He was with his girlfriend."

Dennis blinked, controlling his reaction. So Ashok's wife knew about Susannah. "Your husband had a girlfriend?"

"Of course he did. I can't think of any other explanation for all the nights he stayed away from home. He told me he was at conferences. But he was a quantity surveyor. I don't think they have conferences."

"Did you have any specific reason to suspect your husband was having an affair?"

A shrug. "There's no other explanation. Was he with her, when he died?"

"Ash was in a house in Sandbanks. He was with a woman, yes. But we don't know what his relationship was with—"

"His girlfriend."

Dennis looked around the space. This house was comfortable. But it was nothing like Susannah's. He found it difficult to picture a relationship forming between the owner of this house and a woman like that.

"Did your husband leave his phone at home, on Sunday?"

She shook her head. "He keeps it with him. Kept. Even when he's in the bathroom. More reason to suspect." She wiped her nose.

"Did he go out in his car?"

The woman nodded. "Yes. It's a—"

"It's OK. We have his registration details on our system." He checked his notebook. "A green Passat, is that right?"

"Yes. When will I get it back?"

"We found it in a car park in Branksome. It's in our warehouse right now. We need to go over it for forensics before we can return it to you."

"Oh. I don't have a car, that's all."

"PC Hughes can help with transport, if you need to go anywhere."

"Oh." She looked past him, out of the window. "A police car?"

"If you need a lift somewhere, we can help."

"Thank you." She forced a smile. "The boys would enjoy that."

Dennis looked up from his pad. "Did Ash tell you where he was going, on Sunday?"

"A work meeting. I didn't believe him."

"Did you challenge him?"

She shook her head, her eyes lowered. "No. I wasn't..."

Dennis nodded. He and Pam had never had reason to mistrust each other, thank the Lord. But he could imagine how hard it would be to confront the person you loved. He wondered how many women Ashok had been seeing. And how he'd met Susannah Ramsay.

"Mrs Verma, have you heard of the name Susannah Ramsay?"

"No. Should I?" Her face fell. "Is that the woman? The dead woman? I saw on the news... she was a millionaire, wasn't she?"

"Did your husband mix with wealthy people for his job?"

"Not that I know of. I've got no idea how he knew her. I suggest you talk to his colleagues. I think they knew more about Ash than I did."

"Thank you," Dennis said. "We will."

CHAPTER FORTY-EIGHT

The firm of quantity surveyors Ashok Verma had worked for was based in a nondescript office just outside Bournemouth town centre. Tina and Stanley waited in the reception area, Tina tugging on the sleeves of her jacket. She was still getting used to wearing plain clothes, hoping it would stick if she passed the detective's exam. A middle-aged man with a broad smile and a combover emerged from a battered door.

He surveyed them both.

"Can I help you?" he asked.

"We're here about one of your employees," said Stanley. "Ashok Verma."

The man frowned. "He hasn't come into work for the last few days. Is everything OK?"

Tina exchanged a glance with Stanley. "His wife hasn't contacted you?"

"I didn't know he was married."

Wow. What else had Ashok chosen to keep from his

employers, Tina wondered. "Can you tell me your name, Mr...?"

"Dawes," he said, "Fred Dawes."

"Any relation to Sadie Dawes?"

He laughed. "The BBC woman? Thank God, no."

"I'm very sorry, Mr Dawes, but I have to inform you that Ashok Verma is dead."

Mr Dawes put out a hand as if about to grab Tina, then thought better of it and plunged the hand into his pocket.

"Dead. How?"

"He was murdered on Sunday night," replied Stanley.

"Where?"

"A house in Sandbanks. It belonged to a Susannah Ramsay. Was she a client of yours?"

"Sandbanks, you say? I doubt it."

"It would be helpful if you could check," Tina said.

"Of course. Come with me."

He turned towards the door, standing aside to let Tina and Stanley through. "How did he die, exactly?" he asked.

Tina stopped on the other side of the door. They were in a narrow corridor, offices leading off to both sides.

"He was stabbed," she said.

Dawes put a hand to his chest. "Oh. Dear God. I'm so sorry."

She nodded.

Mr Dawes looked confused. "We worked on office buildings, the occasional school. No residential properties. Who was this woman again?"

"Susannah Ramsay," Tina said.

"I've never heard of her. And Ash was in her house when he was killed?"

Tina nodded.

She saw recognition dawn on the man's face.

"Was it drugs?"

"Like my colleague said," replied Stanley. "He was stabbed."

Tina heard a sound behind her. A woman stood in a doorway, her mouth open.

"Who was stabbed?"

Fred Dawes stepped towards her. "Ash Verma. Sunday night. Rita, we need to—"

The woman approached Tina. "Why? Ash was just..." She shook her head.

"I'm sorry, madam," Stanley said. "What's your name?"

"Rita Parker," she said. "I'm his line manager. Oh God. Does Prisha know?"

"She does," Tina told her.

"Poor woman." She looked down, grasping at her necklace.

She looked up. "Fred, find them somewhere suitable to sit. I don't think we should do this in the corridor."

The man grunted, then gestured for Tina and Stanley to follow him. They did so, the woman following. Fred opened a flimsy side door.

"Here." He looked at Rita. "Will this do?"

"We still need to know if Susannah Ramsay was one of your clients," said Stanley.

"Who?" asked Rita.

"She was with Ashok when he died."

The woman took a step back. "Oh. That... Fred, can you go and check that please? I'll stay with the officers."

"OK." Fred left them.

Rita closed the door and looked between Tina and Stanley.

"There's something I need to tell you," she said. "Something Fred doesn't know."

CHAPTER FORTY-NINE

Lesley threw herself into her car.

She'd detected a change in Dennis during the briefing. Did he know what she'd found? Or had he just picked up on her own mood?

She'd find out later. Meanwhile, she had a case to work.

Half an hour later, she was waiting in the offices of BBC Dorset. She sat in a low, uncomfortable chair, tapping her feet against its front legs. A young woman had offered her a cup of tea which she'd refused. She wouldn't be here long.

At last Matt Crippins appeared.

"Sorry, Detective," he said. "In the middle of wrapping up a VT for later tonight."

Lesley had no idea what he was talking about.

"I need to ask you some more questions," she told him. "Where's the best place to talk?"

"My office."

He turned and led her through a crowded open-plan space. Heads turned as they passed, people pausing phone calls. Let them wonder, Lesley thought. If their minds were on Sadie, they might remember something useful.

This space was very different from the offices she was used to. Desks were littered with paperwork, piles of folders almost tripping her up. People hurried past, calling to each other across the room. There was more energy here than in her own team room, but less privacy. The thought of leaving paperwork out like this made her shudder. And when she reached it, she realised that Matt's so-called office wasn't much better.

Matt closed the door to his low-walled cubicle and gestured for Lesley to take a seat. There were two chairs: one behind the desk, the other next to Lesley, with barely any space to walk around them. Lesley took the free chair. Matt shuffled around the desk, steadying a stack of files as he brushed past them, and sat down.

"Any progress?" he asked.

"I want to talk to you about what Sadie was working on before she died."

He leaned forward. "Yes?"

She glanced round. She could hear voices on the other side of the low wall. "Is there nowhere more private? This is confidential."

He smiled. "They're making such a racket out there, no one will hear you. Don't worry."

Lesley sniffed and pulled her chair closer to the desk. She leaned forward and Matt did the same, clearly drawn in by the sense of conspiracy.

She took a breath. "How much do you know about the death of my predecessor, DCI Mackie?"

"He committed suicide, didn't he? Threw himself off the cliffs up near Swanage."

"Sadie was investigating his death."

Matt slumped back and gazed off to one side. "That was months ago."

"Sadie had reason to believe it was suspicious."

Matt turned back to her. "Was it?"

"The coroner returned a verdict of suicide."

"That's not what I asked."

Lesley had wondered if she would regret this. "Matt, I need to stress that anything we discuss here today is in the strictest of confidence." She lowered her voice. "It can't be reported."

"Not yet."

"I don't—"

He shook his head. "I'm happy to work with you while we're looking for Sadie. If what she was working on means she's at risk then of course I'll cooperate. But once she's back…"

"You're confident she will come back."

"Of course. She's Sadie."

"Does she often go missing?"

"She did it once before, in her last job."

Lesley raised an eyebrow.

"Investigating industrial corruption for BBC Scotland. She went off the radar for a couple of days. Told me about it when I interviewed her for this job. I was impressed by her tenacity."

Lesley turned her hand over in her lap. She was sweating. If this made it onto the news, her posting here would be over.

"Mr Crippins—"

"Matt."

"Matt, if I have reason to believe you might reveal

anything we discuss while our search for Sadie is ongoing, then I will have to caution you before we talk any more. That would involve taking you to a pol—"

He placed a hand on the desk. "It's fine. I'll keep schtum." He mimed zipping his lips, his eyes wide. Lesley pursed her lips.

"Good. This applies after Sadie returns, if there's a criminal investigation relating to her disappearance, or to what she was working on when she disappeared."

"In other words, I can't talk until anything goes to court. Relating to Sadie's disappearance."

"Not just that."

"But DCI Mackie's death has already been concluded, legally."

"Exactly. And that's why you can't reveal Sadie's investigation."

"You know I can't—"

"Mr Crippins." She leaned in. "The two are linked. That's why I'm talking to you. Do you *want* to put Sadie at risk?"

He eyed her. "Why did you move Johnny Chiles?"

"I'm sorry?"

"He was a good copper. Straightforward to work with. None of this threatening to caution me malarkey. Why did you move him to the Met?"

"Johnny asked for a transfer. I—"

"Bullshit."

Lesley clenched her fist. "I don't think that's—"

"Johnny's wife was about to have a baby. And then he moves to London? Why?"

Lesley wasn't about to give this man the real reason she'd requested Johnny's transfer.

"He was your contact, in our team," she said.

"He was. Good guy."

She shrugged. "You came to me, when Sadie didn't return from holiday."

"I would have gone to Johnny."

"You came to me. I'm SIO on this case. So you're stuck with me." She resisted a sarcastic *sorry*.

"Yeah." He scratched his nose. "So what's the link between Sadie's disappearance and your old DCI's death, then?"

"Mr Crippins—"

"Matt."

"Matt, do you think Sadie might have put herself at risk in pursuit of this story?"

He smiled. "She's a bit of a terrier. Once she gets an idea in her head, there's not much stopping her."

"I know that."

"She was a pain to you on Brownsea Island, wasn't she?"

"You could say that."

"Only doing her job."

"But she didn't put herself at any real risk on that case," said Lesley.

"Story. It's a story to us, not a case. And yes, I wouldn't be surprised if Sadie went knocking on doors she shouldn't do. Got anyone specific in mind?"

Lesley met his gaze. "Did Sadie give you any indication of how close she might have been to a breakthrough on the story she was investigating?"

"If she was investigating Mackie's death, then no. I didn't even know what she was up to."

"She didn't make any hints? Maybe say she might have a scoop for you soon?"

He laughed. "Scoop! No one says scoop any more. No. No, she didn't. Is this all you've got to work on? What she may or may not have told me?"

Lesley chewed her nail. Her stomach growled.

"All I can say," continued Matt, "is that Sadie was tenacious and difficult to put off once she had the bit between her teeth. If she thought someone had killed DCI Mackie, she'd keep going till she tracked that person down and got them on film."

"That's what I was worried about," said Lesley.

"Who do you think she might have been trying to track down?"

Lesley shook her head. She had a hunch, but she wasn't about to share it with him.

She stood up. "I want to talk to your other reporters. Find out if Sadie shared what she was doing with them, if anybody else was helping her. And I want her laptop."

"You've already got it," Matt said. "Your CSIs took it away after we reported her missing."

"Good."

She needed to speak to Gail.

CHAPTER FIFTY

Tina frowned at Ashok's colleague.

"What is it you need to tell us?"

"Come with me," Rita said.

Tina exchanged glances with Stanley.

"Just you," the woman added.

"OK." Tina shrugged at Stanley.

Tina followed the woman into the next office. She closed the door behind her and leaned against it.

"Please," Tina said, "was Ash hiding something?"

The woman nodded. She took a couple of steps backwards and gripped a chair, her knuckles white.

"It's awkward," she began.

These things often are, Tina thought.

"Please," she told the woman. "If it helps us find Ashok's killer..."

"But his colleagues will find out."

Tina suppressed a sigh. "If it goes to court, and it's included in evidence, then yes. They might."

"What about Ash's wife?"

"What about her?"

"She doesn't know this. She thinks..." Rita looked away.

"What does she think?" Tina asked.

"She stopped me in the street one day when I was coming out of work, she thought I might know. Ash and I have worked together for years, we were good friends." Her expression dropped. "I'll miss him."

"What did she think?" Tina asked.

"She thought Ash was having an affair. To be honest, she thought the affair was with me." A stilted laugh. "I didn't think about him that way." Her eyes flashed. "Not my type."

Tina nodded. "So, if Ash wasn't having an affair, what is it you're trying to tell me?"

"He had a job on the side." Rita licked her lips. "He'd got himself into debt, some equity scheme that he'd managed to get himself tangled up in a few years back. He needed to pay it off, he was worried he'd lose his house."

"And did his wife know about that?"

"The finances were all in his name. He bought the house before they met, and she didn't know anything about the debt, or the equity scheme."

"OK," said Tina. "So he got himself another job to pay off that debt?" She had a feeling this other job was going be illegal. "What kind of other job?"

The woman looked down. "He was... he was an escort."

Tina hadn't been expecting that.

"An escort?" she asked. "You mean a prostitute?"

"Do they have that? Male prostitutes? But no, no he wasn't a prostitute." The woman's voice was firm. "Ash was good looking, he had charm. He was young, women liked him. He decided to make use of that."

"So, Ash was being paid to go on dates with women?"

"Exactly."

Women who couldn't get dates, Tina thought. Susannah Ramsay had been rich and attractive. It made no sense.

But yes. Yes, it did. Susannah Ramsay was the kind of woman who wouldn't want the complication of a relationship. She was busy, wealthy. She wouldn't want to waste time.

"Women like Susannah Ramsay?"

A nod.

"How long had he been doing this for?"

"Six months, maybe a bit longer?"

"And did he tell you about the women he met?"

"Oh, no."

Tina wondered how you'd go about broaching the subject of becoming an escort with a work colleague.

"The two of you were close?" she asked.

"We were. I found him in his office one day, in tears. Everything came pouring out. The debt, the job."

Would you describe being an escort as a *job*?

"Did he tell you the name of the agency he was working for?" Tina asked.

"Sorry. He was worried he'd get into trouble if he let anybody know that."

"Of course."

Tina took her card out of her pocket and handed it over.

"If you do remember the name of the agency, or the names of any of the women that he saw, call me. Yes?"

"Of course." The woman sniffed.

CHAPTER FIFTY-ONE

Mike leaned back in his chair and took a deep breath. It had been interesting working with the boss on the Sadie Dawes case, however brief. He'd got a glimpse into the way the DCI worked, and the relationship she had with the sarge. Being in a team of two had certainly been eye-opening.

But now, he was back working for the sarge on the Susannah Ramsay case, sifting through the forensics. He didn't know whether this move was permanent, or if the DCI would bring him back into the Dawes case.

He had a feeling not. There was something she was hiding, something she didn't want him to know. He wondered if the sarge knew what it was.

He'd drawn a blank with the forensics, and now he was seeing what else he could find out about Susannah Ramsay. So far, they had plenty on her work – corporate law, big London firm with offices in Paris, Milan and New York. Her ascent in her profession had been less like working her way up, more like flying. Was there something suspicious in that? If there was, he didn't know what it was.

They'd sent a team from the Met to talk to her colleagues and had looked at her tax returns. Everything was above board, not a decimal point out of place.

Now, he was looking for personal information. It seemed that Ashok Verma wasn't a serious boyfriend, so did she have one? He'd been trawling society websites and found one that focused on high-flying businesspeople. Dull as hell, but he was hoping to find Susannah's name in there. Maybe her photo, with someone she'd pissed off.

He was on the fourth page of the search results when he clicked on a link that led him to a regular column in a legal magazine. The kind of so-called journalism that dressed itself up as legitimate business news but was really no more than gossip. According to Google, Susannah's name was in this one.

He scanned it, then stopped. He leaned back, surveying the screen. Then he sent it to print and walked to the printer.

He approached the sarge and placed the printout in front of him.

"This might change things," he said.

The sarge looked up.

"How so?"

Mike drilled his finger into the printout. "Society page from a legal journal, four weeks ago."

The sarge leaned over it. "And?"

Mike bit his lower lip. "Susannah was married."

The sarge looked up. "Married? Who to?"

"A man called Geoff Middleton."

"So why hasn't he come forward? How come we haven't heard about him before?"

"Because she hasn't lived with him for almost two years,"

Mike replied. "And they're in the process of getting divorced."

CHAPTER FIFTY-TWO

"So you never had a laptop?" Lesley asked.

"Sorry, no," Gail replied. "We searched Sadie's flat for one, and went to her offices. No sign of it."

"Matt Crippins thought you had it."

"Hang on." There was rustling on the line. "Sorry, just letting myself into the office. Where are you?"

"Bournemouth. I've just been talking to Crippins."

"Well, there's no laptop I'm afraid. If he doesn't know where it is, then I assume Sadie had it with her when she disappeared."

"Can you find out if it's been used, since last week?"

"I spoke to the IT folks at the BBC, they said her email hasn't been accessed and she hasn't logged onto the server."

"And does the thing have location tracking?"

"Yes, but it hasn't pinged. If it was turned off..."

"Yes." Lesley knew how useless GPS was if a device was switched off.

"Sunil says she could have used it if she knows how to disable location tracking."

"And how would she do that?" Lesley asked.

"It's not difficult. They just had the standard location settings on their laptops. I get the feeling they're going to upgrade them, after this."

Too late, thought Lesley. "So anyone with a basic understanding of IT could disable the location tracking."

"Indeed. But she couldn't hide the fact that she'd logged into the server."

"No." But she hadn't, that was the point. "Thanks, Gail. If you think of anything, call me."

"Will do."

Lesley leaned back in the driver's seat. She was parked up outside a McDonald's in Poole, having finally given in to her grumbling stomach. The remains of a Big Mac sat on the passenger seat, a carton of fries going cold beside it.

Her phone rang again.

"Gail?"

"Boss, it's Mike."

"Mike. You're wondering if I need you for Sadie Dawes. I'm sorry, bu—"

"It's not that. The sarge wanted me to tell you we have a new suspect in the Ramsay case."

Why hadn't Dennis made the call himself, she wondered.

"Oh?"

"I found an ex-husband. Well, strictly speaking, a husband still."

"Susannah was married?"

"She was in the process of getting divorced. Split up almost two years ago."

"But they're not divorced yet?" Lesley asked.

"No, boss."

"What's his name and where does he live?"

"Geoff Middleton, he lives in London."

"Of course he does. I'm assuming that the guy stands to gain everything from Susannah's death. Is there a will?"

"The sarge is on it. We're tracking down her solicitors," Mike said.

"You need to talk to the husband too."

"Of course."

"Good. I know this isn't my case anymore, but tell Dennis to keep me in the loop."

"Will do."

Lesley wondered if Dennis really had asked Mike to update her, or if this was just Mike's way of reminding her that he existed.

"And thanks, Mike. Good work."

CHAPTER FIFTY-THREE

ZOE PULLED SHUT the curtains to her living room. The street outside was dark, the only sound a group of students making their way noisily back from the pub.

She shivered. She didn't like putting the central heating on now that Nicolas had left. It seemed wasteful for one person.

Maybe she could put the gas fire on? She bent over it, screwing up her face. Every year she had this problem, trying to remember how the thing worked. There was a knob on the side and a button somewhere she had to press. She fiddled with it for a few moments, until eventually it sprang to life. The smell of burning dust filled her nostrils.

She felt warmth brush her leg. Yoda, seeking out the heat of the fire. The cat flopped down on the rug and stretched herself out, her stomach taking the full force of the heat. Zoe sat on the rug next to her and stroked her back.

"You've got the right idea, Yoda," she said. "This house is bloody freezing."

The cat purred and gave her a long slow blink. She was

getting bigger: no longer a kitten. Her silver tabby coat glowed in the firelight.

Zoe heard a sound from the kitchen. She stilled her hand on the cat's back.

"What was that?"

Yoda was ignoring her now, gazing into the fire and purring loudly. Zoe heaved herself off the floor and went into the kitchen. She flicked on the light and blinked against the brightness. The room was empty.

"You're going doolally," she told herself. "There's nobody here."

She went to the sink. Might as well make herself a coffee while she was here. Then she heard it again. A scuffling sound, from beyond the back window.

She went to the back door and unlocked it, then eased it open. Her house had been broken into when she'd been working the Jackson case a year earlier and she was still wary of opening this back door. She eyed the rack of kitchen knives beside the oven. Should she grab one?

"Hello?" she called out into the darkness of her back yard.

The space was empty, nothing there but the weeds she kept telling herself she needed to deal with, and her two wheelie bins.

"Is there somebody out there?"

"Shh," came a reply.

Zoe stiffened.

"Who is it?" She pulled herself straighter, ensuring her full five-feet-six was visible to the intruder. "Show yourself."

Movement in the shadows was dimly illuminated by the light from the kitchen window. Someone was in front of the straggly hedge that separated her garden from the students next door.

"Who is it?" she repeated.

A figure appeared from around the wheelie bin. It was a woman. Her hair was blonde and matted and she wore a fleece that had seen better days.

The woman blinked at Zoe. "Can you let me in?"

Zoe felt her mouth hang open. "You."

The woman approached the back door.

"Quickly, I think I'm being followed."

"Followed?" Zoe peered out into the yard. Still no movement.

The woman nodded.

Zoe looked at her. She sighed.

"Sadie Dawes, what the fuck are you doing in my back garden?"

CHAPTER FIFTY-FOUR

LESLEY SHIFTED BETWEEN HER FEET, clapping her hands together for warmth, as she stood outside Dennis's front door. The last time she'd been here had been during the Watson case, when Dennis had been off sick. The conversation had been awkward, Lesley not believing that Dennis had the flu. She'd been right, too: he'd eventually confessed to mental health problems.

This time, the conversation would be even more awkward.

The front door opened and Dennis's wife Pam smiled at Lesley.

"I thought that was your car," she said. "Come in."

"You're sure I'm not disturbing you?" Lesley asked.

Pam smiled. She was dressed in a navy-blue dress, and thin gold bangles jangled on her wrist. Lesley wondered if she was always this well turned out: last time, it had been a red dress and silver chain.

"It's fine, we were just finishing our dinner," Pam replied.

Lesley looked the woman up and down. She certainly

didn't dress like that for dinner at home herself. Elsa was lucky if Lesley hadn't changed from a rumpled suit to her slippers and dressing gown by the time she got home from work.

She followed Pam to the dining room at the back of the house. The table was laid formally: a cloth, table mats, cutlery neatly arranged. Dennis sat at the table reading a newspaper.

Lesley smiled. "Evening, Dennis."

He looked up. Folding the newspaper, he placed it on the table.

"What's happened? Is it the Ramsay case? Why didn't you call me?" He looked at his wife. "Pam, where's my phone?"

"It's alright, Dennis," Lesley said. "You haven't missed a phone call. I wanted to speak to you in person."

Pam cleared her throat. "I'll be in the kitchen if you need me."

"Thank you," Lesley said.

Dennis watched as his wife left the room. He swallowed and blinked at Lesley.

"What have I done?"

"You're assuming you've done something?" she asked.

"It's not normal for you to come to my house in the evening."

Lesley lowered herself into the chair opposite him. In front of her was what she assumed to be Pam's place setting. The knife and fork were gone but there was still a dessert spoon. Lesley wondered what she was missing.

"I'll get to the point," she said. "I can see that you're in the middle of eating."

Dennis shrugged.

"Gail gave me access to the evidence file for DCI Mackie's death today," she told him.

He looked back at her, his jaw clenching.

Lesley cocked her head. "Do you know what I'm about to ask you?"

Dennis placed a hand on the folded-up newspaper. "His mobile phone."

Lesley nodded. "And?"

"The message I left him," he said. "We arranged to meet on the day he died."

"And did you?"

Sounds came through the wall behind Lesley. Pam was moving around the kitchen, clattering pots and pans, trying to drown out their voices.

"No," Dennis replied. "He didn't turn up. I was supposed to meet him in Swanage. I'd been assigned an aggravated burglary case; our suspect was someone the DCI had arrested in the past. I wanted to get some background from him. When he didn't arrive, I tried phoning him, but there was no answer."

Lesley nodded. There had been missed calls on Mackie's mobile.

"So, what were you meeting him for?"

"I've just told you," Dennis said. "The aggravated burglary case. I wanted to show him the location."

"Tell me about the case," Lesley said to him. "I haven't heard about that one."

"It was before you were here, and it wasn't important enough to tell you about. A caravan park outside Swanage. A gang was trying to steal gas canisters, the warden spotted them, it got nasty."

"So why did you want to bring Mackie in?"

"I told you. He'd had dealings with one of the suspects. We caught two of the men, but two others got away. We recognised one of them, and I wanted to find out from Mackie where we might find him."

"Surely that would be on file."

Dennis shrugged. "Sometimes these things are better learned from the horse's mouth."

Lesley looked at him. From the kitchen, she could hear Pam singing, *Waterloo*.

"I don't believe you," she said.

Dennis's nostrils flared. "I don't see why not."

"DCI Mackie had retired. Any information he might have had would have been on file. He wasn't directly involved in the case."

"Mackie had got to know this chap well over the course of many years arresting him. He was one of those sorts who reoffend the minute they're out of prison. You know the type. And a few lenient judges just gave him fines."

Lesley cocked her head. "So you called DI Mackie and he didn't answer. How long did it take you to realise that something was wrong?"

"I waited an hour," Dennis said. "Then I called him again. Still no answer. I thought of calling his wife, but I didn't want to alarm her."

"Who was it that reported him missing?"

"His wife. Gwen. She waited until midnight. I still wish I'd..." He looked down at his fingers, dragging against the tablecloth.

"Arranging to meet a former colleague like that," Lesley said. "It's not normal procedure. Surely you'd go to Mackie's house and speak to him as a witness. He was a member of the public at that point."

"He knew the suspect inside out," Dennis told her. "He wasn't exactly your average member of the public."

"OK," Lesley said. "And was that the first time you were supposed to be meeting him in relation to this case?"

"Yes."

"So he didn't show up, you got worried, but not worried enough to speak to his wife. Did you tell Carpenter about this?"

"No."

"Why not?"

"He and the DCI didn't get along."

"No? They worked together for... how long?"

"Twelve years."

"But they didn't get along."

Dennis shook his head. Lesley thought of what Gwen Mackie had said: Carpenter hushing up the nature of her husband's death.

The door opened. "Can I get you a coffee, DCI Clarke?" Pam asked.

Lesley turned in her chair. "Please, call me Lesley. And no thanks, I won't be long."

Dennis grunted.

Lesley turned back to him as the door closed.

"Why didn't Carpenter and Mackie get along?"

He shrugged. "Personality clash. They were professional about it. I doubt that many people realised. But I was close to Tim Mackie. I saw how frustrated it made him."

"Once again, why did you arrange to meet him?"

"I've already told you. The aggravated burglary case."

Lesley screwed up her mouth. She stood up.

"Gwen reported him missing at midnight. Had she been expecting him home from a meeting with you?"

"She knew we were in the habit of meeting for a pint."

"Did she know you were meeting him that day?"

"I don't think so."

"Why didn't he tell her about your meeting?"

"As far as she was concerned, he'd retired and that part of his life was over."

"OK," she said. "So you were meeting Mackie in connection with a robbery case. That's all, nothing else I need to know about?"

"No, boss."

"It's not got anything to do with your mental health problems?"

Dennis reddened. "No, boss."

"Hmm."

Lesley put a hand on the back of her chair.

"If there's anything you remember, Dennis, that you want to tell me about, you do so. Please?"

"Of course," he said, not meeting her eye.

"Good," she replied, and made for the door.

CHAPTER FIFTY-FIVE

The Ship Inn in Wool was one of those modern establishments that wasn't sure whether it was supposed to be a restaurant or a pub. When Lesley entered, it was full of small groups of people eating quietly, a hum of voices and cutlery clinking against plates. It was nothing like the Duke of Wellington, where Elsa sometimes worked. There, there would be people propping up the bar, chatting to Elsa or her brother. But here, it was all very formal.

She spotted the team at a table in the corner and approached them.

"Evening all," she said, taking the vacant chair. Mike and Tina were next to each other, their hands on the table but not quite touching. Stanley sat opposite them, next to Lesley. His body language was closed, his head bowed.

"DC Brown," she said. "We haven't had much chance to get to know each other yet."

He straightened. "DCI Clarke. Ma'am. Good to meet you."

She smiled. "Just call me boss. Let's just get on with

working out where we're at with this case and then I can go home."

She looked at Mike.

"What have we got on the ex-husband?"

Tina leaned forward. "Before we get to that, boss. I talked to Ashok's colleague."

"And?"

"He was working as an escort."

Lesley stared at Tina. "An escort?"

"That must be how he met Susannah," Stanley said.

"Yes." Lesley ran over what they knew about Ashok Verma. "Did his wife know?"

"She thought he was having an affair," said Stanley.

"Poor woman. OK, we need to confirm if Susannah hired him that night. And who he was working for."

"Boss," said Tina.

"OK. What about the ex-husband?"

Stanley pushed a piece of paper across the table.

"Not quite ex, not yet. His name's Geoff Middleton, lives in Chiswick. We've got the details of Susannah's divorce lawyers but they've gone home for the night."

Lesley eyed the slip of paper.

"You all understand that I'm not taking over this case. It's Dennis's."

"Is the sarge OK, boss?" Tina asked.

"He'll be fine," Lesley replied.

She hadn't told him she was coming to the pub. She felt bad for undermining him, but at the same time, Dennis had been behaving erratically for the last few weeks. Her focus right now was on getting the case solved; dealing with Dennis's problems could come afterwards. She'd received a text from Carpenter on her way here: *Political pressure on Ramsay case. Any progress?*

"In the morning," she said, "I suggest you go and speak to the husband and the solicitor. Find out the situation with Susannah's will. Did he stand to gain everything if she died? If so, he has to be a suspect."

"What about forensics?" Mike asked.

"What about them?" Lesley said.

"They didn't find any other prints or DNA. No sign of another man having been there."

"He might have been careful," she told him. "What's his job?"

"TV producer," said Tina.

"So maybe he's worked on a few crime dramas, picked up some ideas. Do we have his car registration details? He might have driven to Susannah's house."

"Boss," said Tina. She drew a pad out of her pocket and made a note.

"Also," Lesley added, "there's the CCTV. Go back to that."

"The car we saw, the reg was obscured," Stanley said.

Lesley nodded. *Typical.*

Mike leaned forwards. "Do you want us to report back to you or the sarge?"

"Dennis will be in in the morning," Lesley told him. "You tell him what we've discussed and report your progress to him. If there are any problems, come to me, but only if there are problems."

"Understood."

Lesley looked around the team. She knew it was awkward for them. Tina was shuffling in her chair, desperate to know more.

But Lesley wasn't about to tell them her worries about Dennis.

She stood up.

"Have a nice evening," she told them. "It'll all be fine. Don't worry."

Tina smiled up at her. "I hope so, boss."

CHAPTER FIFTY-SIX

Tina kicked off her shoes and lifted her feet onto Mike's coffee table. His flat was pokey, only a studio really, but cleaner than she'd expected. She knew what some single guys could be like, piles of dirty dishes in the sink and laundry in the corner. Mike was nothing like that. His flat could do with a lick of paint, but it didn't need cleaning. It was a relief.

She leaned back on the sofa, arranging cushions – *cushions! In a bachelor flat!* – around herself.

"So, what do you think's going on with the sarge?" she asked him.

Mike shrugged. He sat down next to her and handed her a glass of white wine.

"No idea," he said. "But there's definitely an atmosphere between him and the DCI."

"D'you think he's ill?"

Mike leaned back, causing the sofa to dip. "He was off sick the other week, wasn't he?"

"The flu," Tina replied. "That's what he told us."

Mike raised an eyebrow. "The sarge never takes time off

sick. Even when he injured his leg in the summer, he used holiday leave instead of sick leave."

"How d'you know that?" she asked.

"Johnny told me."

"Johnny and the sarge were close, weren't they?"

Mike pursed his lips, saying nothing.

Tina put a hand on his arm. "It can't have been easy for you."

He shrugged.

"It was fine, that's just how things work. Johnny and the sarge had known each other for years before I joined the team. I was the noob."

"You weren't a noob," Tina said. "You're a bloody good detective. They should have given you the recognition you deserve."

"Well, the DCI is doing that."

"She's not a racist."

Mike frowned. "I don't think the sarge is a racist, T."

"I didn't say he was," she replied. "But there's always unconscious bias. He's an old white guy from Wareham. He may not be doing it deliberately, but don't you think...?"

"Let me fight my own battles, T." Mike put his glass on the table and turned to face her. His mouth was a thin line. Had she annoyed him? "I don't want to talk about the bosses," he said. "We already had to go through that charade in the pub."

Tina shivered and took a gulp of her wine. "I wanted to ask the DCI what was up with the sarge, but I got the feeling she was pissed off with him."

Mike looked into her eyes. Tina smiled at him, waiting for him to smile back.

Mike was cute. He was more than a good detective, he

was a good guy. Genuine, the kind of person you could trust. She was normally wary of going out with other coppers, but she'd got to know Mike over the last few months and felt she could open up to him.

She reached out and brushed the side of his face.

"I really like you, you know?"

One side of his mouth flicked up and a dimple appeared in his cheek. That was something else she liked about him.

That dimple. She wanted to put her forefinger into it, see if it was ticklish.

"I'm glad about that," he said. "Because I like you too."

CHAPTER FIFTY-SEVEN

"DCI CLARKE, HOW'S THINGS?"

Lesley held her phone to her ear. She was in her car, parked outside Elsa's flat. She realised she needed to start thinking of it as *home*.

"Complicated, Petra," she replied.

"Anything I can help with?"

"Not really. But I do have something for you."

"Letters from our friend DCI Mackie?"

"Yes. He wrote to his son, when he was at university. His wife's given me the letters. Apparently he brought them back when he graduated and she was more interested in keeping them than he was."

"Sensible woman."

"She wants them back."

"I can imagine. They'll help me get a feel for how the man used language, though. Can you stick them in an email?"

"I'll scan them and get them to you in the morning."

"Fabulous. I suppose you want my thoughts yesterday?"

Lesley smiled. "I am busy with another case. Two other cases, in fact. But one might be related."

"To Mackie?"

"You don't need to know the details. I'll send you these letters, and you'll let me know what you think?"

"No problem. Leave it with me."

CHAPTER FIFTY-EIGHT

LESLEY WAS WOKEN by her phone ringing. She threw out an arm, almost slapping Elsa in the face.

Elsa grunted.

"Sorry, love," Lesley said.

She withdrew her arm and fumbled for the bedside table with the other one. After a few seconds' frantic scrambling, she found her phone, put it to her ear and opened her eyes. It was dark outside, no light from around the bedroom curtains.

"Who is it?" she said.

"That's not very professional," came the response.

Lesley sat up. Elsa turned over and pulled the duvet over her head.

"It's the crack of dawn," Lesley said. She yawned. "Who's this?"

"It's Zoe."

Lesley let herself relax into the pillows. Her head hit the headboard and she winced.

"Zoe, why are you calling me now? What time is it?"

"Ten to seven," Zoe replied. "I figured you'd want to know what's happened."

"OK."

Lesley sat up and pushed her feet out of the bed. Her slippers were down there somewhere. Elsa put a hand on her back.

"Who is it?" she whispered.

"Just work," Lesley replied.

She found her slippers, heaved herself out of the bed and shuffled to the kitchen.

She yawned. "Go on then, Zoe," she prompted as she grabbed the kettle.

"Sadie Dawes came to my house."

Lesley almost dropped the kettle.

"She *what*? She's not missing, then."

"Well," Zoe said. "Strictly speaking, she *is* missing again. I don't know where she is, anyway."

"What d'you mean you don't know where she is? Isn't she at your house?"

"Sorry, Lesley. I couldn't convince her to hang around. She's scared."

Lesley put the kettle down, carefully this time. She all but fell into a kitchen chair.

"What's she scared of?"

"Whoever killed Mackie," Zoe said. "She reckons that they'll be after her next."

Lesley rubbed the back of her head. That headboard...

"So who did kill Mackie? Does Sadie know?"

"She's got evidence that Mackie was taking money from organised crime."

"Shit. That's all I bloody need. What about Carpenter?"

"Your superintendent?"

"Did she mention him?"

"Sorry," Zoe said. "She didn't say anything about him."

"What evidence has she got?" Lesley asked.

"I'll WhatsApp it to you," Zoe said.

"No," Lesley replied. "Put it in the post. It'll take longer but..."

End-to-end encryption was all very well in theory, but she didn't want photographs relating to the Mackie case going back and forth on police-issue telephones.

"What time did she come to your house?"

"It was about ten," Zoe said. "I was talking to her until after one am."

"What about?"

"She told me what she's been doing for the last month. How she got an inkling that Mackie's death wasn't what it was supposed to be."

"How was that?" Lesley asked.

"She got a phone call."

"Who from?"

"Anonymous."

"Of course it bloody was," Lesley said.

The kettle clicked behind her.

"Give me a minute," she said. "I need caffeine."

"I've got my own mug in front of me."

Lesley put the phone down on the table. She went to the cupboard and fished out a jar of instant coffee. She sprinkled it into a mug, getting half of it on the worktop. She delved into the jar and threw more into the mug. The stronger, the better. She poured water on it then opened the fridge.

"*Bugger.*"

She'd meant to go out for milk last night.

She'd have it black. She stirred it, threw the teaspoon into the sink, then turned back towards the table.

Elsa was standing in the doorway, her dressing gown wrapped around her.

"What's up?" she said. "Who's calling at this time of day?"

She looked at Lesley's phone, sitting on the table. Lesley could hear Zoe's tinny voice issuing from it.

"A case I'm working," Lesley said. "Nothing for you to worry about."

She took her coffee to the table and grabbed her phone. She gave Elsa a look that she hoped would be enough to let her know she needed privacy.

Elsa shrugged and left the room.

"Go on then," Lesley told Zoe. "Fill me in."

"So, yes, she got an anonymous call. She reckons it was from somebody in one of the organised crime gangs down there."

Lesley cupped her hand to her face, covering the phone.

"Arthur Kelvin's lot?" she muttered, her voice as low as she could go and still be heard. Elsa had represented Arthur Kelvin and some of his employees in the past, and Lesley knew how seriously her girlfriend took her duty towards her clients.

"That's what Sadie reckons," Zoe said. "She said there's only really one organised crime gang down there anyway."

"As far as I know, yes. What was this call about then?"

"DCI Mackie didn't kill himself, that's all. The caller hung up as soon as he said it."

"So Sadie's been running around, talking to Gwen Mackie, following you home, all on the basis of a one-line phone call?"

"You're suspicious too," Zoe said. "And your crime scene manager."

"Yeah."

It was Gail who'd originally alerted Lesley to the likelihood that Mackie's death hadn't been suicide. It was too late for the forensics to be of any use, at least as far as the evidence at the crime scene was concerned.

"*Shit*," she said.

"What?" asked Zoe.

"Dennis, he called Mackie the day he died, wanted to meet him. He says it was nothing, just a case Mackie knew about. But what if he's involved somehow?"

"You think he is?" Zoe asked. "I thought he was the height of probity."

"I don't know," Lesley said. "He's been acting weird lately, taking time off, going to a psychiatrist. Maybe the whole thing's freaking him out." She scratched her cheek. "I'm going to have to talk to him."

"I'll send you what I've got from Sadie," Zoe told her.

"You do that," Lesley said. "Where did she say she was going next?"

"Sorry, she wouldn't tell me. I promised her that all this would go no further than you. And even then it was hard to get much out of her. She doesn't trust you."

"I don't blame her," Lesley said. "OK, if she comes knocking on your door again, tell me straight away, yes? I don't care if you have to wake me up or drag me out of another investigation, I want to know where she is."

"Will do," said Zoe.

"And other than that," Lesley told her. "I think you should keep away from this from now. This is getting too hot, we could both get in trouble. Carpenter hasn't said anything yet, but he knows you've been down here."

"We can both get disciplined for that," Zoe said.

"I know, and the very fact that I've not been hauled over the coals makes me more suspicious of Carpenter."

CHAPTER FIFTY-NINE

Dennis sat at his desk, eyeing the other members of the team. When he'd arrived this morning, nobody had made eye contact. Tina had shared a look with Mike, and Stanley had kept his eyes firmly on his computer screen.

Something was going on.

He stared at his own screen for a while, trying to focus. After the conversation he'd had with the DCI last night, he was worried.

Was he about to be disciplined? Was his job at risk? Dennis was only three years away from being able to claim his pension, he couldn't afford to do anything stupid. What would Pam say?

He cleared his throat and pushed back his chair, wishing Johnny was here. Johnny would tell him what was going on.

"You're all very quiet today," he said.

Tina and Mike looked at each other.

Stop doing that, Dennis thought. He didn't like the fact that the two of them were clearly an item.

Stanley raised his head, meeting Dennis's gaze. At least somebody was looking him in the eye.

"What are you all working on right now?" Dennis asked.

"I'm trying to get hold of Ashok Verma's colleague. She told us he was working as an escort," Tina said.

Dennis stared at the PC. "Is that true?"

A shrug. "He had money problems. People get desperate."

"If that's how he met Susannah Ramsay…" He looked through to the DCI's office, and the photos of the victim. She was attractive, wealthy. The thought of women like that hiring men for company made his blood run cold.

But his personal feelings were irrelevant.

"Carry on with that," he told her. "Anything else?"

"I'm looking into Susannah's husband," Stanley said. "I'm on hold to her lawyers, I need to find out if she's got a will."

Dennis cocked his head. "A will?"

"If Susannah's will left everything to her husband, then it stands to reason that he would be the prime suspect. Kill her now before the divorce goes through."

Dennis nodded. "Fair point." He looked at Mike. "What about you?"

"I've been checking records for Susannah's husband's car. It was in London, parked on his street, for the last five days."

"That doesn't mean he didn't use an alternative means to get down here."

"No. We need to talk to him."

"I'll go and see him later. Stanley, you can come with me."

Irritation flickered across Mike's face. Dennis ignored it;

he wanted to get to know the newcomer better, and a trip to London would be a good opportunity.

Stanley put down his phone. "I've got good news on that score. Geoff Middleton is in Poole today."

"I thought his car was in London?"

"Not any more. Seems he's come down here to sort out funeral arrangements."

"There's a funeral already?"

"Not yet. Coroner still has the body. But he's seeing an undertaker this afternoon. We can interview him afterwards."

"So he's her ex, but he's arranging the funeral?" asked Tina.

Stanley shrugged. "Not sure. But it means we don't have to go schlepping all the way to London."

Dennis nodded. "Good." He turned to Tina. "How are you getting along with piecing together Verma's movements before his death? I'm assuming he would have met more women."

"There's a phone number he kept ringing," said Tina. "I've been calling it, but there's no answer."

"Any message? Answerphone?" Dennis asked.

"Nothing."

"You reckon it's a burner phone?" Stanley asked.

Tina shrugged. "Could be. I'll run it past his wife maybe?"

"OK," said Dennis. He turned to Stanley. "Keep digging into Geoff Middleton. I want to know everything we can about him before we meet him."

CHAPTER SIXTY

LESLEY HAD ARRANGED to see Matt Crippins in a branch of Costa Coffee two streets away from his office. He was uneasy about her coming into the BBC offices again; apparently it disturbed his team. She wondered if it was really because a parallel investigation was going on in those offices that they didn't want her to know about.

She took a table in the front window and put down her cappuccino. It was too large – the cup they'd put it in would have been big enough for a shoal of goldfish. She'd picked up a chocolate brownie as well: probably the only chance she'd get to eat all day.

She took a big bite of the brownie as Matt entered the coffee shop. Nodding her way, he made for the counter. She'd finished her brownie and was halfway through the cappuccino, more air than coffee, by the time he arrived at their table.

"So what's in your office you don't want me to see?" she asked.

He smiled. "I told you. It freaks my team out having you there all the time."

"You're journalists. You're not that easily *freaked out*." She waggled her fingers in air quotes.

He sat down and removed his coffee from a tray. He leaned the tray against his chair, checking it didn't slide to the floor.

"They're worried about Sadie," he said. "They're missing her."

"Well, you don't need to worry anymore."

"So you said in your message," he replied. "Where is she?"

"She's safe. Working."

"Where?"

"I don't know. Not right now."

"She's gone back under the radar?"

"She said she didn't want to be found." Lesley eyed him across the table. "Do you have any idea why that might be?"

"No idea."

"Is there anything you're not telling me about the work Sadie was doing before she went missing?"

"She told me she didn't want to let me in on it until she had more concrete evidence."

"And you let her use her work time working on a case – a *story*, sorry – that you didn't know anything about?" Lesley found that hard to believe. She certainly wouldn't let Dennis waste his time on a secret case.

It occurred to her that was exactly what she was doing herself. And Carpenter was humouring her. Why?

Matt took a gulp of his coffee and grimaced.

"Sadie was a damn good journalist. *Is* a damn good journalist. I trust her, she's got a nose."

"Seems her nose might have led her into trouble this time," Lesley told him. "She's scared to be found."

"Hang on a minute," Matt said, pushing his coffee further onto the table. "If you know where she was, how?"

"What do you mean, how?"

"Well, who saw her? Who told you she'd turned up?"

Lesley clenched her fist in her lap. "Matt, I want you to bring me in on what you know about whatever Sadie was up to when she went missing—"

"You said she's not missing."

"You know what I mean. And I need you to tell me if she gets in touch." She paused. "Has she been in touch? You don't seem surprised at the news she's alive."

"No, Detective. She hasn't been in touch. Not with me, anyway."

"Other colleagues, perhaps? Her flatmate?"

He laughed. "Not her flatmate. Colleagues..." He shrugged.

"Ask them. Or I'll have to."

He met her gaze. "Very well. You still haven't told me how you know where she is... was."

Zoe would forgive her for this. It was her investigation, after all.

"If I tell you this," she said, "I need you to share what you know with me. I need you to talk to your team, find out if anyone knows more than they're letting on."

He brought his cup to his lips. It was empty, Lesley knew.

"OK," he said at last. "One of my team got a call."

"Who?"

He shook his head. "Quid pro quo."

She sighed. "She spoke to a former colleague of mine."

"Which former colleague?"

"None of your business."

"In Birmingham?"

Lesley looked at him.

He smiled. "You think I didn't Google you?"

She pursed her lips. "OK. In Birmingham."

"Detective Inspector Finch."

"I'm not giving you names."

His eyebrows rose. "She was the one Sadie was talking to, wasn't she?"

"How did you know Sad—"

"Sadie talked about it. When she called my team member."

Lesley placed her hands on the table, fingers clasped together. "Your turn. Which team member?"

He stared at her for a moment. "Tamara."

"Tamara. Who is she?"

"Member of the production team. Mate of Sadie."

"When did Sadie call her?"

"Last night."

Lesley leaned back. "That's quite a coincidence."

"It was after she spoke to your colleague."

Lesley felt her shoulders slump. "So you already knew she was in Birmingham."

"I'm a journalist."

Lesley wanted to reach across the table and give him a good slap. "Matt, are you aware that I could arrest you for obstructing a police investigation?"

"You won't."

She took two slow breaths, in and out. *Stay calm.*

Bloody journalists.

"I want to talk to this Tamara."

"OK."

"OK? Just like that?"

Matt smiled. "You told me you need my cooperation."

"I do. Good. Thanks."

"So why was Sadie in Birmingham talking to a DI from up there?"

Lesley put her hand on the table. Could she afford to tell him?

She sighed. "The two of them had arranged to meet on the day Sadie went missing. Zoe was following up on a case that Sadie told me she knew about."

"But they didn't meet."

"No."

"Look," he said. "I'm not shitting you this time. I don't know how much Sadie had on Mackie's death. She wasn't ready to share it with me. How much did she tell your DI mate?"

Lesley shook her head. "No way I'm telling you that."

"Worth a try."

She downed the dregs of her coffee. "Sadie didn't leave her laptop behind. She must be using it. But our CSIs say she hasn't accessed your systems. Are there any other systems she might be using, other than the official ones?"

"There might be."

"Come on, Matt. We need to find her. She could be in danger."

"I'll talk to IT."

"Thank you. And Tamara's details?"

He took a notepad out of his bag, scribbled a phone number and tore off the sheet. He pushed it across the table.

"Thank you," she said. "Let me know if she gets in touch again."

Matt looked across the table at her, his eyes narrow. "But you told me. She's safe, doesn't want to be found. Surely you don't have a missing persons case anymore."

Bloody journalists.

"That's for me to decide," she said.

CHAPTER SIXTY-ONE

SUSANNAH'S HUSBAND had asked to meet at a smart new building on the outskirts of Poole. Dennis parked his car in the underground car park and waited for Stanley to get out before locking it.

He eyed the younger man across the roof of the car. Should he give him instructions for this interview? No. The man had five years in CID. If he didn't know what he was doing by now, he never would.

They took the lift up to the ground floor and stopped at the reception. A receptionist stood behind a vast, polished desk and some kind of water feature trickled down the double-height wall behind her.

"We're here to see Geoff Middleton, please."

"I'm sorry, we don't have anybody with that name working here."

"He's from your London office, here for a meeting. He's expecting us." Dennis got out his ID. "DS Frampton, Dorset Police."

"Oh." The woman straightened her shoulders. "Certainly, just wait there, please."

Dennis exchanged a smile with Stanley and walked towards a row of leather chairs beneath a vast oil canvas. It was a semi-abstract painting of Poole Harbour. Dennis wasn't keen on it, he preferred realism. His living room had two nice watercolours of Swanage Bay. The kind of thing tourists liked to buy, but the way he saw it, they were attractive paintings of the place he called home, and there was no harm in owning them if you were a local.

A tall, skinny man wearing a purple jacket and grey trousers came through the turnstile, his hand outstretched towards Stanley. Dennis looked him up and down. He would have expected the man to wear black, at least.

Stanley glanced towards Dennis and the man followed his gaze.

"I'm sorry, who's in charge here?" he asked.

Dennis stepped forward.

"I'm DS Frampton, this is DC Brown. You're Geoff Middleton?"

A nod.

"We're investigating the death of your wife. Thank you for agreeing to meet us."

The man's face darkened. "Poor Susannah."

"Is there somewhere private we can speak?" asked Dennis.

Middleton raised a finger. "Give me a moment."

He approached the reception desk and conferred with the receptionist. After a few moments he returned, pointing towards a door next to the oil painting.

"That meeting room's empty," he said. "We can use that."

Dennis and Stanley followed him inside. The meeting

room had no windows and was lit by harsh overhead bulbs. The table was wooden: not cheap, but not expensive. Not as swanky as the reception area.

"Take a seat," Middleton said.

Stanley had already done so. Dennis took the chair next to him, the two of them facing Middleton. The man sat down, smoothing his hands in his lap.

"Do I need a solicitor?" he asked.

"Not right now," Dennis replied.

"So I'm not under caution."

"We just want to ask a few questions about your relationship with Susannah and the last time you spoke to her."

Middleton nodded.

"Of course, only happy to help."

Dennis watched his face for signs of grief. The skin under his eyes was grey but there was no sign of redness. And that purple jacket...

"How long have you and Susannah been separated?" he asked.

"Nineteen months."

"And was it an amicable separation?"

"Not exactly. I found her in bed with another man." Middleton raised an eyebrow, looking across the table at Dennis. "So, no. We weren't exactly friends when we split."

"Who was this other man?" Dennis asked. He gestured for Stanley to take notes

"Oh, he was nobody. Just one of many, as it turned out. My wife was having casual sex with a string of men. All younger than her, sometimes young enough to be her sons. How I didn't spot it earlier, I've no idea."

"How long had she been doing this?" asked Stanley.

Middleton turned to him. "Five years at least."

"And how long had you been married?" Dennis asked.

"Seven."

Dennis resisted a wince. Susannah had only managed to be faithful for two years.

"Does the name Ashok Verma mean anything to you?" he asked.

Middleton shook his head. "Sorry. Is that one of her boyfriends?"

"Mr Verma was found with your wife on Sunday."

"Dead?"

"Yes."

"Poor chap. Collateral damage, I imagine? Or do you think she was killed because of him?"

"We prefer not to speculate right now," Dennis replied. "Can you tell me when you last saw Susannah?"

"That's easy. Two months ago. Her father's birthday, she insisted that I come along. He's ill, you see. She hadn't told him."

Stanley leaned forward. "So, Susannah's parents didn't know that you and she had split up?"

"My wife was a habitual liar. She didn't want people knowing what was going on in her life. Her family certainly didn't know about her eventful sex life."

"Can you tell me the exact date?" Dennis said.

Middleton leaned back. "Eighteenth of September."

"And when was the last time you spoke to Susannah?" Dennis asked.

"Same date. We're not in the habit of chatting on the phone, if that's what you're thinking."

"Where were you on Sunday night?"

Dennis watched the man closely, monitoring his reaction. Middleton looked back at him, unblinking.

"At home, in my flat. I had to buy a place in Islington after we split up. Susannah's got a pad in Richmond. Gorgeous place, garden going down to the river. After the split, my means were a little straightened, you might say."

"What are the terms of your divorce?" Stanley asked.

"I don't know yet," Middleton replied. "Our two years aren't up."

"Do you have to wait two years, if she—"

"I preferred not to air our dirty linen through the divorce courts."

"Fair enough. But do you expect to get half of her assets?"

Middleton shook his head. "She insisted on a prenup. I get what I brought into the relationship, she gets what she brought. We've both done OK over the last nine years, but obviously she's done better than me. I won't have much more than the flat I'm living in in London, and a few shares. And my pension, for what it's worth."

Dennis grunted.

"And what about a will?" he asked.

A shrug. "If I know Susannah, she'll have changed it the moment I told her I was leaving. If you're thinking I killed her to get all her stuff, I'd imagine you'll be disappointed."

"We'll need to verify that," Dennis said.

"Do you know who Susannah's lawyers were?" Stanley asked.

"Yes. Nevin, Cross and Short, in Bournemouth." Middleton glanced at Stanley's notepad.

Dennis took a breath. *Of course.* Why did Lesley's girlfriend have to come into everything?

CHAPTER SIXTY-TWO

GAIL OPENED a large evidence bag containing Ashok Verma's belongings. There were tests that she needed to run on his clothes, chemical analyses to conduct.

She laid the items out on the bench in front of her. A pair of grey trousers, slightly shiny on the seat. A matching jacket, also with some shine. A blue shirt, House of Fraser: expensive but not ridiculously so. Underwear, Marks and Spencer. A ten-pound note and a pack of mints had been in the inside pocket of the jacket; they were in a separate bag. No wallet, no mobile phone: not surprising Lesley hadn't been able to identify him for a while. Inside another bag were a watch and three rings. Gail tried to remember if any of them had been on his left ring finger in the crime photos; probably not. One of the rings was shiny on the inside, from being removed and put back on repeatedly. She could imagine Ashok shifting it from one hand to the other when he left the house.

They'd already combed the clothes for hairs and other fibres, and found only Ashok's own hair and a single strand of Susannah's. Now she wanted to check for drugs.

She bent over the jacket and used a scalpel to cut off a small section of the pocket. She took two more sections: one from the lapel and another from the belt of the trousers. She mixed up the testing solution in a shallow dish and split it between three containers. She placed each of the samples in a container and stood back to wait for a result.

A couple of minutes later, the fabric from the lapel was beginning to show signs of a reaction. She bent over it, squinting.

She lifted the dish carefully and carried it over to a microscope. If this was what she thought it was...

Gail peered through the microscope, scanning the fabric sample for signs of crystallisation. Sure enough, it was doing what she expected.

She returned to the other two samples. The belt of the trousers was showing no sign of change, but the sample from the pocket was developing crystalline structures like the one from the lapel.

She'd have to repeat this with more testing solutions, check for different drugs.

But for now, she had a positive result.

Ashok Verma had taken cocaine while he was wearing that jacket. Maybe in the hours leading up to his death

CHAPTER SIXTY-THREE

LESLEY LEFT the BBC offices feeling frustrated. She'd overruled Matt Crippins to speak to Sadie's colleague and the IT people. The IT team had no record of Sadie accessing any systems via another machine, or any of the non-BBC systems they used. If she'd picked up another machine or used different systems, they'd told her, they'd have no way of knowing. Sadie was clever enough to create multiple email addresses and online aliases.

Wherever Sadie was, she'd clearly found herself another laptop or was using internet cafés. Either that, or she'd gone so deep undercover that she wasn't even accessing the internet. Lesley had asked for them to look for her phone, but that, too, hadn't been used. Lesley wondered where the laptop and phone were. Did Sadie still have them with her, or had she dumped them? She would call Zoe later and find out if she'd noticed either of them.

And Sadie's colleague, Tamara, had drawn a blank. She'd told Lesley that Sadie had called to tell her she was safe, and not to worry about her. Other than mentioning Zoe, she'd said no more about what she was working on. Lesley had checked Tamara's phone: withheld number.

She made for her car, her mind churning. She needed to speak to Carpenter. He'd asked her to keep him updated on both cases, and she didn't want to put his nose out of joint any more than was strictly necessary

The Susannah Ramsay case looked like it was edging closer to a breakthrough, with the team focusing on Ashok Verma's escort job and Susannah's divorce, but the Sadie case was running dry. She wanted to warn Carpenter in case there was a risk of Sadie turning up in Dorset with information that could embarrass the force.

She stopped in the Lower Gardens in Bournemouth and found a bench. The illuminations were lit, despite it being just gone lunchtime. The air was heavy with the threat of rain, and no one was out admiring the lights.

Carpenter answered after two rings.

"DCI Clarke," he said. "I hope you've got good news for me."

"Yes and no," she replied.

"Give me the bad news first."

"The team working the Susannah Ramsay case are making progress. They're looking into the other victim's movements during the days before he died. And we've also discovered that Susannah was getting divorced."

"The husband's a suspect?"

"Dennis has gone to see him. I'm not sure of the outcome."

"Keep me updated, I'm still getting political pressure. And what about Sadie Dawes?"

"The good news is that she's alive and well."

"Where?" asked Carpenter.

Lesley ran a hand down the back of her neck.

"She's in Birmingham."

"*Birmingham?*"

"She turned up at the house of my former colleague."

"That DI that you brought down here to help you?"

"Yes, Sir."

"You do know that bringing in an officer from another force could get you disciplined, or worse?"

"Yes, Sir."

She waited. If Carpenter was going to discipline her, he'd have done it already. She sensed that there was something he was trying to keep quiet, too. Had Gwen Mackie been right?

"Sir, she told us she doesn't want to be found. She's not missing, she's just gone undercover."

A sniff. "Very well then. I guess that case is closed."

Lesley allowed herself a long breath.

"Yes, Sir."

"So you need to go back to the Susannah Ramsay case. Take over from your DS."

"Sir."

Lesley hesitated.

She wanted to talk to Carpenter about Dennis. She wanted to ask him what he knew about Dennis asking Mackie to help him after the former DCI had retired.

"I need to ask you about something that DCI Mackie might have been working on."

"Mackie?" Carpenter said.

"Yes, Sir. I'd rather not do it over the phone though."

Silence.

"Sir?"

"I was just checking my diary," he said. "I'm busy with meetings for the rest of today, but come and find me later, yes? I'll be in my office at around six pm."

CHAPTER SIXTY-FOUR

DENNIS STOOD up from his chair in the meeting room and gestured for Stanley to follow him.

He nodded at Susannah's husband, reaching into the inside pocket of his jacket for his card.

"If you remember anything that might be useful, anything Susannah said to you about people who might have wanted to hurt her, please call me."

"Like I told you, Susannah didn't talk to me."

"Still." Dennis knew that people sometimes remembered things when they didn't have a police detective sitting in front of them. "Keep that safe, just in case."

The man shrugged. "I won't be using it. But yes, of course."

As Dennis and Stanley left the office building, Dennis's phone rang.

"DS Frampton."

"Dennis, it's Gail. You're in charge of the Susannah Ramsay case still, aren't you?"

He felt himself bristle. "Yes, Gail. How can I help you?"

"I've been analysing Ashok Verma's clothes. There was cocaine on his jacket."

Dennis stopped walking. He cupped his hand over the receiver and turned to look at Stanley.

"Cocaine?" he said.

"Unmistakable," she replied. "In the fibres of the jacket. I did some more tests, and found it deep in the material. I don't think it was just from the night of the killings, he'd been doing cocaine for a while."

"Thanks." Dennis hung up.

"Let's go back in there," he said to Stanley.

He pushed the door open again. Geoff Middleton was by the lift, tapping his foot and watching the display.

"Excuse me, Mr Middleton," Dennis said as he approached.

The man turned and frowned. "What's wrong?"

"I need to ask you another question."

He ushered the man away from the lift, towards a corner where they stood by a large plant.

"Are you aware of your wife having taken illegal drugs?" Dennis asked the man.

"Drugs?" Middleton looked between Dennis and Stanley.

"We found traces of cocaine on her companion's clothes."

The man's frown deepened.

"She'd been attending Narcotics Anonymous. I thought she was clean."

"Maybe she was," said Stanley. "It's not her clothes they found the drugs on."

Dennis glanced at his colleague. He found it hard to believe that if Ashok Verma had been taking drugs on Sunday night, Susannah wouldn't have been taking them too.

"Where did she get her drugs?" he asked Middleton.

He shrugged. "She had a phone, kept it hidden, but I saw her with it a couple of times. Cheap thing. She told me she'd thrown it away, when she started at her last job."

Dennis dug his fingers into his leg through the fabric of his trousers.

"And why didn't you think to tell me this?"

"It didn't occur to me."

"This phone," Dennis asked, "where did she keep it?"

He ran through his memories of what the CSIs had found in the house. There had been a mobile phone, but it had been a high-end smartphone. Not what Middleton was describing.

"No idea, sorry. I thought she'd got rid of it, like I said."

Dennis nodded.

"Was there somewhere in the house that she would have hidden it?"

Middleton shook his head.

"I'm not familiar with that house, she bought it after we split up."

Dennis nodded. "Very well."

He pointed at his business card, which was still in the man's hand.

"If you do remember anything about this phone, call me straight away. Please."

CHAPTER SIXTY-FIVE

Tina and Mike were at their desks when Mike's phone rang. Tina glanced at him as he picked it up, and he gave her a smile.

"Everything alright, Sarge?" he said into the phone. He frowned and nodded. "Ashok?"

A pause. Tina watched Mike place his hand on the desk, his fingers splayed. What was happening?

Mike nodded, his fingers shifting on the desk.

After a moment, he hung up and looked at Tina. "Sarge wants us to go talk to Ashok Verma's wife."

"Why?"

"CSI found cocaine in his clothes. We need to check if she knows anything."

"Did they find it in the house, too?"

"Nothing."

"Then how d'you think she's going to know?"

"Worth a shot, isn't it?" He stood up and grabbed his jacket. "You coming, or not?"

"I am." She followed him out of the office.

Two minutes later, Tina was behind the wheel of an unmarked car, Mike beside her in the passenger seat. She was getting used to driving these cars; they could be as high-powered as squad cars, but didn't have the disadvantage of everyone slowing down the moment they saw you in the rear-view mirror.

"The sarge says we're to go at it carefully," Mike said. "Bereaved widow, and all that."

Tina nodded as she took a left turn. "Maybe she won't know anything about it."

"Maybe not, but Gail thinks he'd been doing it for a while. Surely you'd notice, if the guy you lived with was a regular cocaine user?"

"The effect on his septum, if nothing else," Tina said. She slowed at a roundabout.

"Was there evidence of that?" Mike asked.

"If there was, it wasn't apparent in the crime scene photos."

"So he was sensible."

"Maybe he was dealing," she suggested.

Mike grunted as they pulled up outside the house.

Poor woman, Tina thought.

Mike put a hand on her arm. "You take the lead on this, please."

"You sure?" Her arm felt like it had been scalded where he'd touched her. She looked at his face. He needed a shave. It suited him.

"Sure," he replied. "You're good at this stuff."

Mike was right. But she didn't want to be pigeonholed. The young female constable who could do the touchy-feely stuff. She'd need to show herself capable of more than that if she was to make a success of CID.

"It's not all I'm good at, you know."

He grinned. "I know."

She pulled her arm away, her face hot. "I didn't mean that!"

"Sorry. You meant..."

"I meant professionally." She put a hand on the door handle. Had it been a mistake, taking up with Mike? She'd thought he was different.

"I don't think we should talk about our relationship while we're at work," she told him.

"Is that what it is? A relationship?"

"I just *told* you I didn't want to talk about it at work."

He leaned towards her. She wondered if Mrs Verma was in there, watching them from her front window.

"I want it to be," Mike said.

Tina felt her chest clench. *So do I.*

"We've got a job to do, Mike. We can talk later." She gave him a look. "Keep things professional, yes?"

He smiled. "Of course. Sorry."

She grunted and threw the door open, trying to assume a professional expression.

CHAPTER SIXTY-SIX

Lesley pulled over at the side of the road. She couldn't do this while she was driving and she didn't want to do it back at the office. She found a lay-by just outside Wareham and sat for a moment, considering what she needed to do. Cars hammered by, buffeting hers as they passed.

She shivered. It was cold today and she hadn't worn the right coat. She got out her notebook, sighing as she did so. She'd made a note of the numbers from Mackie's phone. Calls received, calls he'd made. There were three numbers that she hadn't been able to trace. One of them had made calls to Mackie's phone on numerous occasions in the two weeks before his death. Not every day, but not far off.

She wasn't using her own phone; she didn't want whoever answered to trace her. Instead, she'd borrowed one of a rotating set Dorset Police used for this purpose.

She tried the number that had made plenty of calls first. It rang out, no answer. Then she tried the other two. The first one was unobtainable, the second engaged. Voicemail kicked in, a male voice she didn't recognise.

"I'm not available right now, leave a message."

Lesley wasn't about to leave a message. She hung up and held her phone in her lap.

That first number, the one that had made multiple calls, it was familiar. Was it from a case?

She'd go back to the office, run it through HOLMES. Hopefully, she'd find a match.

CHAPTER SIXTY-SEVEN

"So, what did you think, Constable?"

Dennis and Stanley were in Dennis's car, driving back to the office. Approaching the roundabout where the A35 met the A351, Dennis slowed and looked across at the DC.

Stanley shrugged. "I don't think he did it, Sarge."

"No?"

The roundabout was clear. Dennis pulled out, turning left. The road was straight here, quiet at this time of year.

"Why not?" he asked.

"He didn't stand to gain financially, did he?"

"Not from what he tells us," Dennis replied.

Stanley's hand was on the dashboard. Was he trying to get Dennis to slow down, or speed up? "He's hardly going to lie, is he? He knows full well that we'll be able to find out the details of her will."

Dennis nodded, glancing in his rear-view mirror. The DC had half a point, but only half: even if it turned out, somehow, that Susannah Ramsay hadn't changed her will, there was nothing to stop her husband pleading ignorance.

"I'd be interested to see how Mike and Tina get on with Ashok Verma's wife," he said.

"The drugs?"

"I'm still not convinced Susannah was the intended target."

Stanley shook his head. "Tina's got a theory that way too. Still, she's only a PC."

Dennis felt his jaw tighten. "And what's that got to do with anything?"

Stanley looked at him.

"Well, she's not CID trained, is she, Sarge? I mean, she's bright and all that, but until she passes the detective's exam and gets her formal training..."

Dennis tightened his grip on the steering wheel. Tina had been a member of the team for five months. She might still officially be in Uniform, but she'd learnt plenty about working on murder cases.

He shuffled in his seat.

"How many murder cases have you worked, DC Brown?"

"One," said Brown, his eyes on the road.

"And which one was that?" Dennis asked.

"Two years ago, fight outside a pub in Bournemouth. It got nasty, a guy was bottled."

"Did you have many suspects?"

"Just the one. Fella he was fighting with. There were at least a dozen witnesses."

"So not much of an investigation, then."

"We had to take thirteen witness sta—"

Dennis slammed his hand on the steering wheel. "You had one suspect, multiple witnesses. Hardly a tricky investigation."

"No, Sarge." Stanley's voice was low.

Dennis cleared his throat. "Well, then, perhaps you won't judge PC Abbott until you've had a bit more experience yourself."

Dennis could sense Stanley stiffening in the passenger seat next to him.

"Well?"

"Yes, Sarge."

CHAPTER SIXTY-EIGHT

"Oh." Prisha Verma looked shocked as she answered the door. "Are you...?"

Tina held up her ID. *PC Abbott*, it said. Hopefully that would change soon. "I'm sorry, Mrs Verma. We just had a few more things we wanted to talk to you about, if you don't mind." She glanced at Mike. "This is my colleague, DC Legg."

The woman nodded. "Come in, I suppose. PC Hughes will make you a cup of tea."

Tina and Mike followed her in. PC Hughes was a good family liaison officer, he knew how to blend into the wallpaper. Tina had heard that he'd been entertaining the Verma boys. What must it be like, telling your kids their dad was dead?

Mrs Verma led them past the kitchen. PC Hughes was in there, moving around. Keeping busy.

He turned to them, then looked at Mrs Verma. "Anything I can do?"

"Cup of tea please, mate," Mike said. PC Hughes nodded and grabbed the kettle.

They continued into the living room. It was a wide room looking out over a small patch of grass, a football in the centre.

"PC Hughes said it would be a good idea to send the boys back to school," Mrs Verma said.

Mike raised an eyebrow. "Already?"

"Just for the afternoon. The school have been wonderful, they've assigned each of them their own member of staff to support them." She looked down at her hands. Her nails were bitten. "And it helps them to be with their friends."

Tina took a step forward.

"Do *you* have any friends who can help you?"

A side door opened and an elderly woman entered. She smiled at the two detectives.

"Don't mind me." She took a seat at the dining table and picked up some knitting.

"That's my mother," Mrs Verma said. "She's been here since..." her voice trailed off.

"Pleased to meet you, Mrs...?" Tina said, looking at the older woman.

"Acharya," the woman said. "Geeta Acharya. Nice to meet you too, dear."

Tina looked back at Prisha Verma.

"We'll be quick," she said.

She looked at Mike. He was the full member of CID, he should be taking the lead. But she sensed that here, in a room full of women, he was letting her take over.

Mrs Verma sat in an armchair, smoothing her hands over her trousers. "What is it you want to know?"

Tina lowered herself onto the sofa next to the woman.

"Were you aware of your husband taking drugs, Mrs Verma?"

The woman's brow furrowed. "Drugs? What kind of drugs?"

The sofa dipped as Mike sat next to Tina. "We found traces of cocaine on his clothes," he explained. "Did he talk to you about taking the drug at all?"

The woman shook her head. "Never. Ash wouldn't, he wasn't that type of..." She hesitated, then looked towards the dining table. "Mum?"

Tina turned towards the older woman, who looked up from her knitting.

"Don't ask me," she said. "I hardly knew your husband."

Prisha's face darkened. "Yes, you did, Mum. He was always here when you came to visit."

Mrs Acharya put her knitting down. "He always went out when I came. He had some excuse or other. Work, meeting up with a friend."

Prisha frowned. "Did he?"

Her mother rose from her chair and went to her daughter. She perched on the edge of the armchair and lifted her daughter's hand, stroking the fingers.

"I always assumed he didn't like me, darling. Maybe he thought your old mum was a bit dull."

"You're not dull, you're..."

A smile. "I'm dull, sweetheart." The woman stroked her daughter's face. "Maybe Ashok didn't like the company of women?"

Prisha's face darkened.

"I think he liked the company of women too much, that was the whole problem."

She turned to Tina. "He was having an affair with that woman, yes? The one with the house?"

"We've found no evidence of a prior relationship," Mike said. "But..."

"But what?"

Tina leaned forward. "We spoke to one of Ashok's colleagues. According to her, your husband was working as an escort."

"An escort?"

Mrs Acharya jolted. Prisha shook her head. "Why?"

"He needed the money, Mrs Verma," Mike said. "Did he talk to you about money problems?"

"He told me we were fine." Her mouth dropped open and her eyes narrowed. She tugged at her ear.

At last she turned to Tina. "I saw messages on his phone, I smelt perfume on his coat. Sometimes it was cheap, sometimes expensive." She licked her lips. Her mother had hold of her hand. "I thought it was another woman. But... an escort?"

The older woman cleared her throat. "He's dead, let's let him rest—"

"I'm sorry, Mrs Acharya," Tina interrupted. "But we think the escort work might have been connected to his death. Mrs Verma, is there anything you might know about this? The name of the agency? Where he was going?"

Prisha shook her head.

"What about the drugs?" Mike asked. "Were you aware of your husband taking drugs?"

"There were women, but there were no drugs. You're wrong." She gripped her mother's hand tighter. "The boys. Ash would never..."

Tina nodded. "Do you mind if we take some of his

clothes?" CSI had been here, but they hadn't taken any of Ashok's belongings.

Prisha lowered her eyes. "Help yourself. None of it matters any more."

CHAPTER SIXTY-NINE

TINA WAS elbow-deep in a chest of drawers when she realised there was somebody behind her. She straightened up and turned to see Prisha Verma standing in the bedroom doorway.

"Everything alright?" she asked.

Mrs Verma nodded, tight-lipped. Her hand was shoved inside the pocket of her trousers. It looked like she was holding something.

"Is there anything you want to give me?" Tina asked.

Prisha stared back at her. She nodded, then shook her head. Tina approached her, placing a hand on her shoulder.

"Do you want to sit down?"

She guided the woman to the bed. Prisha stumbled towards it, her hand still buried in her pocket.

Tina flicked her eyes towards it.

"Is there something you want to share with me?"

The woman hunched over herself. She was crying.

"I'm sorry," she said. "It's too..."

"Too what?"

Prisha looked up. "Humiliating."

She pulled her hand out. In it was a phone.

Tina looked at it, her breath catching.

It was a cheap phone, not a smartphone. The kind of phone drug dealers used. Or men who were arranging meetings with women.

"Was that Ash's?"

Prisha glanced towards the door. "I didn't want to…"

"It's OK," Tina said.

She reached out and waited for the woman to place the phone in her hand. After a moment, she did. Tina pulled an evidence bag out of her pocket and slipped the phone inside.

"Thank you," she said.

"What's happening?"

Tina looked up to see Mike standing in the doorway.

"It's alright," she told him. "Mrs Verma has just given us another piece of evidence."

He stepped inside. "What evidence?"

"Mike…" Tina said. "It's OK."

She held out the evidence bag.

"Is this Ashok's?" Mike asked.

Prisha nodded.

"Why didn't you tell us before?"

Go easy on her, Tina thought. Yes, she'd withheld evidence. But what if she had more, and they scared her enough to stop her opening up?

The woman drew in on herself. "I'm sorry."

"Have you looked at this phone?" Mike asked her. "Have you checked it?"

Prisha shook her head.

"There's a PIN. I tried his birthday, our wedding anniversary." Her voice caught. "Nothing worked."

"It's OK." Mike took the evidence bag from Tina. "Forensics will find a way to access it. Thank you."

CHAPTER SEVENTY

LESLEY LEANED back in her chair.

She needed the rest of the team here. She wasn't used to trawling through HOLMES; that was normally Tina and Mike's job. The number from Mackie's phone that she'd thought she recognised wasn't on the system. She peered at it, scrawled in her pad.

"Who are you?" she asked herself.

There was only one thing for it: try again. She picked up the borrowed phone and dialled. It rang out again.

She sighed. She'd try the other number, the one where voicemail had kicked in last time.

After a few rings, it was picked up. Lesley sat upright in her chair. She hadn't been expecting that.

Silence.

"Hello?" she said. "Who am I talking to?"

"Sorry?" came a voice on the other end. It was a woman.

"Who am I talking to?" Lesley asked again.

"Boss?" the woman said.

Lesley frowned. She gripped the arm of her chair. "Who is this?"

"Boss, it's Tina. You've just rung Ashok Verma's phone."

CHAPTER SEVENTY-ONE

INES HAD ALREADY FILLED two suitcases, and there was more piled up on her bed. Over the three months she'd worked here she'd accumulated too much stuff. She'd come from Spain with two suitcases and bought a rucksack in Bournemouth. There wasn't enough space.

The second suitcase was on the floor. There was no way she was going to fit it all in.

She looked towards the door. Susannah had suitcases and Ines knew where they were. At the top of her wardrobe, out of reach. Ines would have to take a chair in there to get them down.

She shivered, remembering the room. The blood stain on the carpet, the bed stripped of its sheets, the dull stain at its centre.

Maybe she'd go out and buy herself another bag instead. Or just use a bin bag. And how was she going to get all this stuff to Vali's flat? Perhaps she should just go straight to his flat, leave her stuff. How much of it did she really need?

She slumped down on the bed and rested her head in her

hands. She wished her sister was here. Sophia would know what to do.

She jerked her head upwards. There'd been a sound downstairs, a door closing.

Ines put her hand to her chest. She tiptoed to the bedroom door, which was open. She stood next to it, listening. This house was designed to deaden sound: footsteps were silent, door handles turned without a creak.

But she'd heard somebody downstairs. That had been the front door closing, a sound she knew. She'd listened to Susannah coming home in the night enough times.

Holding her breath, she pulled her bedroom door so that it was almost closed. She swallowed. Her phone was on the bed, but she couldn't tear herself away from the door.

Her heart was racing, her breathing shallow.

More noise. Things being moved around. The sound of objects being placed on surfaces.

Susannah was dead. Ines was the only person with a key.

So who was down there?

CHAPTER SEVENTY-TWO

"Tina, where are you?"

"I'm at Ashok Verma's house, boss."

"You're on his phone?"

"It's a burner phone. His wife gave it to us. She reckons he was using it to arrange meetings with women."

Lesley dragged her hand through her hair.

"She waited until now?"

"Yes, boss."

"*Shit*. OK, Tina. I take it you've bagged it up?"

"We have. I'm holding it through the bag."

"Good. Bring it in, I want CSI to go over it."

Silence. After a moment, Tina spoke. "Boss?"

"Yes?" Lesley replied.

"How did you get this number?"

"We'll worry about that later," Lesley said. She hung up.

CHAPTER SEVENTY-THREE

THE TEAM WAS in Lesley's office, the board now almost full. It felt like old times.

Lesley perched on the edge of her desk. Ashok's burner phone was on the desk beside her in an evidence bag. She stared at it. *Why did Mackie have that number?*

Gail was with them, leaning against the wall at the back. Tina and Mike were in the two chairs, while Dennis and Stanley stood either side of the board.

Lesley tugged at her fingernail.

"Right," she said. "So we've got three pieces of information about Ashok Verma. First, he was working as an escort. Second, the drugs, and third, this phone."

She looked across the room at Gail. "Can you take the phone? See if you can crack it. Trace any numbers you can. Let me know if any familiar faces crop up. And we need the number of the agency."

Gail straightened up. "Of course."

Dennis stepped away from the board.

"Er, boss, shouldn't—?"

Lesley raised a hand to stop him.

"This is forensic evidence, Dennis. I want CSI on it. We've got enough to keep us busy with the escort business and the drugs."

"And there's the husband too," Mike added. "Susannah's."

"Where are we at with him?"

"His alibi checks out," said Stanley. "He was at home on Sunday night, nowhere near Sandbanks. We checked his phone records and he gave us access to the recording of a video call he made around the time Susannah was killed."

"Couldn't he have made that from somewhere in the Sandbanks area?"

Stanley shook his head. "IP address is West London. He definitely wasn't anywhere near her when she died."

Lesley gritted her teeth.

"OK. So it's looking increasingly like the intended victim was Ashok Verma. I still don't believe Susannah was an innocent bystander, though. The way she was laid out on the bed, him slumped on the floor next to her. From that alone, it feels like *she* was the target and he got caught in the crossfire."

She raked her fingernails across the desk. Dennis watched her, his expression stern. She knew this was supposed to be his case now. But the two cases had collided. And besides, Sadie Dawes was no longer missing.

"I need to bring you up to speed on something else, as well," she said.

She sensed them tensing in anticipation.

"Sadie Dawes reappeared last night. She's told us not to look for her, she's working on a story and she's gone undercover."

Mike whistled.

"I knew it," said Dennis.

Lesley looked at him. "I'd still like to know where she is. I'm worried the woman's at risk, which is why she's gone to ground."

"We're not here to babysit wayward journalists," the DS told her. "There's been no crime committed."

"You're right." She looked down and took a breath. After a moment, she looked back up to make eye contact. "And that means I'm back with you on the Susannah Ramsay case."

Irritation flickered across Dennis's face.

"Is that alright, Dennis?"

"Of course. I knew it was only temporary."

"Good. So, Gail's got the phone. We need somebody to check out this escort agency. Do we know of any escort agencies locally?"

"Sorry, boss," said Tina.

"Right. Well, in that case, I want you and Stanley following that up. Find this agency, speak to them. Find out what they know about Ashok and how he came to be in Susannah's house."

"No problem." Tina glanced at Stanley.

"And Mike, I want you on the drugs," Lesley said. "I want to know if it was Susannah or Ashok who bought the drugs and where they got them. Talk to Drugs Squad, find out if there's a match with anything they've brought in recently."

"My lot can help with that," said Gail.

"Good," replied Lesley. "But focus on the phone, yes?"

"OK."

Lesley leaned against the desk. Finally, she could focus on a case that they had a chance of cracking.

"OK everybody, get to work. Gail, can you stay back a moment?"

Lesley spotted Dennis looking at Gail. He wasn't happy. She would deal with that later.

"Of course." Gail leaned against the wall and watched as the rest of the team filed out.

When the door was closed, she approached Lesley. "They're pissed off with you, you know that?"

"It's not my job to make friends."

Gail cocked her head. "Sure, but you want them working with you, not against you."

"They're professionals," Lesley told her. "It won't be a problem."

"Fair enough, not my job to tell you how to do yours. What is it you need to talk to me about?"

"This phone of Ashok Verma's," Lesley said. "Did you know that I rang it while Tina was at Verma's house with it?"

"No, how?"

"I got the number from DCI Mackie's phone."

Gail took a step back.

"Mackie's?" Her voice had lowered. "The phone you were looking at in the evidence store yesterday?"

"That's the one," Lesley said.

"But how did Mackie have the number of Ashok Verma's burner phone?"

Lesley shrugged. "I can't think of any connection between the two of them. Unless this escort agency's a cover for something."

"What about the drugs?"

Lesley nodded. "Ashok could have been getting his drugs from someone Mackie was investigating."

"It was a personal phone. He was retired."

Lesley leaned against the desk. Outside, Dennis kept looking up from his computer and towards her.

"Ashok must have been given that phone by someone else," she said. "But who?"

"Beats me," Gail replied. "I'm just a CSM."

"You're more than just a CSM." Lesley smiled. "But let's keep this between us for now. Tina's going to want to know how I got that number, I'll need to think of something."

"You haven't told them you're still investigating Mackie's death?"

"Dennis is suffering mental health problems. I think it's related to Mackie's death. I don't want to make things worse."

Gail looked through the glass to the main office. "Poor Dennis."

Lesley grunted.

"Thanks, Gail. I appreciate your help."

Gail looked at her. "I just hope I'm not going to regret this."

CHAPTER SEVENTY-FOUR

LESLEY HEAVED herself away from the desk as Gail left the room. No sooner had the door closed than it opened again, and Dennis came in. He shut it behind him, his movements jerky.

Lesley sighed.

"Everything alright, Dennis?"

"What's going on?"

"I beg your pardon?"

"Tina told me you rang that phone when she was at Ashok Verma's house. His wife had just given Tina the phone, and you rang it. How?"

"What do you mean, how?" Lesley asked.

He took a step forward. His hands clenched and unclenched at his sides and he was sweating.

"Where did you get the number from, boss?" he asked.

Lesley looked at him. "This goes no further than you and me. I don't want the rest of the team involved in this."

He frowned. "I can't..."

"In that case, I can't talk to you about it."

Dennis looked out through the glass wall. Mike was watching them. He quickly looked away.

Dennis chewed his lip. "How can I promise to keep a secret if I don't know what it is?"

"Dennis..."

He stared at her. "Or if it will get us both into trouble?"

She met his gaze. "Superintendent Carpenter is aware of the work I'm doing."

"What? What work?"

Lesley looked out at the team. Gail had her phone to her ear. She put it down and spoke to Tina. Tina turned to Stanley, who rose from his chair. The two of them headed for the door, hopefully following up a lead. Mike was staring into his computer screen. Gail picked up her phone again.

She had to trust Dennis. He knew more about Mackie than she'd been able to discover, and even if his behaviour had been odd lately, there was no doubt that he could be an asset.

She turned her back to the glass wall.

"I got that number off Tim Mackie's phone," she said. She closed her eyes. She was going to regret this.

"DCI Mackie?" Dennis asked.

"The very same."

"I don't understand. What do you mean, you got it off his phone?"

"There were various numbers that Mackie had been calling in the days before his death, and that was one of them. As was your number, as we've already discussed."

A muscle by Dennis's ear twitched. "Ashok Verma?" Dennis said. "Mackie was calling him?"

"The phone might have belonged to someone else at that

time," Lesley told him. "I've asked Gail to look into it. I don't want the rest of the team knowing about this."

Dennis nodded. "But you're bringing me in."

"Yes."

"You trust me."

"You're my DS, Dennis. Of course I—"

"You know what I mean."

Lesley raised an eyebrow. "You were friends with the man, he was your mentor. Are you sure this isn't going to be too painful for you?"

He stiffened. "I'm fine."

"Dennis. We both know you've been having mental health problems. I need to know if it's related to Tim Mackie's death."

He blinked. "It's just what comes of thirty years in this job."

Lesley didn't believe him.

"If you decide to tell me what's really going on, Dennis, I'd be very grateful. I want to bring you in on this, I want to involve you. I don't think you've done anything wrong, but you're not telling me everything, and that makes me uneasy."

"I'm fine, boss."

She grunted.

"Anyway, we've got a murder case to solve. I suggest you get out there and put the team's worries to rest."

CHAPTER SEVENTY-FIVE

Tina got out of the car. They were parked just along from Full Hearts dating agency, in a business park in Boscombe. Gail had cracked Ashok's phone and found this number. Tina had run it through Google. Sometimes the internet could be a hundred times more useful than HOLMES.

There was a small sign beside the door. No advertising, no logo. She imagined their work was all online.

She was about to press the intercom buzzer when she realised that Stanley was still standing next to the car. She turned.

"What's up?" she called. "Did I not lock the car?"

He shook his head.

"I need to talk to you."

Tina shivered. She hadn't got to know Stanley well enough yet for serious conversations with him. She approached the car, her footsteps slow.

"We need to get inside, Stan," she said. "If this dating agency is the escort service Ashok was working for..."

"Don't call me Stan," he replied, his voice low.

She shrugged. "Sorry. Stanley. What's the problem?"

"I owe you an apology."

Tina searched her memory. "What for?"

"Something I said to the sarge. I was rude about you, about you being in uniform."

She sighed. "I'm used to that, Stanley. I get it all the time. I can't wait to get past the CID exam."

"I heard you're in with a good chance."

"Let's hope so," she said. "Come on, they'll be watching us."

She turned and started walking. Stanley hurried to catch up with her.

"I think you'll be a good DC," he told her.

She was at the door again, Stanley next to her. She'd only just registered just how tall Stanley was. He must be six foot four. Willowy and gangly, he reminded her of her cousin Paul.

"Let's not jinx it, eh?" she told him. "Wait until the exam results come in."

He smiled and gave her a nudge on the shoulder.

"Good luck, Tina," he said. "Not that you'll need it."

She frowned.

"Stop jinxing it, I said."

He laughed.

The dating agency's door was of scuffed metal. A window in the wall next to it had a crack running down it.

"And to think a woman like Susannah Ramsay used the services of this place," said Stanley.

"We'll see," replied Tina as she pressed the button.

The intercom buzzed. So someone had been watching them.

"Full Hearts, can I help you?"

"I'm PC Abbott from Dorset Police."

"What's it about?"

"An ongoing investigation."

"We ain't done nothing wrong."

"No. But I'm sure you'd rather we talked indoors."

A pause. "Well don't hang around."

Tina pushed the door open as it buzzed again.

"I take it you want to do the talking?" she asked him as she stepped inside.

"Why?" He gestured for her to go in first.

"You're a DC."

He shook his head. "I think your skillset's what we need here."

CHAPTER SEVENTY-SIX

LESLEY STEPPED out of her office, Dennis behind her. She nodded towards Tina's desk. "I take it they're following up a lead?"

Gail, still on her phone, nodded. Mike looked up.

"Gail got numbers off the phone," he said. "One of them's a dating agency."

"Where?"

"Boscombe. Full Hearts."

"Good. Escort agency too?"

"Not according to their website, but that doesn't mean—"

"No. What about the drugs?"

"I've put a call into the drugs team. Gail's getting her guys to send them over the analysis, so they can check for a match."

"OK. Keep me updated."

"Boss."

Lesley turned to Dennis just as her phone rang: Elsa.

"One moment," she told him.

She turned her back to Dennis and Mike as she picked up.

"Hi, love. I've been trying to call you. Is your phone playing up?"

"Sorry," Elsa replied. "I changed the settings, voicemail isn't working properly. I'll fix it when I can work it out. But I was checking for tonight."

"What about tonight?"

"I booked a table at Café Branksome, my parents are coming down."

"Shit. Sorry, I'd forgotten. It's just I'm in the middle of—"

"It's OK." Elsa's voice was flat. "I know what it's like when you're on a case. I'll just go with them on my own."

"No," Lesley said, "I want to meet them. This is important."

She glanced back at the team.

"The team can deal with this. I'll be there. What time?"

"Seven-thirty."

7:30 pm. Carpenter had asked her to come to his office at 6pm. "I promise you I'll be there."

She hung up and frowned. Elsa's number was programmed into her phone, she couldn't even remember what it was, but something was niggling at her.

She brought up the contacts and scrolled through. There was Elsa, right at the top, her number beneath.

Lesley felt her jaw hang open.

That was where she'd seen it before. The other number on Mackie's phone, the one that had been familiar. And the voicemail that was playing up...

Why had DCI Mackie been calling Elsa?

CHAPTER SEVENTY-SEVEN

INES KNEW her breathing was too loud.

She'd squeezed herself under her bed, hoping that the shadows would hide her.

Every muscle in her body was clenched, and her senses were on fire. She could hear the intruder roaming the house, opening and closing doors, tossing the contents of drawers onto the floor. It was claustrophobic under here, dust was in her nostrils. *Don't sneeze.*

Don't cough, don't move, don't make a sound.

In her head, all she could see was the memory of Susannah lying dead on her bed.

Was it her turn?

It had to be the same person. They'd come back to shut her up. Maybe they thought she'd seen them.

Had she? Had someone been leaving the house as she'd arrived with Vali? She didn't remember anything.

She swallowed and coughed, champing her hand over her mouth to muffle the sound.

Shut up, she told herself.

The house was quiet. Had he gone?

But if he was moving around without opening things, she wouldn't hear him. The floors were solid, the carpets thick. He could be climbing the stairs right now and she wouldn't know.

She dug her fingernails into her palms and held her breath. Why hadn't she thought to grab a weapon? There must be something in her room she could bring under here with her.

Jump out if he came in, startle him?

No, the best thing to do was to lie low. Stay put. Wait.

He'd leave eventually and she'd be safe.

But what if he'd seen her coming in? What if he'd been watching all this time, waiting for her to return? What if he knew she'd been released?

She felt a sob rise in her throat. *Stop it*. It would be fine. She just had to stay here, out of sight, and it would be OK.

She wished Vali was with her. Where was he now? They'd let him out before her. Had he gone home? She should call him.

Mierda. Her phone was on the bedside table. It gave her away. If he came in here...

What else had she left up there? There was the bag she'd been packing. Bags. The empty suitcase was on the floor, next to her.

Ines thought of her mother, her sister, her friends at home. She'd been raised to be independent. She'd come to England alone and had begun to make a life for herself. She was not someone things like this happened to.

If Susannah's killer had come back, she couldn't just lie here and wait for them to do the same to her.

She took a deep breath, then propelled herself out from

under the bed. Not stopping to look at the door, she reached up and grabbed her phone. It fell to the floor next to her face.

She grasped it and scooted back under the bed.

She stared up at the bottom of the bed, her breath short. She hadn't dared look out of the room. What if he'd seen her?

Quick. Make the call.

The detective had given her her number. It was in the pocket of Ines's jeans.

She pulled the card out and squinted at it in the darkness.

She couldn't see it.

Could she risk shining her phone at it?

She turned on her phone and tilted the screen towards the card. This would have to be enough, there was no way she was turning the torch on.

It was enough. She memorised the number, then turned the screen back towards her.

No signal.

What? There had always been a signal here. She'd phoned Vali from this room, phoned her mum, used the internet. The wifi was fast enough to watch movies on.

But now there was no wifi.

Of course. The bill wouldn't have been paid. Eventually the electricity would be switched off, and the water, everything else, too.

The wifi had been the first to go. Just her luck.

She let her head fall to the floor. What was she going to do now?

She'd have to try. If she sent a text, it would go as soon as she picked up a signal. Even if she didn't have the phone at that point.

She bit down on her tongue and started to type.

CHAPTER SEVENTY-EIGHT

"Boss," said Mike.

Lesley was on her way out of the office, trying to ignore what she'd just discovered about Elsa. Before she spoke to Carpenter later, she needed to know whether Elsa was connected to Mackie, and if so, how.

"What is it, Mike?"

"I've been going through the rest of the phone numbers on Ashok Verma's phone. I've found a match on the system."

"Go on." What she'd been planning would have to wait. She stood behind him and gripped the back of his chair. Dennis joined her.

Mike pointed to the screen.

"Jake Griffin," he said. "He was arrested last year, drugs possession. He got a fine, first offence."

Lesley narrowed her eyes.

"Where does he live?"

"Weymouth," Mike replied.

"Typical. Weymouth's miles away."

"An hour by road," Dennis said. "Longer, at this time of day."

"What else have you got on him?" Lesley asked.

"He works for Harrison's Plumbing," Mike said.

"Doesn't mean anything to me."

"It's one of Arthur Kelvin's businesses. A legit one, supposedly."

"So he's a part of Kelvin's gang?"

"Hang on."

Mike clicked on his screen to bring up the case notes. He scrolled through them. Lesley peered over his shoulder, her jaw clenching.

"Cannabis and cocaine. He should have been done for intent to supply, with those quantities," she said. "He's done a deal, hasn't he?"

Mike shrugged.

"Think he might have provided evidence on Arthur Kelvin?" Dennis suggested.

Lesley nodded. "Who to?"

"I'll ask Drugs Squad," Mike said.

"They might not be able to tell us anything." Lesley cursed under her breath. "But we need to try."

CHAPTER SEVENTY-NINE

TINA FOLLOWED Stanley up a flight of narrow stairs. There was a smell of decaying food and sweat. The place needed a good clean.

She turned to Stanley. "I don't imagine they do a lot of face-to-face trade, do you?"

He shook his head. "Dating agency, it'll all be online. I'm surprised they even had a phone number."

She grunted and carried on walking.

At the top was a tiny hallway, no wider than the stairs. A green door with paint flaking off was to the left. She knocked on it, then tried the handle.

"It's locked," she said.

"Hang on a minute," came a voice from inside.

Tina exchanged glances with Stanley as scuffling noises came from behind the door. At last it opened and a short, overweight woman with thinning black hair stared back at them.

"What's happened?" she asked. "We file all our tax returns, we don't do nothing wrong."

Tina tried to give her a reassuring smile.

"We're working on a murder investigation," she said. "Ashok Verma. He was a client of yours, I believe."

The woman shrugged. "I'd have to check the system."

"I'd be grateful if you could do that, please," Tina said.

The woman peered around the doorframe to look at Stanley.

"Who's he, your boyfriend?"

Tina shuddered.

"He's my colleague."

Stanley held up his ID. "Detective Constable Brown."

The woman looked back at Tina. She pointed at her chest. "And you're just a PC?"

"For now," Tina replied, her toes clenching in her shoes. "Can you check for a record on Ashok Verma?"

"Oh, yeah. Come in then."

They followed the woman through to a cramped office. A scuffed table sat in one corner, the chair behind it skewed at an angle that looked ridiculously uncomfortable. On top of the table sat a large monitor. A video was running: a woman chasing after a cat.

"Is it on there?" Stanley asked.

"Give me a minute," the woman said. She clicked her mouse a few times and brought up a spreadsheet.

"Ashok what?" she said.

"Verma," Tina replied. "V-E-R-M-A."

The woman sniffed. She wiped her nose with the back of her hand then returned her hand to the mouse, squinting into the screen.

"Here he is," the woman said. "Oh, hang on a minute." She leaned back. "That's odd."

"What's odd?" Tina asked.

Stanley had put a hand on her shoulder. Tina looked up at him. "What?"

"There's someone coming up the stairs. You wait here."

He turned away and put his head through the doorway. Tina heard footsteps clattering up the stairs. A pause, then the sound of them hurrying back down again.

Stanley turned back to her. "I know him," he said.

"Who?" Tina asked.

"You wait here."

Stanley ran out of the room.

Tina looked after him. What the hell was going on?

"What's your mate doing?" the woman asked.

"Don't worry about that," Tina said. "What is it that's odd about Ashok's record?"

"There's an asterisk here by his name."

"What does that mean?"

"Not sure," the woman said.

"Has anybody else got an asterisk?"

The woman scrolled through the database.

"Four more. Three women, one other guy."

"Bring up their records, please," Tina told her.

The woman clicked on the names and brought up photos of three young women and a man. The women all had long, shiny hair. The man was slim with short dark hair. They were all attractive.

"They're all clients of yours?" Tina asked.

The woman shrugged. "Looks like it," she said. "But they've all got asterisks by their name, just like your Ashok Verma."

"Why?" Tina asked.

"Beats me. I just look after the office. I don't deal with clients."

"Maybe they were all working as escorts."

"Escorts?" The woman laughed. "Don't talk bollocks. We're not that kind of outfit."

"OK," Tina said. "So who's going to know?"

The woman gave her a wary look. "I'm not sure."

"I need the name of your boss," Tina said. "I can get it from Companies House."

"You do that then."

"Really? You're going to stall a murder investigation because you don't want to give me your boss's name, when I can get it in five minutes online?"

The woman grunted.

"Cheryl Zayne," she said. "You'll find her in the phonebook."

"No I won't," Tina replied. Nobody was in the phonebook these days. "Just give me her contact details."

The woman stared at her. "That's confidential."

Tina gritted her teeth. "Again, I can get her address from Companies House. Just give me the phone number, please."

The woman grabbed a pad of post-it notes and slapped it on the table. She scrawled a number onto one of them, ripped it off and handed it to Tina.

"There you go," she said. "Don't tell her I gave it to you."

CHAPTER EIGHTY

"Ah, Lesley." Superintendent Carpenter turned towards her. He'd been reading a file on his desk. He snapped it shut. "Take a seat." He gestured towards the easy chairs in the corner.

A pot of coffee sat on the table. So it was going to be that sort of meeting.

Lesley took the chair closest to her and waited.

"Help yourself," he said, sitting down.

She poured a cup for him and another for herself.

"Milk?" she asked him.

"Please."

She poured milk in his and left hers black. She left the cup where it was.

"So," said Carpenter, picking up his own cup and blowing on it. "Sadie Dawes has turned up and your friend Zoe Finch is back in Birmingham."

She nodded.

"All those rabbits are back in their hats, yes?"

"I hope so, Sir."

"What about Sadie Dawes? Is she going to give us any trouble?"

"She's still undercover," Lesley replied.

"Why?"

"She wouldn't say."

"You've spoken to her?"

"She spoke to Zoe."

"Where?"

Lesley drew in a breath.

"She went to Zoe's house, Sir, in Birmingham."

"What's Sadie Dawes doing in Birmingham? She got a story she's working on up there?"

"I doubt it, Sir," Lesley said. "I think she was trying to get away from Dorset."

"You don't need to go to Birmingham to get away from Dorset."

"I think she was also trying to warn Zoe off."

Carpenter drummed his fingers against his mug. He shook his head then slurped noisily.

He turned to look at her, his gaze sharp.

"You broke a fair few rules, inviting a colleague from your old force down here to work on an investigation."

Lesley opened her mouth to speak.

"An investigation that didn't officially exist," he continued, "into a death that was recorded as suicide."

Lesley closed her mouth. She had a feeling she'd be better off waiting for him to finish.

"I'm not going to discipline you," he said. "So long as you can assure me that it's all over now."

Lesley swallowed.

"I'm not sure I can give you that assurance, Sir."

He placed his coffee down, wincing as it spilled onto the table.

"Damn." He pushed the spill away from his cup with his hand. It dripped onto the floor. Lesley resisted the urge to help him.

"You have to stop this now," he said, finally, giving up on his forlorn attempts to clean up the mess. "DCI Mackie committed suicide, the coroner recorded it in his report. I don't see why you have to go sniffing around when you weren't even here."

"It was only eight months ago, Sir."

"Nine months," he said.

"Not exactly ancient history and his wife isn't—"

He raised a forefinger. "Gwen is fine. She's a highly strung woman who was extremely upset by the death of her husband. I don't think she's a reliable witness and I certainly don't think you should be having people from the West Midlands talking to her."

"Sir."

She thought back to her conversation with Gwen Mackie. The widow was convinced Carpenter was covering something up.

But Lesley needed to keep her boss sweet. Mackie's death wasn't the only thing she was here to discuss.

"So," he said, leaning back, "we'll say no more about DCI Mackie. I'm assuming you haven't involved your team in any of this, that was the whole point of bringing the Finch woman in?"

"No, Sir," Lesley said. Dennis hadn't been involved in her investigation, so strictly speaking, she wasn't lying.

"Good," he said. "Now, that's not the only thing we need to talk about."

"No, Sir."

"I've had a call from your superintendent in West Midlands, new man, name of Woolworth."

"Yes, Sir," Lesley said.

It was a name she recognised from East Midlands Police. So they'd parachuted someone in.

"What did he say?" she asked.

"He's happy for you to do whatever you prefer."

Good.

"And what about you, Sir?"

He licked his lips.

"You're a good detective, Lesley. You've developed loyalty from your team and you've cracked some difficult cases. As long as you can promise me that all this nonsense with DCI Mackie is behind us, then I'll be more than happy to keep you on."

Yes. Elsa would be happy. Maybe now they could stop arguing about the future.

Carpenter walked to his desk. He picked up the file she'd seen him looking at, and allowed it to drop the few inches to the coffee table.

"Your file," he said.

She nodded.

"Your mental health has improved. Barely any episodes for the last month."

It was true. Coming down here had done her good. She'd almost forgotten the terror attack on Birmingham that had traumatised her.

"Not completely cured though, I see."

She realised she'd put a hand to the back of her neck, where she'd been injured. She dropped it.

"Just a reflex, Sir. I'm fine."

"Good." He sat down. "There are formalities to go through. We can't just move you here permanently without a process."

"I understand."

"But it's not as if people are chomping at the bit to come and work here. You're unusual." He gave her a smile.

She shrugged. "In that case, I'd like to formally apply for a permanent transfer to Dorset Police."

Carpenter smiled and nodded.

"Glad we have that sorted. You leave the formalities with me. And forget about DCI Mackie, yes?"

CHAPTER EIGHTY-ONE

INES STOOD NO CHANCE.

Light fell across the carpet inches from where she lay.

She held her breath, her throat tight.

The door was open. He was here.

She crossed herself, then regretted it as her hand hit the bottom of the bed. Had he heard her?

Ouch. She pulled her hand to her mouth and sucked on it. She'd scraped it, making it bleed. She was breathing too heavily. He'd hear her.

Ines closed her eyes then opened them again. The light kept changing. He was moving around between the bed and the door. What was he looking for?

He stopped. She heard the sound of breathing.

Querido Dios. She was dead. Her turn next.

Why had she come back here? It was just stuff, a few belongings, nothing worth anything. She should have fled, gone straight home to Spain. What had she been thinking?

She swallowed. A lump in her throat made her want to cough. Her eyes watered and her head was heavy.

A pair of feet was next to the bed, right by her face. Wearing shoe covers.

Shoe covers?

She stared at them, blinking. She had slippers like that. She'd been given them when she...

The bed dipped above her. The heels were facing her, their owner sitting on the bed above her head. She stared upwards. He knew she was here. He was taunting her.

The bed sprung up again and she let herself breathe. A pair of knees appeared on the floor beside her.

She gasped in a breath. The valance moved, a hand pulling it upwards. A face appeared.

She closed her eyes, then forced them open again to find a pair of brown eyes looking into hers.

She stared at them.

"Ines," a voice said. "You're Ines, right?"

She nodded.

"Come out, you silly girl."

A hand reached under the bed.

Was it the police? Had they come to rescue her?

"Who are you?" she asked.

"Just get out from under there."

The hand hauled her out.

Ines brushed herself down and coughed.

She looked up at the person who was about to kill her.

She blinked. She knew that face.

"You?" she said. Suddenly the shoe covers made sense. "What are you doing here?"

CHAPTER EIGHTY-TWO

TINA HURRIED out of the office and down the stairs. Behind her, the woman was shouting. She ignored her.

"Stanley!" she called. "DC Brown!"

Where the hell was he?

She landed at the bottom of the stairs and shoved open the front door. Outside, she scanned the street. It was dark now, shoppers replaced by people heading for pubs.

"Stanley, where the hell are you?" she muttered under her breath.

She spotted movement at one end of the street, somebody running around the side of a building. She started to run, hoping this was Stanley and the man he'd been chasing. She wished she was in uniform. A radio, body cam, her pepper spray. Being in CID, she was going to have to get used to not being kitted out.

She turned the corner of the building to find Stanley standing over a man. The runner had found himself at a dead end, and it looked like he'd crashed into a bank of wheelie bins.

"Everything alright?" Tina called. "Do we need backup?"

Stanley raised a hand, not turning to look at her.

"It's fine," he said. "I can deal with this."

Tina stepped forward. "*We* can deal with this, you mean."

If there was one thing she knew how to handle, it was an arrest following a chase. This was bread and butter to a uniformed PC.

But was an arrest required?

"Who is he?" she asked Stanley.

"Stand up," Stanley said.

The man eased himself up, his hands out in front of him. Tina recognised him.

"You're on their books," she said.

"Who are *you*?" he spat. "Why did you chase me?"

"I'm PC Abbott," she said, "This is DC Brown. Why did you run?"

The man leaned on the bins. They stank.

"I asked you a question," she told him.

Stanley put a hand on her arm. Tina resisted an urge to shake it off.

"Charlie Ibbotson," Stanley said. "I arrested him last summer. You got a caution, didn't you, mate? Not a good idea to run away from me."

The man shrugged. "I haven't done anything wrong."

"Why's there an asterisk by your name on their files?" Tina asked, waving back towards the agency.

Stanley looked at her. "What are you on about?"

"This guy," she gestured at Ibbotson, "had an asterisk on his record. Ashok Verma had the same thing." She turned to him. "Why?"

He clenched his jaw. "Are you arresting me?"

Tina forced herself to relax. "No. But we've got questions for you."

"You'll have to caution me."

She rolled her eyes. "Just answer the questions. Easier for all of us."

The man wrinkled his nose. "Why?"

"Look, just tell us why the dating agency's got an asterisk by your name."

"It's not illegal, you know."

"Good. We still need to know."

Stanley put a hand on her arm: *calm down*. She could feel the adrenaline coursing through her.

She looked at Ibbotson. He was medium height, well-built. He looked like he worked out. His hair had been neatly styled, but was dishevelled because of the running.

"What were you doing at the dating agency?" Tina asked. "You're not a client, are you?"

He stared back at her. "I work for them."

"Doing what?" Stanley asked.

"None of your business."

Tina sighed. "Look, we can do you for resisting arrest, if we're in that sort of mood, or alternatively you can help us. We're working on a murder investigation. Ashok Verma."

The man paled. "You're looking for whoever killed Ash?"

"You knew him?" Stanley asked.

"Ash was a good guy. Poor bastard."

"Was Ash an escort?" Tina asked.

The man looked between the two of them. "It's not illegal, you know? We don't have sex with the customers."

"What customers?" said Tina.

"Hang on a minute," said Stanley. "You're an escort too?"

The man squared his shoulders. "So what if I am?"

"Was Ash an escort?" Tina asked.

The man stared at her. He breathed in and out a couple of times. He seemed to be coming to a decision. Slowly, he nodded.

"So Ash met Susannah Ramsay through Full Hearts?"

The man took a step forward.

"Yes." He paled. "He took the job cos I was busy. If I hadn't had to look after my kid, it would've been me."

CHAPTER EIGHTY-THREE

"How ARE you getting on with the drugs lead?" Dennis asked.

Mike looked across the desks at him. "I've trawled HOLMES, but there's nothing else on Jake Griffin." He scratched his cheek. "Should we go and talk to him, find out how well he knew Ashok?"

"I don't want to alert his suspicions. Or those of the people he works for. Let's wait till we hear back from Stanley and Tina."

"Fair enough."

"There's something here I'd appreciate a second pair of eyes on, though."

"Sarge." Mike pushed himself up and approached Dennis's desk. "What you got?"

Dennis pointed at his screen. "Ashok Verma's bank records."

"This the first time we've seen them?"

"It's the first time we've seen this set. His current

account's in order, a joint savings account he has with his wife. This one's with a building society. High interest."

"And?"

Dennis zoomed in on a transaction. "Eight days ago, ten thousand pounds was transferred into his account."

"Where from?"

"That's what we need to find out." Dennis sniffed. "Let's check the current account again."

"In case he'd been saving, moved it across."

"Exactly that." Dennis opened the file with Ashok's current account statement for the last month. There was no corresponding transaction. Only fifteen hundred pounds had been deposited.

"That's his salary. Name of his employer," said Mike.

"It is." Dennis switched back to the savings account. "So where did this money come from?"

CHAPTER EIGHTY-FOUR

"Are you going to arrest me then?" Ibbotson said.

Tina looked at Stanley. He shook his head.

"No, mate," he said. "Even if you were sleeping with the women, it wouldn't be you committing a crime. It would be them."

"It's not always women," the man replied. "Susannah was unusual. They set me up with men mostly."

"How did they set you up?" Tina asked.

They were still standing in the alleyway by the bins. A group of people passed at the other end, laughing.

Tina looked at the man. "How did they set you up?" she repeated.

He looked back at her. "The agency gives me names. Wealthy guys. Good-looking normally, not what I was expecting when I signed up for it. They take me out, pay for dinner."

"And then?" asked Stanley.

Ibbotson gave him a hard look. "I don't shag them, if that's what you mean. I'm not even gay."

"So the men think you're gay?" Tina asked.

"I don't tell them one way or the other. I have a nice time, they get a bit of company, I go home, the agency pays me."

Tina grunted.

"So was Ashok Verma paid to go on his date with Susannah Ramsay?"

The man shrugged. "Probably. Ash would have been perfect for her. You've seen his photo, haven't you?"

Ashok had been a good-looking man. Like the man standing in front of her, Tina could tell from his photos that he worked out. She could imagine why a woman like Susannah, wary of gold diggers, would prefer to hire the company of a man from time to time instead of trying to weed out the dodgy ones.

Tina looked at Ibbotson. "How much did you get paid?"

"It varied. Normally a hundred or so. Sometimes more. Ash told me he had a big paying job about to come in."

"Money that a woman was paying?" Stanley asked.

"You'd have to ask the agency."

Tina looked at Stanley. "We need to do that."

They turned away from Ibbotson.

"What d'you think?" she asked Stanley as they walked back to the agency.

"Sounds dodgy to me," he said. "Maybe they were getting paid extra to sleep with the clients? Maybe that's why Ashok was expecting more money to come in, he'd been paid to go back to Susannah's house with her."

"But it all went wrong," Tina said.

Stanley nodded. "Poor guy."

Tina smiled at him. "Wasn't expecting you to be sympathetic."

"The guy was murdered. He was paid to do a job and he

was killed in the process. Not much different from coppers who die in the line of duty."

"Really?" she asked. "You think it's the same?"

"Ashok Verma was just unlucky, I guess," he said. "Found himself in a line of work that most people wouldn't want to do."

They were back at the dating agency. Tina buzzed the intercom: no answer. The door was locked.

She bent down and looked through the letterbox. The space beyond was dark.

Stanley banged on the wood while Tina shouted through the letterbox.

"This is PC Abbott. We've got more questions."

No answer. She stood up.

"Typical," she said. "They've gone."

CHAPTER EIGHTY-FIVE

LESLEY WALKED into her office and slumped into her chair. It was just Dennis and Mike in the outer office; Tina and Stanley were still out at the dating agency. It was late now, long since dark.

So Carpenter was going to let her stay in Dorset, but on the condition that she dropped the Mackie case.

Could she do that? It had been niggling at her since the day Gail had taken her up onto that clifftop. That had been her second case here, only a matter of weeks after she'd arrived. She'd been sucked into investigating the death of her predecessor before she'd even got her feet under the table.

Maybe she should leave it alone? Maybe it was none of her business?

Bollocks.

She'd leave it for a while, let things die down, wait for her appointment to become official. And then, well, perhaps then she'd return to it. Bringing Zoe in might not be such a good idea next time.

Her phone rang: Gail.

"Hi, Gail," she said. "I thought you'd have left by now."

"Just on my way out."

Lesley needed to leave too: the dinner with Elsa's parents.

"How did you get on with Ashok's phone?"

"I've got messages from the dating app," Gail said. "Women that he was meeting."

"OK," Lesley replied.

"There's one here you're going to find interesting."

"How so?"

"One of the women was burgled," Gail said. "A house in Christchurch. Big place, wealthy owner. Woman living alone. It was burgled ten days before Susannah Ramsay and Ashok Verma died."

Fifteen days ago. "I don't see the connection," Lesley said.

"You will," Gail replied. "The burglary was on the evening Ashok Verma met the owner for a date."

CHAPTER EIGHTY-SIX

"Let's wait," Stanley said. "See if she comes back."

"She's gone," Tina told him. "She saw us chasing after that guy and she knew better than to hang around."

Stanley wrinkled his nose. "We've got her boss's details. We can talk to her instead."

"We need to call into the office," Tina said, "tell the boss what's going on. She'll want to know about the money."

Stanley nodded.

Tina walked away from him and dialled the DCI's mobile. It was engaged. She left a message and turned back towards Stanley. He was standing with his back to her, beckoning her to approach him. She did so, her footsteps light.

"What is it?" she whispered.

He pointed across the road.

"There," he said. "That car."

She squinted, it was dark now. A dark coloured hatchback had pulled up a few doors along from the dating agency.

"What about it?" she asked him.

"We've seen it before," he said. "The logo."

She squinted. The car was parked between streetlights and she hadn't noticed. But the car had a logo on its side.

Tina nodded.

Stanley put a hand on her arm. "Shh."

The door opened and a figure emerged. A woman. She approached the door to the dating agency, rang the buzzer, and waited.

Tina held her breath, hoping the woman wouldn't look round. She looked back at the car.

She knew that logo, alright.

Mayfair Domestic Services. The company Ines Perez worked for.

CHAPTER EIGHTY-SEVEN

"WHAT ARE YOU DOING HERE, you stupid girl?" Bernard asked.

Ines stared back at him, clenching and unclenching her fists at her sides.

"I live here," she told him. "But you know that, it was you who sent me to live here."

He curled his lip. "Just sit down."

"No." She folded her arms across her chest. "I need to know why you're here. Are you hiring another housekeeper?" She frowned. "You've brought in a team for deep cleaning, haven't you? Susannah's bedroom."

He looked at her for just a beat too long.

"None of your business, girl," he said. "But what the fuck are you doing back here? I thought you'd scarper, bugger off back to Spain after everything that happened to you."

She swallowed.

"You still owe me my last month's pay. I'm not going anywhere, and you should find me another job."

He shook his head. "You're tainted now. These rich

bastards talk to each other. I know the police let you out, but none of them will trust you." Bernard cocked his head. His piggy eyes gleamed at her. "Did you do it?"

"Do what?" She glared back at him, forcing herself not to blink. She'd never liked Bernard, but at least he'd found her well-paying work. She'd put up with the sexist remarks and the sideways glances at her bum. She'd needed work. Still did. And she liked this job.

"Of course I didn't."

"You were with a boy, weren't you?"

"A man." Her face felt hot. "His name is Vali."

"He was arrested too."

"They let him go. We were in Bournemouth when she died, we had our phones. Nowhere near the house."

He grunted. His gaze flicked up and down her body. She kept her arms folded over her chest.

"Still," he said. "It's a bit suspicious, isn't it? You being the only person with access to the place, and then your boss dies."

"Boss and her boyfriend," Ines said. "There was the man too. Ashok."

"Did you know him?"

"I never saw him before."

"Good. Anyway, I'll sort out your last month's pay and then I suggest you fuck off back to Spain."

"No." She took a step forward. "I'm staying here, you owe me another job. Find me another house to clean."

He laughed. "Fat chance."

He turned away from her. She stared after him as he hurried down the stairs.

What was he doing here? Why had he turned up just as she'd arrived back? Should she be worried?

CHAPTER EIGHTY-EIGHT

Lesley stood in the doorway to her office and looked at Dennis.

"How are you getting on?" she asked him.

He turned to her. "We've found another bank account. Ten thousand pounds was deposited in it ten days ago."

"Ten days ago? Who from?"

"That's what I'm working on now," said Mike.

"Gail found messages on his phone," Lesley added. "Dates he went on. One of the women was burgled ten days before he died."

"Could it be connected?" Dennis asked.

"It could be a coincidence. But we need to follow up with other women he met."

"This burglary... was there any violence?"

"Just a burglary. Big house over in Christchurch, break-in was reported the next day. But here's the thing, the woman who owned it was out on a date with Ashok at the time the house was burgled."

"Shi..." said Mike. He stopped himself when he saw Dennis's look of disapproval.

"What do you want us to do, boss?" Dennis asked.

"I want to go to that house," she said. "We need to find out exactly what happened. Speak to the homeowner."

"I can get contact details from HOLMES, call ahead."

"Good," Lesley replied. "Mike, keep us updated if you find out any more about the women he was meeting or the source of that money. Maybe we can kill two birds with one stone."

CHAPTER EIGHTY-NINE

LESLEY WAS RATTLING down the stairs towards the main entrance when her phone buzzed. She pulled it out of the inside pocket of her jacket, glancing behind her to check whether Dennis was following.

It was a text, unknown number.

She flicked it open.

Help. Susannah house. Intruder. Ines.

She looked up the stairs to see Dennis behind her. "Everything alright, boss?"

"I've had a text from Ines Perez. She may be in danger."

"Where is she?"

"Susannah's house. I'll alert Uniform, get them to send a car round. But I want to go myself, too. She says there's an intruder."

"I'll come with you."

"No. One of us has to speak to the burglary victim. You take Mike to that one, I'll have Uniform as backup with Ines."

"Are you sure?"

"It might be nothing. I imagine she's jumpy."

"Let's hope so."

Dennis turned and took the steps two at a time, on his way to fetch Mike. Lesley blew out a couple of times then hurried out of the building.

She made the call to the switchboard on her way out. Uniform would send cars from Poole. She was backing out of her parking space when her phone rang.

"Boss, it's Tina."

"Tina, what have you got for me? Are you at the dating agency?"

"It's more than a dating agency, boss, it's an escort agency. Ashok Verma was being paid to go on dates with wealthy women. We spoke to another guy, he was being paid to go on dates too. Mostly with men, some women."

"OK," Lesley said. "We've got another burglary, happened while Ashok was on a date with the homeowner."

"Maybe he was keeping them away from home while they were broken into."

"It looks like it." Lesley turned out of the car park. *Ines, I hope you're OK.*

Uniform were sending cars on blue lights, they would arrive before she did.

"Tina," she said. "Get back in there. I want the names of everyone involved with that dating agency. We've got some doors to knock on."

"The place is locked up," Tina said. "Nobody there."

"Typical."

Lesley turned left at a roundabout, leaving Wareham behind her and heading towards Poole.

"But there's another thing," Tina said.

"Yes?"

"A car turned up, with the housekeeping company logo."

"Which housekeeping company?"

"Mayfair Domestic Services. The company Ines works for."

Lesley gripped the steering wheel. "When you say a car turned up, has its driver gone into the dating agency?"

"A woman got out, knocked on the door, got back in the car."

"Did you recognise this woman?"

"No. Sorry. It was a man at the agency, wasn't it? Bernard Timms?"

"Yes. Watch the car."

"Ye... hang on."

Lesley heard Stanley's voice in the background as she turned onto the A35, heading towards Poole. At last, she was able to speed up.

"What's happening?"

"The car's moving."

"Follow it," Lesley said.

"Yes, boss."

CHAPTER NINETY

DENNIS AND MIKE pulled up outside the house that had been burgled.

"Let's hope there's somebody in," Mike said.

Dennis nodded. "She's expecting us."

He sat for a moment, his hands on the steering wheel. He looked at the house. One of the windows at the front was lit. The place was impressive, set back from the road with four perfectly symmetrical windows and a broad front door.

"How long ago was this burgled again?" he said.

"Fifteen days," replied Mike.

"What have we got on the nature of the burglary?"

"Professional job," Mike said. "Whoever did it knew what they were up to. The woman who owns the place didn't even know the break-in had happened until the next afternoon."

"How so?" said Dennis.

"Her laptop was taken."

"That's all?"

Mike shook his head. He was scrolling through his phone, texts from Bournemouth CID.

"There was a safe as well. They managed to break into it, take jewellery. Twenty grand's worth."

Dennis almost choked. "Twenty thousand pounds' worth of jewellery in a safe?"

Mike raised his eyebrows. "They're wealthy women that these people are targeting. Look at Susannah Ramsay, that house."

Dennis nodded, peering up at the house. "The discerning burglar."

He pulled his shoulders back and straightened his tie.

"Right, let's speak to this woman. See what we can find out about her date with Ashok Verma."

CHAPTER NINETY-ONE

LESLEY'S PHONE rang as she turned onto the road leading alongside Poole Harbour to Sandbanks.

It was Petra. She didn't have time for this.

"Petra," she said. "Great to hear from you, but your timing isn't brilliant. I'm just in the middle of—"

"I thought you might like to know what I thought of those letters."

Lesley glanced at her satnav. She would be there in four minutes.

"We'll need to be quick," she said.

This was important, too. She wasn't sure if she was still really working on the Mackie investigation, but it didn't hurt to have more information.

"What have you got for me?" she asked.

"So, these letters that you sent me..."

"Yes?" *Get on with it.*

"Well, they're definitely written by the same person. The handwriting is virtually identical. You can tell by the line quality and the connecting strokes, as well as the loops of the y's and g's."

None of that made sense to Lesley, but that didn't matter. "I sense there's a 'but' coming."

"Well done." A chuckle. "The tone of the writing itself is completely different, the sentence construction, the use of adjectives."

"You can get all that just from a few letters?"

"And a suicide note," Petra said. "Don't forget the suicide note."

Lesley grimaced.

"OK. So you're saying that DCI Mackie didn't compose his own suicide note?"

"That's my conclusion. I wouldn't swear to it, these things are never a hundred per cent accurate, but there are significant differences in the style. The use of adjectives and dangling prepositions. I think the suicide note was dictated to him by somebody else."

CHAPTER NINETY-TWO

Tina started the ignition.

Hopefully, whoever was driving that car hadn't spotted them. This part of Bournemouth was quiet, but not deserted. Three cars had passed while they'd been sitting here. She gritted her teeth as the car pulled away.

"Follow that car," said Stanley, casting her a grin.

"You've been waiting to say that, haven't you?"

He laughed. "You don't get to do a lot of this in my normal job."

"No?"

He shook his head as they pulled out.

The car was a hundred metres ahead, no vehicles between them. She'd hoped another car might pass to hide them. It wasn't as if a car with *Mayfair Domestic Services* plastered all over it was difficult to keep up with.

But no, the road was too quiet, and she couldn't afford to wait any longer.

"The occasional burglary," Stanley said. "Plenty of paperwork. No chasing possible murder suspects."

"I'm used to high-speed chases," she told him. "At least, I was in Uniform."

"You were response vehicle trained?"

"I was." She stroked the steering wheel of this car. Would she be required to bring her skills to play? "Still am, I suppose. Can't resist a high-powered vehicle."

"You're going to miss it?"

"No. I love this job. Anyway, I need to focus."

He leaned back as they followed the car. It headed west, along the coast.

"So, what do you reckon," Tina asked him. "House-keeping company and the dating agency all messed up in this together?"

The car indicated to turn left. Tina hung back, waiting to indicate until she reached the turning. When she did, she took it briskly, enjoying the feel of the car's wheels gripping the road.

"Maybe the two companies are owned by the same people?" Stanley suggested.

Tina licked her lips, her fingers tight on the steering wheel.

"Can you look it up?" she asked him.

"Not here."

"Yes you can. Get your phone out, go on the Companies House website. Find out who the directors are for those two companies. You never know, might be the same people."

"That would be convenient."

She shrugged. "Worth a try. People are stupid, or at least most criminals are."

They came to a roundabout. The car went straight on and Tina followed, waiting for another car to come in from the left and place itself between them. She relaxed a little.

She didn't like following immediately behind a target. OK, so her car was unmarked and nondescript. And it was night. But they could end up on a deserted road, the only two vehicles on it.

"No joy," said Stanley.

"No?"

Tina glanced in her rear-view mirror. The road behind was busying up. They were leaving Bournemouth behind, heading into Poole.

"Director of the dating agency is a Cheryl Zayne, the name her employee gave us. Cleaning company is Bernard Timms – not the same people."

"Google them," Tina told him.

He eyed her. "You're enjoying this, aren't you?"

"Two people died," she told him.

"That doesn't mean you're not enjoying it."

She said nothing.

Tina couldn't stop thinking about the CID exams. The result was due in tomorrow. She hoped to God she'd passed. If she'd failed, would they send her back?

They were driving through Canford Cliffs now, making their way down towards Poole Harbour.

"Are you thinking what I'm thinking?" Stanley asked her.

Tina nodded.

"Sandbanks," she said. "Susannah Ramsay's house."

"And I've got a Google hit."

"Anything helpful?"

"Hang on. It's not easy reading when you're in a car."

"Not carsick, are you?"

"No comment."

How could someone make it to DC if they suffered from

carsickness? Maybe when Stanley had been in uniform, he'd had a walking beat.

How old-fashioned.

They came to the bottom of Haven Road. There were two cars between them and the target now, but it was still easy enough to follow. The logo, blue on a yellow background, showed up under every streetlamp. Sure enough, the car turned left.

"It's heading for Sandbanks," she said.

"Could just be making for the ferry," Stanley replied.

"That would be a hell of a coincidence," Tina told him.

"We'll know in a minute."

"What about this Google hit?"

Stanley held his phone out towards her.

"I can't read it while I'm driving."

"Sorry." He pulled it back. "I've found a link between Bernard Timms and Cheryl Zayne."

"Which is?"

"They're married."

CHAPTER NINETY-THREE

LESLEY MUTTERED to herself as she drove towards Susannah Ramsay's house. She couldn't afford to be distracted by the Mackie case now. But if the suicide note was a fake, then who had dictated it to him? The same person who'd pushed him off the cliff?

The road alongside Poole Harbour was busy, cars stopping and starting, nobody in a hurry. It was almost eight o'clock in the evening, rush hour long since over.

"Get out of the fucking way." She grimaced, imagining what Dennis would make of her language.

At last she arrived at Susannah Ramsay's house. A squad car was parked outside. She pulled up behind it, her car halfway up the pavement. She was on double yellows, but that didn't matter.

She slammed the car door closed and ran to the open gate. A car was on the drive. A blue Golf, not one she recognised. Susannah Ramsay had driven a Mercedes, her friends would have similar cars. Ines didn't own a car. So whose was this?

Lesley rushed up the driveway. Two uniformed officers were standing at the door.

"How long have you been here?" she snapped.

"Just arrived," said the younger of the two women. "No one answering."

Lesley pushed past them and hammered on the door.

"Police!" she shouted. "Ines, it's DCI Clarke!"

After a few moments the door opened.

Standing in front of her was Ines Perez, her face pale. She blinked back at Lesley and then swayed. Lesley stepped forward and grabbed the woman's arm.

"Ines, are you OK?"

"She's fine," came a voice.

Lesley looked past Ines to see a man step into the hallway. He'd been standing on the stairs up to the first floor, which went off to the side. He wore a heavy coat and clutched a hat. A flat cap?

"Who are you?" she asked. "Is that your car?"

"I'm Ines's employer. I came to offer her some support."

Lesley looked into Ines's eyes.

"Is that true?" she asked the young woman.

"He is my employer, yes."

"And the support? I got a text from you, you said you were in danger."

Ines's arm stiffened in Lesley's grip. "I'm fine."

"You don't look it."

Lesley turned at the sound of a car entering the driveway. It bore the logo of the housekeeping company that Ines worked for.

She felt her jaw hang open. Was this...?

She looked back at the man standing behind Ines.

"We cleaned the place already," she told him. "The CSI's

gave it a good going over." Gail was known for her pride in leaving a place tidy.

The man stepped forward and put his hand on Ines's shoulder.

"It's fine," he said, "You can leave it with us now."

Lesley heard a car door slam. She turned to see a woman emerge from the housekeeping company car.

The woman smiled, ignoring Lesley and looking at the man. "Darling. I thought you were going to take care of things."

He shook his head. "This is DCI Clarke. Ines texted her."

The woman's gaze flicked to Ines. "Stupid bitch."

"Hey," said Lesley. She looked at the woman. "Who are you? What are you doing here?"

"Her name's Cheryl Zayne! Arrest her, boss!"

Lesley looked past the woman to see Tina running up the driveway, pulling cuffs out of her pocket. Stanley followed behind, holding out his phone. He plunged it into Lesley's hand: a photo of this woman, with her name in the caption.

"Boss," Tina panted. "She runs the escort agency. They were paying men to go on dates with homeowners, then burgling them while they were out." She looked up at the house. "This one went wrong."

Cheryl Zayne looked at Lesley, her mouth tight. "You can't prove anything."

Lesley put a hand on the woman's wrist. "Let's go inside. If you're as innocent as you say, you won't mind answering some questions."

CHAPTER NINETY-FOUR

Felicity Beauman was a slim, dark-haired woman, wearing subtle makeup and an expensive suit.

Dennis held up his ID as she opened the door.

"Ms Beauman," he said.

She frowned. "Is this about the burglary? Have you arrested someone?"

"We have a lead," he said. "This is DC Legg, I'm DS Frampton. We spoke on the phone."

She nodded and stood back.

"Come into the kitchen," she said. "I was just cooking dinner."

Dennis walked past her, through a wide door and into a vast, gleaming kitchen. The work surfaces and units were in the same tasteful shade of beige, and everything sparkled. A pan sizzled on the stove, and Ms Beauman hurried past him.

"Sorry," she said. "I'll turn this off. What's happened?"

She turned to them, her face expectant.

"Sorry to intrude on you of an evening," said Dennis,

"but we need to know more about where you were on the night of the burglary."

Her face darkened. "I was meeting a friend."

"A friend?" Mike asked.

Dennis gave him a look.

She stiffened. "OK, a date. A blind date, if you must know."

"And how did you come across the man you were on the date with?" Dennis asked.

Her gaze was hard on his face. "A dating app. I'm assuming this is all confidential?"

"Of course." Dennis gave her his most reassuring smile, trying to hide the fact that he was repulsed by the idea of dating people you met online. He'd met Pam through a mutual acquaintance, and it had taken five meetings with friends before he'd asked her out to the cinema.

"Which dating app?" Mike asked.

She pulled her phone out of her pocket and flicked through screens. She held it up.

"It was a website," she said. "Not an app."

Dennis peered at the phone. *Full Hearts*.

He exchanged glances with Mike. The woman shifted her weight between her feet. "What's that got to do with anything?"

"What was the name of the man you were meeting?" Dennis asked.

She swallowed. "Ashok Verma."

Dennis felt his jaw clench.

"You may have heard his name in the news recently," he said.

The woman shook her head. "I don't watch the news, too busy with work."

"What is it you do?" Mike asked.

"I'm a radio producer," she replied. "Drama, I don't need to know about current affairs."

"And did you meet Mr Verma for any other dates?" Dennis asked. "Or was this the only one?"

"It was our first date, if you must know," she said. "It went well, I enjoyed myself. I tried contacting him again through the website a couple of days later, but he'd deleted his account. The phone number he gave me rang out." She curled her lip. "Just my luck. It's not easy to meet someone when you have money."

"Surely they'd be flocking after you?" Mike asked.

Her head snapped round towards him. "Men are threatened by women like me."

Mike raised his eyebrows and looked back at the screen.

Dennis sucked in a breath. "I think you were the victim of a scam," he told the woman. "They set you up on a date and then they burgled you when they knew you'd be away from home."

"What the fuck?" she said.

Dennis felt his muscles tense. "If you don't mind..."

"I do bloody mind," she snapped. "So Ash was just keeping me busy so somebody could nick my stuff?"

"I'm very sorry," said Dennis. "But it does bring us closer to catching the people who did it. Did the CSIs tell you if they got any prints?"

"Of course they didn't get any prints," she spat. "These people wore gloves. They didn't leave a bloody trace. It was only the following afternoon I realised I'd been burgled."

"They took jewellery?" Dennis asked.

"Yes," she replied. "Irreplaceable. So, are you going to arrest them?"

"Thank you for your time," Dennis said. "It's been very helpful."

She frowned: he hadn't answered the question.

Dennis gestured for Mike to follow him and made for the front door. He spotted a card on the hall table: Mayfair Domestic Services. He picked it up.

"Excuse me?" the woman said. "That's mine."

Dennis turned it over in his hand. "Does this company do any work for you?"

"Yes. They're good. More than just cleaning, they look after the place like it's their own. My regular girl just left, went back to Ireland. That's why I'm cooking for myself, normally she prepares my meals."

Dennis looked at Mike. "We need to tell the boss about this."

CHAPTER NINETY-FIVE

THEY WERE in the hallway of Susannah Ramsay's house when Lesley's phone rang.

"Dennis," she snapped. "I'm busy."

"This is important."

She eyed Cheryl Zayne. "Be quick."

"We're at Felicity Beauman's house. The burglary victim. She was on a date with Ashok Verma when it happened. The next day he'd disappeared from the website, she couldn't track him down."

"So it definitely wasn't just Susannah."

"No. And there's more. Ms Beauman uses Mayfair Domestic Services to look after her house. Isn't that the company that looked after Susannah's house?"

"It is." Lesley felt a smile flicker on her lips.

"There was jewellery taken, from a safe. The cleaner could have passed the combination to her employers."

"So she could. Thanks, Dennis. Head back to the office. I'll be bringing two suspects in. Tomorrow morning you can help me with questioning."

"Tomorrow morning," he replied. "We'll do it now, surely."

"Won't Pam be waiting for you?"

"Pam understands how it works when we've just arrested a murder suspect."

"OK."

Lesley was worried about overworking Dennis.

"I'll be fine, boss," he told her.

"I'll see you at the office shortly," she said, checking her watch.

Shit. She should call Elsa. She'd long since missed the dinner.

Not now.

She plunged her phone into her pocket and turned towards Zayne and Timms.

"Bernard Timms and Cheryl Zayne," she said, "I am arresting you both for burglary and conspiracy to murder."

"What?" said Zayne. "You can't do that."

"You've been using your cleaners to feed you information about what's worth stealing, no doubt getting safe combinations and the like, and then sending people on dates with the homeowners and breaking into the houses while they're out."

"That's not murder," Timms said.

Lesley cocked her head. "What went wrong with this one? Did they come home when they shouldn't have, and you killed them?"

He scowled at her. "I have no idea what you're talking about. You search this house top to bottom, you won't find my prints."

Lesley shook her head.

"Just because you weren't physically here on the night of the killing, doesn't mean you weren't responsible."

Zayne grabbed Timms's hand.

"Don't say anything."

Lesley looked between the pair of them.

"Anyway," she said, nodding at one of the uniformed officers to put cuffs on them, "I haven't finished. You do not have to say anything, but it may harm your defence if you do not mention when questioned something which you later rely on in court. Anything you do say may be given in evidence. Do you understand?"

"Yes," Timms muttered.

"Ms Zayne?"

"Yes."

"You might be getting somebody else to do the break-ins for you, but you're responsible for Susannah Ramsay and Ashok Verma's deaths. Our CSI team will have your phones and computers, they'll get to the bottom of it." She gestured towards Tina, who took out her phone to call Gail.

Sorry, Gail, Lesley thought. She'd be at home with her son. But Gail knew what this job entailed, and she had a good team.

Zayne stared at her. "You're wrong. It was Ines. She knew what was here, she knew when Susannah would be out."

Ines stood behind Cheryl Zayne, firing a look at the woman that could melt steel. She stepped forward.

"They asked me questions about the house. There was a form to fill out. An inventory. I thought it was for insurance."

"Can you still access that form?"

"Yes."

"Good." Lesley looked at Zayne. "Not looking so good for you." She nodded at the two uniformed officers. "Take them to Winfrith."

As the pair were led away, Lesley looked at Ines.

"Ines, we will need to question you again. Under caution."

Ines nodded. "You don't think I...?"

"I don't think so. But we need to ask you some more questions, just to be sure. And we'll need to talk to other people working for Mayfair."

A nod.

"You'll come with us?"

Ines looked around the hallway. "I never want to set foot in this house again."

"I don't blame you. Come on, you can ride in my car."

CHAPTER NINETY-SIX

LESLEY YAWNED. It was half past ten and she and Dennis had just finished interviewing Bernard Timms followed by Cheryl Zayne.

The pair had refused to say anything, but the evidence was mounting up. Gail had computers and phones from the dating agency and housekeeping company, and there was plenty of documentation indicating a conspiracy to identify targets for burglary, then get the homeowners out on dates.

They still needed more to pin the murder conspiracy to the couple, but Mike was already following up on phone records, and they were hoping to find the people who'd been employed to break into the houses. Even without that, if they could find evidence of Timms and Zayne selling the stolen goods, that might be enough for a charge.

Felicity Beauman's house wasn't the only one that had been targeted. So far they'd unearthed six wealthy home-owners who'd hired the cleaning firm, used the dating agency, and been burgled while out on a date. There were three other escorts, all women.

Lesley expected that they would uncover more, burglaries that hadn't been reported. The very wealthy often kept items they preferred the authorities not to know about.

They would keep digging and they would build a case. Hopefully, the CPS would have enough to press charges.

"OK, everybody," she said. "You've done enough for tonight, let's head home."

"You sure, boss?" asked Tina.

"I know you want to show willing, with the CID exam result coming up. You don't need to prove anything to me, none of you do."

She looked at Stanley. "Not even you, DC Brown."

He straightened in his chair. "Thanks, boss."

Lesley smiled. Stanley had got off to a difficult start, but judging by the body language between him and Tina when they'd returned, they were getting along well now. Maybe she'd ask for him to be assigned to her team permanently. Tina would fill Johnny's slot if she passed the CID exam, but she was inexperienced. A Major Crime Investigations Team needed more resources.

"What about Ines?" asked Mike. "What's happening to her?"

"We let her go," said Dennis. "There's no evidence that she knew she was feeding information to Cheryl Zayne. And she's handed over all the information she has."

"It's understandable to be asked for an inventory," added Tina. "When you have to keep everything clean." She laughed. "Not that I'd know, my place is a tip."

Lesley's cottage in Wareham had been pretty squalid at times too. But now, she was rid of the place. Elsa's modern, light-filled flat was a whole different ballgame.

"Gail's team will be trawling through computers and phones over the next few days. They'll need help."

Four hands went up: everyone was volunteering.

"Thanks, folks," Lesley said. She stood up. "Home, now. You need your beds. I'll see you in the morning."

CHAPTER NINETY-SEVEN

Lesley let herself into the flat, expecting to find darkness and silence. Instead, Elsa was sitting in front of the TV, drinking a glass of wine and nibbling on pistachios.

"That looks nice," said Lesley.

She walked to the kitchen and helped herself to a glass. Elsa smiled up at her as Lesley returned to the living room and took the seat beside her. Elsa placed a warm hand on Lesley's knee. It had been cold in Lesley's car on the way home.

"How was your day?" Elsa asked. "Did you get your arrest?"

Lesley nodded. "I'm so sorry. The dinner. How did it go?"

Elsa's hand stilled. "My mum wasn't impressed."

Lesley didn't blame her. "I'm so sorry, sweetheart."

Elsa shrugged. "It's OK. You're a detective, comes with the territory." She squeezed Lesley's knee.

"Thanks. I owe you."

"You do that. So, your arrest?"

"It was a couple. Between them they were running a housekeeping company and a dating agency. Setting people up to be burgled when they were on dates. The housekeepers fed them information about the contents, without even knowing what they were doing. Susannah Ramsay's burglary went wrong when she came home."

"And they killed her because of that?"

"We still need to winkle out the details, but, yes, that's what it looks like. Ashok Verma, they were employing him to go on the dates, they killed him too. Didn't want a witness, I imagine."

Elsa winced. "Poor guy."

"Poor guy indeed." Lesley sipped at her wine.

The two of them sat in silence for a moment, the TV volume low. It was a home improvement show.

"Since when was this your thing?" Lesley asked.

Elsa yawned. "I wasn't really watching it, just thinking over some stuff from work."

"Anything you want to talk about?"

"No, definitely not."

"OK."

Lesley shifted in her seat, turning to look at her girl-friend. "I need to ask you about something."

Elsa placed her glass on the table and turned to Lesley, her hand still on Lesley's knee. "OK. Sounds serious."

"It could be."

"Go on then."

"How well did you know DCI Tim Mackie?" Lesley asked.

Elsa's hand stiffened on Lesley's knee. "Tim Mackie?"

"The one who died," Lesley said.

"I know who he was, why do you ask?"

She hadn't answered the question, Lesley noted.

"I found a number on his phone."

She looked into Elsa's face, her heart was racing. If Elsa lied to her now...

"And?"

"It was your number."

"You found my number on the old DCI's phone?" Elsa asked.

"The phone you used to call me the other day," Lesley told her.

"It could have been relating to a case." Elsa frowned. "I've got more than one phone, which one was it?"

"I don't know. Who has more than one phone?"

"Criminal lawyers. Call the number," Elsa told her. "Then I'll know."

"OK."

Lesley stood up. She went to the kitchen table where she'd left her jacket and pulled her phone out of her inside pocket. She dialled the number.

There were two phones on the coffee table; one of them rang. Elsa picked it up, clicked the off button and replaced it.

"That's not my phone," she said.

"Yes, it is. It's sitting there right in front of you."

"Yes, but it wasn't my phone when Tim Mackie died."

"So whose phone was it?"

Lesley stared at the phone. She sat back down, her movements stiff.

Elsa looked at her. "At the time that Tim Mackie died, that was my old boss's phone. Harry Nevin."

CHAPTER NINETY-EIGHT

LESLEY WAS first in next day. She walked into her private office and stared at the board. So Ines and Vali had had nothing to do with it, after all, and nor had the ex-husband. The whole thing had been a scam. They would spend weeks unpicking the various burglaries that had taken place, finding out how culpable the men and women who'd worked as escorts and housekeepers had been.

Were they innocent bystanders, or did they know what was going on? They'd certainly received money for their trouble. Ashok, of course, was dead. But then there was Charlie Ibbotson, his friend. He'd been arrested before.

She looked up as the outer door opened and Dennis entered. She went to the door of her office.

"Morning, Dennis. How are you?"

"Fine, boss," he said. "You don't need to worry about me."

"Are you still seeing the psychiatrist?"

"We've reduced our sessions, once a fortnight now instead of weekly."

"And is that because you're on the mend, or because you're trying to get out of it?"

His mouth twitched. "You're not subtle are you, DCI Clarke?"

Lesley cocked her head. "I thought you'd have noticed that by now."

He smiled.

"About that thing we talked about." Lesley put her hands in her jacket pockets. "I've been told to leave it alone."

He nodded. "I don't want to, though."

Lesley felt her chest tighten. "Really, Dennis? You want to risk your career and your pension for this?"

"DCI Mackie was a good man, he deserves justice."

Lesley let out a whistle. "Blimey. When I met you six months ago, I'd never have expected this."

He shrugged. "People change. Your influence, it's rubbed off on me. On all of us."

Lesley wasn't sure if that was a good thing.

"Well, let's wrap up this case first and then talk. I don't want you doing anything foolish."

"No, boss."

Dennis flinched as the door opened behind him: Mike and Tina. The two of them were laughing, falling over each other as they came in together.

Dennis flinched, but Lesley smiled. It was good to see them like this. She knew it was risky having a couple on the team, but for now, she liked seeing the pair of them happy. And there was an envelope on her desk that she hoped would make Tina even happier.

CHAPTER NINETY-NINE

Tina caught herself as she entered the office. The boss and the sarge were watching her and Mike. The sarge was frowning, while the boss, Tina could tell, was laughing at them silently.

Shit.

Tina liked Mike, but she didn't want this to affect her career.

"Sorry, boss." She gave Mike a look.

He nodded and retreated to his own desk.

"We were just—" Tina said.

"It's OK," the DCI said. "You're allowed to have fun. The work you did tracking down those escorts and matching the cleaning company and the dating agency made all the difference."

"Stanley played a part, too. If he hadn't recognised Charlie Ibbotson..."

Lesley put a hand on Tina's arm. "Take credit where it's due, PC Abbott." She looked back towards her office. "That reminds me, I've got something for you."

Tina tensed. She watched the boss go into her office, pick something up from her desk, and return with it.

She handed the envelope over. Tina stared at it, her mouth dry.

"Is this...?" she asked.

"Detective's exam results," the DCI replied. The sarge looked up from his desk.

"I thought they'd email it," Tina said, swallowing.

"They do that too," the boss told her. "You'll have something in your inbox, but they sent this to me as a formality."

"Do you know?" Tina asked.

The boss shook her head. "I wanted to wait for you to open it."

Tina swallowed down the lump in her throat. She felt air on the back of her neck and turned to see Stanley enter. He'd be gone soon, they'd only brought him in because they'd had two cases to work on.

She gave him a smile and waved the envelope. "My CID exam results."

He stepped forward. "Go on then, open it."

Tina cleared her throat. She slid her finger under the flap of the envelope and pulled it open. She could sense everybody's eyes on her.

If she'd failed, this was going to be the most humiliating moment of her life.

She slid the sheet of paper out and started to read.

"I am pleased to tell you..."

The office erupted into cheers.

Tina clenched her fist and carried on reading.

"... that you have passed the CID exam. Congratulations, DC Abbott."

She looked up and into the boss's face.

DC Abbott.

The DCI was beaming. Tina knew she was beaming right back at her.

She felt a squeeze on her hand and realised Mike was standing next to her.

"This means you can stay as a permanent member of the team," the sarge said.

Tina looked at him and nodded. She felt like she was about to explode.

"Yes, Sarge. Thanks, Sarge."

CHAPTER ONE HUNDRED

"First round's on me," Lesley said as they entered the pub.

They were in the Ship Inn, the same pub she'd sat in with Tina, Mike, and Stanley, and found herself discussing Dennis's mental health.

She looked at Dennis, whose face kept flicking between pleasure and unease. Mike had just used language that Dennis didn't approve of, and Dennis was clearly trying to tamp down his reaction.

Maybe he was doing OK, maybe not. Lesley would keep an eye on him either way. And his suggestion that he should follow up on DCI Mackie's death, well, she didn't know quite what to do with that. She'd risked her own position here in investigating. Dennis was three years off pension age: could she let him throw all that away to find justice for his old colleague?

She shook her head. *Think about it when this case is done.*

She went to the bar and waved a twenty-pound note.

The barman came over just as her phone pinged, a text from Elsa.

Will you be home earlier tonight sweetie?

Lesley fired off a reply.

Quick drinks to celebrate Tina's CID exam result and then I'll be right with you.

Lovely, let's order a curry.

Great.

Lesley put her phone in her pocket. She watched the barman as he poured Dennis's pint of Jurassic Dark.

Then she frowned. She pulled her phone out again and brought up the text from Elsa. It was the same number she'd used the other day, the one Lesley had recognised from Mackie's phone. Elsa had told her that it had been Harry Nevin's number before the man had died. Was it common for businesses to pass mobile numbers over to other partners after somebody died?

She scrolled through the texts, working her way back to the very first. If what Elsa was saying was true, this would date to some time after Nevin's death. When Lesley had been in Dorset for about a month.

She landed on the first text. It was coy, not as familiar as the ones she was used to receiving now.

Thanks for a lovely evening on Friday, hoping we can do it again sometime.

Lesley felt her breath catch.

Elsa had sent that after their first date, only three weeks after she'd arrived in Dorset. At that point, Harry Nevin had been alive and well.

Which meant that this had been Elsa's number all along. And that DCI Mackie had been contacting her.

"You OK?" the barman asked.

Lesley looked up.

"Do you want a tray?"

The five drinks were arrayed on the bar.

"Yes, please," she replied, her mind racing.

She put her phone back into her pocket and grabbed the tray. As she turned away from the bar, she watched the team laughing and joking. Mike had his arm around Tina.

Elsa, she thought, *what else haven't you been telling me?*

READ A FREE NOVELLA, DEADLY ORIGINS

It's 2003, and Zoe Finch is a new Detective Constable. When a body is found on her patch, she's grudgingly allowed to take a role on the case.

But when more bodies are found, and Zoe realises the case has links to her own family, the investigation becomes deeply personal.

Can Zoe find the killer before it's too late?

Find out by reading *Deadly Origins* for FREE at rachelmclean.com/origins.

READ THE DORSET CRIME SERIES

ALSO BY RACHEL MCLEAN: THE DI ZOE FINCH SERIES

Made in the USA
Las Vegas, NV
01 February 2022

42835640R00203